Dragon CYCLONE

AIR DRAGONS BOOK 5

CHARLENE HARTNADY

CHAPTER 1

A BIG GUY WALKED UP to her as soon as she climbed out of the SUV. Big as in tall and built, not overweight. In fact, there wasn't an ounce of fat on him. He was raw power. He smiled broadly.

"Good morning, Sergeant Stanger. I'm—"

"I'm going to stop you right there. I was discharged from the US military due to an injury." She rolled her shoulder, feeling the now familiar dull pain. "I would prefer it if you called me Angie." She smiled back.

"Noted. My name is Tyrone, but my friends call me Typhoon." He had striking green eyes, which were very unusual.

Typhoon. Strange name.

Vivid eyes. Almost otherworldly.

Such a big guy.

A prickle raced down her spine, but she ignored it. She was seeing things that weren't there.

"You would be most welcome to do the same and to call me Typhoon." They walked towards a large country-style home. It was sprawling and very impressive. It had large bay windows and a wrap-around patio. The sign at the entrance called it a bed-and-breakfast.

There was a small landing strip nearby, occupied by two small jet aircrafts. To the right of the house was a helipad, but no bird in sight. Then there was a large barn with huge double doors.

What was she doing here? This wasn't what she had expected at all. Where was the shooting range?

There were several more men standing to the side of the main building. They were all just as big and built as Tyrone… make that Typhoon. Another prickle made its way down her spine, slowly this time. There was an icy edge to it. Who were they?

She was just being paranoid. Angie needed to stop!

"Is this my end destination?" It didn't feel like it was. "Or is there another leg to this journey?"

"That depends. This is where you sign the paperwork you were sent, and then we'll take the final flight—if you sign."

She nodded once. "The NDA."

"Yep, the NDA. Then there's your basic information sheet, just to be sure that everything we have on file is accurate. And then I need you to fill out a short questionnaire. It's all standard."

"Before we go any further, I need you and your superiors to understand that I won't do anything illegal. I'm not—"

"I assure you that isn't the case. Once you've signed the necessary documents, all will be disclosed, and then it's up to you to decide whether or not you wish to proceed. The SUV is waiting outside. It will remain there until such time as you make a decision."

"That is acceptable." She nodded once.

"This way." He led her inside. The interior was just as lovely as the outside. It was shabby chic. A little over the top for her taste, but still great.

"That's the documentation." He pointed at a stack of documents on a big desk. There was a gold ink stick on the stack. "The NDA is the same one that was emailed to you two weeks ago, but feel free to take a closer look. Take all the time you need."

It took her a couple of minutes to initial all the pages of the thick document. She signed the pages where applicable. It was lengthy and tedious, but pretty standard. She'd lose everything and then some if she opened her mouth about whatever it was that she was about to find out. She'd had a lawyer look at the thing, just to be sure. As long as she didn't disclose anything, she'd be fine.

Many of the missions she'd been on over the last few years had been classified. Need to know only. She was good at keeping her mouth shut. Angie signed the last page with a flourish.

No problemo!

Then she double-checked that her information was correct. She crossed out Sergeant, putting Miss instead. Then she signed that too.

The questionnaire had a couple of strange questions, like whether she was on birth control. She answered everything. Most of the questions were yes or no, so it didn't take long. Then she signed that too. She dropped the pen on the stack of documents.

"All done?" Typhoon asked.

"Yep." She nodded.

"Perfect." After spending a few minutes checking that everything was in order, he handed her a one-page document. "This is your contact back at our base. As well as the requirements for this assignment."

"I'm giving basic arms and munitions training, right? I mean, that's what I signed up for."

"Yes, that is correct." He nodded.

Angie glanced down at the document, and that shiver down her spine happened again, this time lifting the hairs on her arms. "Mr. H. Cyclone."

Typhoon.

Cyclone.

Big. Built.

Those eyes!

Danger alert!

Danger!

Abort mission!

Abort!

"What does the H stand for?" she asked, trying to keep cool.

"Actually, I don't know." He shrugged. "We call him Cyclone."

"Crap! Craaaaaap!" She dropped her head into her hand. Then rolled her head back and sighed.

"What is it?"

Maybe it wasn't him, and maybe they weren't what she thought they were.

Maybe, just freaking maybe… Oh yeah, and pigs could fly.

"Nothing," she mumbled. "I have this rule about not working with guys called Cyclone."

"Cyclone?" Typhoon looked taken aback. "Why Cyclone?"

"I have a phobia of that name, that's all."

"Cyclone?" His eyes had this confused haze. "Do you know other people called that? I thought it was pretty unique. Too unique for a phobia."

"I know one person. Just one." She squeezed her eyes shut. "At least I used to know a Cyclone."

Crap! This was bad.

Maybe she was wrong. She might be wrong.

"Are you okay with proceeding?" Typhoon asked. "I'm sure it's not the same person."

"Yes, let's proceed for now." She nodded once.

"You're probably right to have the phobia. I must warn you that Cyclone is a little… difficult. He gets moody and—"

"It's fine," Angie said. "I can handle a grumpy asshole."

Typhoon laughed. "Okay. I like you."

"Fill me in on the details so that I can decide whether or not I'm doing this thing."

"No problem," Typhoon said. "Let's go outside, and I'll show you. Some things can't really be explained. You'll have to see for yourself." He turned and started walking.

I'll bet!

Angie stood up. "I'm right behind you," she deadpanned as she followed him. This was going to be interesting.

They walked out onto the front lawn. One of the guys was pulling off his shirt.

Shit!

She held back a groan.

"Don't be alarmed," Typhoon said. "This is Gust; he's going to take off his clothes. It's—"

"Gust?" She shook her head.

Nooooooo!

This was not a coincidence. Angie knew what was going to happen next. She'd seen it twice before.

"I just told you he's going to get naked, and you're worried about his name?" Typhoon pushed out a laugh. His green eyes twinkled in the sunshine.

"I've seen naked men plenty of times before. Your names are weird."

Typhoon chuckled and pushed his hands into his jean pockets.

"They *are* a little weird. I guess we're a little weird. Then again," he turned and grinned at her, "you're a little weird yourself. Most females would be running for the hills."

By now, Gust was completely in his birthday suit, dick swinging in the wind. Actually, his dick wasn't swinging because there wasn't any wind, but it would be big enough to swing if a breeze suddenly hit.

Angie tried to act astonished as he shifted into his dragon form. She watched scales push out on his skin. She heard his bones popping as they reformed. His face grew longer, as did his teeth. Wings and a forked tail slowly appeared, unfurling from his massive body. She took a step back, made her eyes wide, and her mouth gape open. Since she wasn't much of an actress, she didn't try for more. "Well, would you look at that?" she said when Gust flapped his great wings, lifting off the ground a few feet before coming back down.

"I have to say, Sergeant… um, Angie, you're taking this very well; better than most. Though, I guess you are ex-military, so I'm sure you've seen some hectic things during your tours."

"I've seen a whole lot and then more."

"We're dragon shifters."

"You don't say." She finally took her eyes off the dragon. It was actually exciting to see one again after all these years. She'd forgotten how massive they were.

"I *really* like you," Typhoon chuckled. "Anyway, we need some training on how to use human weapons. We're under threat. There is a potential goblin war looming. The situation is currently under control, but I need to warn you that they could attack at any time. We can't guarantee your safety while on dragon soil. Suffice to say, you would be safe from the dragons residing within the Air Lair." When she didn't say anything, he went on, "I realize that this is a lot to take in. If you don't feel comfortable proceeding, we have a replacement all lined up. I would ask that you honor—"

"How common is the name Cyclone among your kind?" she interrupted. "I mean, you get plenty of Johns and Sarahs. I'm sure that there are tons of Angelas out there." She chewed on her bottom lip. "Is Cyclone common as well?"

Typhoon looked at her like she had lost her mind for a second or two. He even cocked his head to the side and narrowed his eyes. "There are far fewer of us than humans, but since we generally name our children after things to do with the weather—things like wind, rain, storms, ice, and so on—it isn't uncommon to find that names are reused. I think that there are a couple of Cyclones. I'm sorry to have to say, but it's a popular name, as is Typhoon." He winked at her.

There was more than one.

What were the odds that it was her Cyclone? Maybe really low? It was possible.

Good!

Great even, because Murphy had a sense of humor and life liked to kick people in the ass like that.

"Are you okay, Angie?" Typhoon asked. "We're desperate to get trained up as quickly as possible, but if you're not comfortable, we can go with our second option.

Abort!

Danger!

Argh!

The money was so good. It was going to give her the push-start she needed once she decided what to do with the rest of her life.

"No, it's fine. I'm good to go."

Typhoon grinned, and a couple of dimples popped out.

"I'm glad to hear it."

Angie knew she should leave. No, she should run. But that's not how she was going to tackle this. Firstly, it might not be the Cyclone she once knew.

If it was, she was sure he would act like a professional. Years had passed since she last saw him. Years! Surely, they could move forward and work together? Surely! He had more than likely moved on. He was probably married with half a dozen kids. He'd always wanted a big family. Angie felt a pang and quickly squished it.

If it was him, and if—a big "if" since it wasn't going to happen—he tried to pull some fast moves, she'd explain to him using no uncertain terms exactly where they stood as a couple, which was nowhere. There was nothing there. Zero. Less than zero. If he crossed the line, she would cut him off at the knees.

CHAPTER 2

*B*LAH, BLAH, FUCKING BLAH.

As far as he was concerned, all of these upgrades were bull. Nothing would beat good old-fashioned eyes on the ground... and in the air. Just like nothing would beat a set of sharp teeth and claws.

CCTV systems, access control, arms, and ammunition were a hard fucking no from him. They didn't need it. Never had and never would. Cyclone would make sure that this so-called arms expert knew his feelings on the subject right off the bat. What could a puny human teach him about defense and offense strategies? Nothing! That's what. Sweet fuck all!

Cyclone held back a sigh, trying not to move around in his chair while Vortex's female went on and on about the installations thus far. Just when he was sure his ears might bleed, she finally concluded.

"We're ahead of schedule." Amy closed the cover on her iPad, smiling broadly. Like hanging a few cameras was something special.

He grunted in annoyance. Eliciting a hard stare from Vortex, who could kiss his ass.

"Thank you for the update, Mrs…" Storm sighed. "*Miss* Winters. It's going to take me a while to get used to that."

"Please call me Amy."

"Amy will be mated soon, and she will retain her last name since dragons don't have one, so don't get used to 'Miss' either, Sire," Vortex interjected, getting this sappy expression that made Cyclone want to slit his own damn wrists. He'd totally do it if it weren't for his healing capabilities. As it stood, there would be no point.

"Or just call me Amy," she repeated and smiled… looking just as happy. The adoring couple reeked of sunshine and rainbows.

"Your scent is agonizing," Cyclone growled. "Stop! We're in a work meeting." He kicked Vortex's shin. *Fucker!* They irritated him to no end.

"Enough," Storm sighed. "I'm glad we're well on track with the installation and that you have tendered your resignation at Trivector," he said to the female, then turned to the others. "I am officially announcing that Amy has been appointed as our Security Manager here at the lair. She'll start in a month."

Oh, joy!

His life was complete. *Not.*

"We hope that you will be very happy in your new role," Thunder added, eyes on the female.

Cyclone grunted. "I suggest that you start training your replacement," he told the human.

"I haven't even started in my new position yet. Why would I train someone to take over?" Amy made a face.

"I give you three months." Cyclone pushed his chair back; he needed to get to his meeting. It was time to make a human piss himself. He'd feel marginally better with life after that. Nothing like the smell of pee on freshly ironed clothing in the morning. That would put him in a better mood. Always did. "If you'll excuse me…" he spoke to the royals.

"Three months until what?" Amy asked, voice hard. Eyes on him and unwavering. He'd give it to her; she had guts. More than most humans. He had a grudging respect for that.

"I give you three months before you're with whelp," he told Amy, holding her gaze. "So, you may as well start training a replacement."

Amy smiled, and her eyes softened. Then she straightened her shoulders.

"No." She shook her head. "Not that it's any of your business, but Vortex and I have decided to wait until the various potential threats are well and truly behind us before starting a family."

Yeah, right! He'd heard that one before.

"There has been no further vigilante activity from the goblins." Storm was frowning. "I mean, don't get me wrong, I speak for Thunder and myself when I say we don't particularly want our new Security Manager pregnant, but the goblins are not a valid excuse." Storm looked at Vortex. "Before you say anything, we will move forward with all of our precautions, every last one of them. Cyclone over here is meeting with an arms expert in a few minutes. He and a select group of males are going to receive training in arms and munitions. I think you should receive training too," he told Vortex. "We're still going through with the full installation. An upgrade of our defenses was overdue. Having said that, I think that the goblin leaders have the situation under control. We're no longer doing this because of an imminent threat."

Vortex tensed up a whole lot. Didn't look happy at all.

"Yes, we have relaxed some of the restrictions, and you can be fucking thankful for that." Storm looked from Vortex to Amy and back, his eyes narrowing. They were about to get their wrists slapped. There wouldn't be any blood, so Cyclone wasn't interested in staying to watch.

"I'm going to be late for my introductory meeting with the human who thinks he can teach me how to kill," Cyclone growled. Bastard had it coming.

Cyclone looked down at the file in his hands as he left the meeting. He briefly considered reading up on the male but decided not to, with the shake of his head. What was the point? He didn't give a shit who this person was. It couldn't be that hard to shoot a gun or throw a bomb. Hand-to-hand combat was a true skill.

Claw on claw.

Anyone could shoot a gun. He'd done it before. Big fucking deal.

Hand-to-hand was the way to go full fucking stop. And no one would change his mind about it. It was the right way to fight. The honorable way. Cyclone stopped dead as he caught a spicy yet distinctly feminine scent. It had his dick hardening. It was a scent he knew well.

It couldn't be her. It couldn't! Not a fuck.

Cyclone growled low, gritting his teeth. He fisted his hands as he rounded the bend, even more pissed off with this human. How dare she carry this particular scent?

And then he saw the source of it. Cyclone staggered back a step. It felt like he had been bitch-slapped; that, or like he'd had a bucket of ice-cold water thrown over him.

It was her.

His Angie.

His female.

She was dressed in fatigues and big-ass boots. The clothing was bulky, a thick leather belt around her waist. Her hair was drawn into a tight ponytail. She turned, stopping dead as well. Her mouth fell open for half a second before she pulled herself together.

She was nothing like he remembered. This Angie was hard, toned, and… battle-ready. Her face was devoid of makeup. Her eyes flared brighter than they already were. There was no more softness. No more smiles or eyes dancing with humor or lust. In fact, they narrowed on him, her jaw tightening.

She was even more fucking beautiful than ever. His heart sped up. His blood turned hot in an instant.

"Angie?" His voice was soft and sappy, but fuck, it was *her*, dammit.

"So, it *is* you," she stated. "I had hoped that there was another Cyclone." She closed the distance between them.

"Fuck." He could hardly believe his eyes. After all these years of searching, of hoping, she was here, on dragon soil. She had come to him.

Better yet, she didn't scent of another male. There was no ring on her finger. No jewelry to speak of at all. Her familiar scent cloaked him… embraced him… held him ransom.

Cyclone breathed her in, feeling a tugging at the corners of his mouth for the first time in fucking forever.

"Spice," he used his nickname for her. "It's so good to see you." He stepped forward, wanting to hug her. Wanting so much more, but he would start there.

Angie threw up her arms to block him. "Don't!" she warned. "No hugging or any of that stuff. I'm here on business. This needs to remain professional, or I'm leaving."

Fuck that. He was hugging her, whether she liked it or not.

"I missed you so—" Cyclone doubled over as white-hot pain exploded between his legs. His balls felt pulverized. He fell down onto one knee, his hand cupping his junk. Even though pain sliced through him, he chuckled. It was the first sincere laugh that had left his lips in years. He looked up at her. Rage was etched into her features. Her blue eyes blazed.

"If you wanted to touch my cock, all you had to do was ask," he said through clenched teeth.

Charlie Foxtrot!

Was it too late to abort the mission?

Crap! It was too late.

It was him. It was Cyclone. *Her* Cyclone. Not damn-well hers. Nope. That ship had sailed a long time ago. It was over between them. Done! Dead and buried! She'd worked hard over the years to get over him. Angie had reached a point where she felt nothing. Less than nothing, dammit.

Arghhhhh! What the hell? She should never have come

here. She was an idiot. An idiot who needed money to move on with her life. She could do this, and then she'd leave.

Get the hell out, and fast.

Easy money. Except, nothing in life was easy. Nothing! This proved that sentiment all over again. Why, oh why, did it have to be him?

Cyclone was bigger than she remembered. Muscle packed on hard muscle and then beautiful too, in the most exquisitely masculine way. Most big guys had that overdone 'roid look. It wasn't the case with him. He had a body made from granite and the face of a freaking angel. His eyes looked even bluer. So vivid they still took her breath away. His full lips hung open for a few seconds as expressions of confusion and shock crossed his face.

"Angie?" as he said her name, goosebumps rose up on her flesh… everywhere.

Screw that!

She was over him!

"So, it *is* you," she stated. "I had hoped that there was another Cyclone." Oh, how she'd hoped. A Cyclone phobia. Oh yes, it was all true. Angie closed the distance between them. She needed to set a couple of records straight. There was no way she could be here, training these shifters—training *him*—without boundaries. Boundaries that would be reinforced with barbed wire and electric fencing.

"Fuck." His whole gaze softened… which wouldn't work for her. His eyes moved down the length of her body. Her skin felt like it tightened as he looked her over. There were definitely more of those irritating goosebumps that popped up. What was it about him? Even after all these years, her body still remembered his. Remembered what he could do to her. Yep, boundaries were paramount. She gave him what she hoped was a scathing look. He was being too familiar. The way he was looking at her had her feeling things she had no place feeling.

Those doors were closed!

Cyclone's nostrils flared. Now he was smelling her. It's what shifters did. It used to turn her on. Those days were over!

She folded her arms across her chest and took the scathing look to new heights as she watched his mouth twitch with the start of a smile, even though his forehead was still lined with a frown.

"Spice," he used his nickname for her. How dare he? He used to call her that during sex. While he was buried deep inside her.

Not a fuck!

"It's so good to see you." He stepped forward, reaching for her.

Hell to the no!

Angie used a classic defensive move to block him. "Don't!" she warned. "No hugging or any of that stuff. I'm here on business. This needs to remain professional, or I'm leaving."

Instead of listening as she'd hoped, he got this look. When he had looked at her like that before, she felt like they had a future. Like they could be together. It simply wasn't true.

"I missed you so—"

It happened on instinct. She'd warned him, and he

hadn't listened. It was his own damned fault when she kneed him in the groin… hard. She knew how tough he was and how much he was packing, so she didn't hold back one iota. Her knee had the desired effect, and Cyclone went down on a hard grunt. Most men would be writhing in agony. Some would even have passed out. Not Cyclone. The bastard laughed, looking up at her with those gorgeous blue eyes now pinched with pain around the edges.

Good!

"If you wanted to touch my cock, all you had to do was ask." He winked at her.

Winked.

"Overlord!" There was the sound of running footsteps. "Are you okay? This female struck you." The guy who appeared looked angry. "I can—" He lunged for her, so Angie used the same move she had on Cyclone, hitting his hands away.

"No!" Cyclone jumped to his feet. "Don't you dare touch her." He put himself between her and the guy.

Angie stepped to the side. She could fight her own battles.

"My apologies, Overlord. Miss." The guy inclined his head at each of them, looking confused. "So, everything is fine, then?" He didn't look like he bought it. "The female kicked you in the balls, but you're okay?" His mouth twitched.

"Yes," Cyclone growled, narrowing his eyes, taking a step toward the guy. "Everything is fine. You can go."

"As you wish," the shifter said, then turned and left.

Cyclone gave the tiniest grunt. There was a light sheen of sweat on his brow. Otherwise, you would never say that he was in any pain, which she knew he was.

"Where were we?" His eyes lit up. "Oh, yes. I'd just told you that if you wanted to touch my cock, all you had to do was ask." His gaze drifted to her mouth for a moment.

This was going to be a long two weeks. Boundaries. Big ones. High ones. Cyclone wasn't seeing anyone. He hadn't married then, after all. A selfish part of her was happy. The rest was… indifferent. *Good!* That's how it needed to stay!

Angie needed to put him in his place. Stop this right now before one of them got hurt, and she wasn't talking physically either.

"Not if your cock was the last little bastard on this planet."

"Little?" His lips curled into a sexy half-smile. At least, it would be sexy if it was on any other man… shifter… person… If it was on just about anyone else, it would have been sexy. He took the smallest step toward her.

"We might need to refresh your memory," he said in that deep baritone of his. The one that did things to her.

Oh, hell no! He was flirting. So much for being professional. This had to stop!

"Stop that right now, or I'll introduce you to my other knee."

"Stop what? We have a history. I'm happy to see you."

"*History* is right. It's gone. Over. Dead and buried. It's done. *We're* done! There's a reason why the past is called the past. You can get unhappy really quickly because I am here to do a job, and then I'm gone. I'm going to request someone else. It's becoming clear that we won't be able to work together."

"There is no one else to take my place." He grinned, infuriating her.

Not sexy!

"There is another Overlord. I'll request that he—"

"Vortex is heading up another aspect of security at the lair. I'm it." He touched his chest.

No! No! No! This wouldn't work. This was a big problem for her.

"When I left, I planned on never seeing you again." There. It was out.

"When you left, I planned on never giving up on finding you… Turns out you found me."

"I *will* shoot you if you keep talking like that! I will fucking shoot you with silver bullets and never look back."

"You won't shoot me."

She pulled in a deep breath, trying to calm herself down.

"I will! I'll dance around your dead body and smear your blood all over my face." Angie could never shoot him, but he didn't need to know that; he just needed to stay away from her because she was weak… so, so weak. As weak as ever where Cyclone was concerned.

"I love it when you talk dirty." He bit down on his lower lip. "Turns me on."

"That's it!" She threw up her hands. "I'm out of here," Angie growled as she walked away. "You're insufferable!"

"More dirty talk," she heard him mutter.

Angie glanced back, and, yep, his eyes were glued to her butt.

No! This most definitely was not going to work for her.

CHAPTER 3

Later that day…

MEETINGS WITH THE ROYALS WERE his worst, followed closely by writing reports. Actually, it was writing reports and then meetings. Reports sucked monkey balls.

"Thanks for coming at short notice. There has been a complaint lodged against you," Storm got straight to the point.

Cyclone leaned back in his chair and smiled. "What was the complaint about?" He could guess.

Storm frowned, cocking his head and looking at Cyclone strangely.

"What the hell is wrong with your face?" He continued to look at him like he'd grown an extra nose or something. "Is that a smile? Can't be!"

Cyclone sobered up. "With all due respect, Sire, I have work to do. A lair to protect. Guns to shoot. Things to learn." That was only tomorrow, but hey, he was excited.

"Talking about guns," Storm laced his fingers together, "Angela Stanger has issued a warning against you for inappropriate behavior. She said that you were coming onto her."

"Me?" Cyclone frowned. "Are you sure she had the right male?"

"I asked her the exact same question because, let's face it…" Storm widened his eyes, "you wouldn't hit on a human female. It just wouldn't happen." He shook his head.

"I sometimes bounce my pecs. Perhaps she took that as flirtation?" Cyclone looked down at his chest for a moment.

"Probably but go easy on the female. I had to talk her into staying. She demanded someone else, or she was leaving. I had to agree to give you a severe talking to. Actually, she mentioned corporal punishment." Storm made a face. "But I'm sure she didn't mean it."

Holy fuck, but that turned him on. Especially since she had totally meant it.

"Try to treat the female with… respect. Be nice to her," Storm warned.

"I can be nice." He could be very fucking nice. Unbelievably nice.

"Don't go bouncing your pecs and walking around naked unnecessarily. Humans see things differently than us."

"Sure thing, my lord." He nodded.

"You're being too agreeable." Storm narrowed his eyes. "What's going on?"

"Nothing! We can't delay. We need to get our defenses up to the desired level. Also, you mentioned her wanting to work with someone else?" Cyclone narrowed his eyes. "I would hate to have Vortex's assignment overseeing the installation of cameras. It would bore me to shit. No, I should be on arms and munitions. I can shoot things and blow stuff up. Far more my style. That's why I'm being agreeable."

"Okay, then. That means we're on the same page. Be nice to her. No flirting."

"No flirting." He was going to skip the flirting part. They were way past flirting, anyway. "Now, if that's all, my liege? I should get back to work."

"That's it. Close the door behind you. I don't want to hear one more peep from our arms expert." He looked back down at his laptop.

Cyclone stopped at the PA's desk on his way out. "Hi, Sarah."

She stopped typing, looking up at him with a confused expression on her face.

"Are you talking to me?" She touched a hand to her chest.

"Yes… Your name is Sarah, right?"

"Yes. It's just that you only ever growl at me, even when I say something nice to you, like 'hello.'"

"I have my good days and my bad days." This just happened to be the first good day in a long time. "Can I ask you to look something up for me, please?"

"Sure thing."

"Am I still on the mating list? It's been a year or two since I was put on there. Since I don't even go on Stag Runs, I figure I might have been removed."

"Let me see." Her eyes were on the screen. Her hands flew over the keys. "Just a sec," she added, typing more keys. Then she was scrolling. Sarah smiled. "There it is. Yes, you're still eligible to take a mate."

"Thank you." He grinned at her.

"No problem," he heard her say as he started to walk out. "Hey, Cyclone," she called after him.

He stopped.

"You should have good days more often."

"I intend to," he said as he walked away.

CHAPTER 4

The next day…

THERE WAS A SECTION OF chairs and tables at the firing range. The team was seated at the tables. Angie had her own table more to the front of the makeshift classroom. It worked well enough for training purposes. There was even a whiteboard for her to put notes down for the class.

So far, Cyclone was behaving. He'd introduced her to everyone this morning, and aside from a broad smile that looked like it was just for her, he hadn't done or tried anything untoward. Then again, they were in a class full of his subordinates, so it made sense. The key was to make sure it stayed that way. They could never be alone together. Back to being weak. Oh, so damned weak.

Angie stood in the front of the class with a gun in her

hands. She wore the same outfit as yesterday. Fatigues, laced-up boots, with her hair out of the way in a high ponytail. The only makeup she'd worn this morning was some lip-gloss because she wasn't trying to be cute. That wasn't her MO. Not anymore.

Cyclone sat in the first row; his eyes followed her every move. It was a little disconcerting, which was strange since she wasn't normally rattled so easily. There was nothing normal about this. Maybe she shouldn't have come here. It was too late now.

"Remember to always keep your firearm pointed away from yourself and others, even if it isn't loaded." She demonstrated with the weapon in her hands.

"We don't die easily," one of the shifters pointed out. Angie couldn't remember his name, only that it had something to do with wind.

"You will if it's loaded with silver bullets," she responded. "Don't get complacent. We're training with regular bullets, but it won't be long before we graduate to silver. You will want to get into some good habits from the start; if not for yourself, then for your teammates."

"Don't get clever, Gust," Cyclone growled. "Our instructor is a human. What if you hurt her?" His voice went so deep and so low that she could barely understand what he was saying. His blue eyes glowed dramatically. "As to us not dying easily… That's a moronic thing to say, since we can get hurt, too. One more comment like that, and I'll shoot your dick off, just to remind you of that fact. You can tell me how you like it as it grows back painstakingly slowly. I'll use you as an example of how accidents can happen."

This comment elicited several sniggers.

"It's not a joke. Listen to Angie," Cyclone snarled. All of them instantly stood to attention, eyes wide. "Pay attention, or you won't pass the test and graduate to the fun part."

"This is boring," another shifter grumbled.

"How about I break your arm? You can dismantle the weapon, clean it, and put it back together with your humerus sticking out through your skin since I wouldn't do a half job. Would that make it more interesting for you?"

Why did his gruff tone make her heart beat a little faster? His words should sicken, not excite her. Not for the first time in her life, Angie wondered what the hell was wrong with her. She wasn't like normal women. Never had been.

"No, Overlord. I mean, yes, Overlord. Please don't, Sire." The shifter bowed his head. "I'm sorry, Angie, ma'am."

"That's okay." She bit back a smile. "I also found this part boring, but it's essential that you learn how to take care of your weapon and the basic rules surrounding weapon handling. What you have in front of you is a stripped-down weapon." The shifters looked down. "Those are the separate parts. The booklet to your right contains all the firearm basics we are going to discuss over the next two days. You'll learn all about parts of a firearm. How to take apart and reassemble your weapon. As well as basic care and safety. I'm going to give you half an hour to study the booklet. By the end of the allotted time, you must know the parts and the safety sections by heart. You may also read through the rest of the booklet should you have time remaining."

"No problem," one of the shifters at the back said.

"On it," another guy said.

The others picked up their booklets and got reading.

"I'll be over there if any of you have any questions." Angie sat down at the desk.

Shit! She'd realized at the start of this lesson that she hadn't paid for the winter range of clothing she'd ordered for her father's hunting store, where she currently worked. Angie was supposed to have paid for the delivery by end-of-business the previous day. A certain shifter had messed with her mind, and she'd forgotten all about it. If she didn't pay right now, they'd cancel her order, and the store would be late with the winter display. This was her father's livelihood. He was relying on her. Normally she wouldn't leave the class like this, but she needed to make the payment and double-check that she hadn't forgotten anything else. She looked up at the cause of all this mess.

Cyclone was looking at her. *Damn!* Her cheeks heated. Angie keyed in her password. It wasn't the end of the world since most of these shifters knew absolutely nothing about firearms. Perhaps a bit of theory first wasn't a bad idea. She'd quickly get this done. Send an email apologizing, and then they could move on to taking a weapon apart.

Her fingers racing, Angie logged into the business account… and her laptop went dead. She pushed a few keys, and the flashing red battery sign appeared in the center of the screen.

"Dang it!" she murmured. What now? This payment had to be made. Her dad wasn't great with computers. He still did everything manually. Since he was manning the store, there was no one who could make that payment but her. It needed to happen now with an apology email, or no winter stock was coming their way.

"I need to leave my desk for 10 minutes. Will you all be alright to continue without me?" she addressed the group. They could read a booklet alone for a few minutes. Their weapons were fully dismantled so no one would accidentally shoot themselves or others. She needed to fetch her charger and get this done. Angie was irritated at herself for letting Cyclone get to her like this.

There were several muttered replies of "yes."

"Why? Where are you going?" Cyclone asked.

"I need to fetch something from my… I won't be long." He didn't need to know her every movement. They were no longer together. It had been years. He was acting like he still had a stake in her, and he didn't.

"I'll accompany you."

"No, you have a task to perform. I'm quite capable of walking down the hallway on my own." She looked down at the weapon in front of him. "Get on with it. My apartment isn't far from here."

Her mouth unhinged as she watched him put the weapon together like a freaking pro. It made her face feel warm. He had always been a quick learner. That, and good with his hands.

Bastard!

"There! I don't need to read the booklet. I've already done my homework. I like to be prepared."

"You were only supposed to read the booklet." *Not be a damned show-off.* She didn't say it out loud, even though she wanted to.

"I don't need to read it. I insist on accompanying you.

I'm sure Storm mentioned that you need an escort at all times. Vortex will keep an eye on things here." He looked over at the Overlord in question.

"No problem," Vortex said, looking back down at the booklet in his hands. The whole class was busy. No one seemed interested in them.

An escort. *Pfffft!* Angie wasn't a little girl anymore. She could handle herself, even against a shifter, goblin, or other.

"Fine," she pushed out, walking ahead of him. "Suit yourself." She walked fast, trying to stay ahead of him.

Unfortunately, Cyclone had long legs and could keep up easily.

"I took a look at your file."

"Good for you." Angie would have picked up the pace, but it would have meant jogging.

"Three tours of Afghanistan, a silver star for extraordinary heroism. Those are phenomenal achievements. I'm proud of you, Ange."

She got this warm feeling inside her. A feeling she hated. There was no future for them. Not anymore. She muttered a "thank you" anyway, since her mother had raised her right.

"No, really… I mean it. From working in your father's hunting gear shop to—"

"I'm back working at his shop. There's nothing wrong with that."

"I didn't say there was. I'm just trying to tell you that I'm so fucking proud. I—"

"That's enough, Cyclone." She stopped and turned to him. "This has to stop."

"I'm making basic conversation. I don't understand

where all the animosity is coming from. I know I messed up." His eyes flared with pain. "But I want a chance to—"

Shit! He was blaming himself for her leaving. It was probably for the best. She didn't want to get into it with him. "No! No chances." She shook her head.

"We were good together. Better than good. I loved you. I still—"

"Don't even say it!" He never said the words back then. It made leaving that tiny bit easier. Cyclone didn't get to say them now. She would die if he said them. She'd turn into a puddle on the floor. *No!*

"It's true, though. I—"

"You don't even know me. You never did." She shook her head. "Can we just drop it? It's been years, Cyclone."

Nothing had changed.

"I'm not dropping it. And how can you say that I never knew you?" More hurt bled into his expression. His eyes darkened. His mouth tightened, as did his jaw.

"We spent a couple of stolen moments together. That's all it was." It was a lie. At least, the second part was a lie. Even though they had been together for a year, they had only had stolen moments. It had been enough, though. Special in every way that counted, but she couldn't tell him that.

"That's not all it was. You can keep telling yourself that all you want." His voice was rough.

"Okay, that's all it was to me."

"Bullshit! I know when you're lying, Angie. Always did. Not that it happened much when we were together. You have a tell. You're lying now. You don't mean that. Why would you lie about something like that?"

"I do not have a tell." What was he talking about?

"You do. You're lying." He was grinning. His eyes brightened right up. He ran a hand over the thick, dark stubble on his jaw. Darn, but he was gorgeous when he was all brooding, and impossibly sexy when he smiled like that.

Look away!

Look away right now, Angela!

She did. She carried on walking. The conversation was over.

"We had something real. Something you walked out on," he said to her retreating back.

"Really?" She spun around, her finger up. Angie hadn't realized how close he was. So close that her finger skimmed his chest. She took a step back. "Seems to me like you were the one always leaving." It was a low blow. One she had to take. She had to get him to drop this already.

Weak.

Getting weaker.

"It wasn't what I wanted. You know that. I was coming back. I always came back."

"But for how long? A day? Two days? Hours? You had just been promoted to Overlord." She remembered how proud she had been of him. "It wouldn't have worked." She meant that wholeheartedly. It would not have worked then, and it wouldn't work now.

"I would give it all up for another chance with you." He cupped her cheeks. "I would…"

"Don't!" She moved away. "You worked hard. You got your promotion. You shaped your path, and I shaped mine. They just happened to go in opposite directions."

His throat worked. "I would give it all up if I had the chance to do things over," he repeated.

"You'd be miserable, and I'd be the one you would blame." True damned story!

"I've been fucking miserable without you. A real grumpy bastard since you left me. You should have said something. Told me what was on your mind. I would've moved mountains to change things. I would never have let you go."

And there it was.

If she'd told him, he would've convinced her to stay.

No! It was done!

She'd made her choices, and she was sticking with them. Nothing had changed. Not a single damned thing.

"I know," she acknowledged. Though it didn't make a difference. Leaving had been the best thing for both of them.

"Everything has changed," he said. "Things are different. We can try again. We can be together."

"No. I don't want you, Cyclone."

"A lie." He gave her a half-smile. "Why are you lying to me?"

Insufferable dragon. "I'm not lying." She turned on her heel. "Leave me alone."

"Still lying." He chuckled.

Angie really should pack her bags and leave. Those goblins sounded like a bunch of pricks, though. If she left the dragons in the lurch and something happened, she would never forgive herself. Also, she needed the money. She couldn't work for her father forever. Angie was trying to convince him to sell the store and retire, which would never happen if he thought she needed him. That way, her mom and dad could move to California and live near the beach like hippies. It was something they'd talked about often over the last few years. Angie wanted that for them. They deserved it.

"Two weeks," she muttered to herself. Two lousy freaking weeks. She could get through it. She had to.

"What was that?" Cyclone said from somewhere just behind her.

Angie kept her eyes on the hallway ahead.

"Nothing," she murmured.

"I think you said two weeks. Two weeks for me to get you to admit that you still have feelings for me. That you miss my big cock."

Angie almost choked on her tongue.

"Yep, you heard me," he added. "I plan on doing my best to get that to happen. To get you to tell the truth. I'm going to give it everything I have and then some."

Angie could well believe that. Cyclone could be stubborn.

"I said two weeks, but I was talking about two weeks of torture," she threw the words back over her shoulder.

Cyclone smirked, "Torture? Hell, yeah! You know how I can draw out your orgasm. How I can keep you on the edge for—"

Thank god they reached her apartment. Angie opened the door, throwing it closed in his face.

She leaned back against the wood, sighing softly.

Two weeks of this.

Lord help her.

"Do you need help in there?" Cyclone said through the door. She could hear that he was smiling.

"No!" she shouted in a voice that was too shrill to be hers. When she looked in the mirror, her cheeks were pink. Flustered. It had been years since she had felt like this. Off-balance. Hot. Bothered. Angie didn't like it one bit.

CHAPTER 5

Three days later…

THREE DAYS OF WEAPONS TRAINING.

Three days of seeing her without being able to get close. Three days of being a level 5 stalker. Of watching. Waiting.

Three days of hell!

Of torture!

Three whole fucking days less to convince her that he was the male for her. That they had a future. Three wasted fucking days. Three days too many.

Cyclone wasn't one for inaction. That was why he was at her door now. He knocked. Then he knocked again.

"Go away!" he heard her say when he knocked a third time and called out her name.

"No!" he growled.

"Leave me alone!"

"I'm not leaving until we talk. So, you might as well let me in. I'll knock all night if I have to. Hell, I'll camp outside this door. That'll get the whole lair talking." Stubborn female.

"What the hell is wrong with you?" She pulled the door open as she spoke. Angie wore a pair of Lycra tights and a little top that barely contained her tits. Her body might be more toned, but she was still all curves where it counted. Some things hadn't changed at all.

"Holy fucking shit!" he ground out. "Looks like I came at just the right time."

She swiped a hand over her glistening forehead, panting softly. "I was working out. I'm busy! What do you want?"

"You look fucking amazing."

"You look…" she folded her arms over her chest, "average." Her eyes widened. "And don't you dare tell me I'm lying, because I'm not."

"Okay, I won't." He smiled. It was happening more and more. Even when he wasn't around her. Just thinking about Angie made him fucking happy. He just needed to get to the bottom of this. Make her talk to him. He could understand why she had left him, but she needed to know that everything that had kept them apart was gone. All the barriers. Every last fucking one. All gone! If there was something else bugging her, he needed to fix it. Angie was his female. She was the only one for him, and he knew, fucking knew that deep down inside, she felt the same. Even if she wouldn't admit it to herself. "I won't tell you that you're lying because you already know that you are. You think I'm sexy as fuck."

Angie rolled her eyes. "Please go away. I want to finish my workout. I've said everything there is to say to you."

"I'm not leaving until we talk." He folded his arms to prove a point.

She groaned in frustration. The sound went straight to his cock because he was a sick bastard. That groan sounded exactly like the ones she used to make when he was toying with her. When he brought her close to orgasm, and then eased off. The same frustrated note was there. It did things to him. His balls tightened.

"You are going to talk fast, and then you're leaving." Angie turned, giving him a full view of her heart-shaped ass in those tight-as-fuck pants. They molded to her like a second skin. It was his turn to groan in frustration.

"Fast was never my style," he pushed out, eyes still on her sexy ass.

She whipped around, pointing a finger at him. Still something she did when she was mad. That finger would always come out, and he'd know he was in real trouble. Then they'd have make-up sex. The best kind of fucking, in his opinion. "Stop with the flirtatious comments and stop with… that… What the hell is that?" She pointed at his cock, which was hardening up.

"Have you seen how you look in that outfit? Holy shit, Angie. I'm not apologizing. You could wear a sack, and my cock would take notice, but in that…" He whistled low. "Not to mention that your scent still drives me insane."

"Stop looking at me like that. Get your… y-yourself under control. Don't sniff me." She waved that finger, and he wanted to suck on it. Suck on her. "That's just… It's…" Her eyes were glued to his erection, which was growing by the second.

"Admit that you still want me." He advanced on her. "No!"

"No, you don't still want me, or no, you won't admit it?"

"I *don't* want you." Her eyes flicked to his.

"Lying... still lying, Ange. Just like the night I met you when you said you didn't want to go back to my place."

"Don't bring that up now," she whispered, her big blue eyes pleading.

"I *will* bring it up, because it happened. You went back with me, and I made you come so hard your eyes watered." It was a night he would never forget.

"I was crying with pain. Your massive cock hurt my tiny vagina." She took a step back. "You have a terrible memory."

He took a step towards her, trying to bite back a smile. "It hurt for a second or two; after that, it was pure bliss. Those were tears of pure joy."

"Agony," she whispered.

"Ecstasy. You told me you didn't do one-night stands. You said you were appalled at yourself. Do you still remember what I told you?"

Her eyes clouded, and she swallowed thickly. "No." She shook her head.

"I think you do," he pushed.

"I don't." She was lying. Fooling no one.

Cyclone decided that he would help her memory along. "I told you not to be upset about it because it wasn't a one-night stand. And I meant it. You were everything to me from the moment I first set eyes on you. Nothing has changed since."

"I want you to go." She took another step back, her thighs hitting the back of the sofa.

"No, you don't."

"I really do!" she said it with venom. Her beautiful eyes flaring with anger.

"No… you really don't." He cupped her jaw. "You want me to stay. You want…" His eyes were on her lush lips.

"Don't you dare kiss me." Her chest heaved. Such a little liar.

"Okay, I will." He covered her mouth with his, and she whimpered; her body melted into his. Angie opened up for him immediately, and their tongues intertwined. Cyclone grabbed hold of her ass using both hands. He growled low in his throat, and she groaned.

Angie pulled away, though her hands clasped his biceps tighter. "You should go."

"No." He took her mouth back, deepening the kiss, asking for more.

She pulled away again, seconds later, panting. "You really should. This isn't—"

He kissed her to shut her up, but also because he loved the taste of her. Some things definitely hadn't changed.

"I'm fucking you," he said against her mouth. "Reminding you…" he kissed her again, "how good we are … together." He tugged at her pants, shredding the Lycra as he pulled the garment down. Yanking at her top, too. There was a rip, and her glorious tits spilled free. "Fuck!" he growled, taking back her mouth to keep her from talking. He didn't want lies. He was going to make her body speak the truth.

He cupped her pussy, getting started on her clit right

off the bat. Cyclone knew he was on thin ice. If he gave Angie half a gap, even a moment to think about this, she would kick him out. He had to show her. They *were* good together. They belonged together. Of course, it was more than just sex, but this was a good start. Her body wasn't lying to him. It never did. Her nipples were hard, reaching for him, so he sucked on one while he finger-banged her, sure to keep his thumb firmly on her swollen nub.

"Oh… ooooooh!" Angie groaned and then panted with each thrust of his finger. He had to get inside her. Had to hear her scream his name. He needed her. Needed to be close to her. She needed to see. Needed to forgive him.

"Ange," he groaned as he kissed her again, keeping his finger on her nub. Keeping her there… right fucking there.

The table.

Now.

He picked her up, and in three short strides, he was there. Cyclone put her down, pulling her legs over his shoulders, baring her to him. *Fuck!* Her pussy was flushed a deep pink. It was a little swollen and already glistening wet.

His balls pulled tight just looking at her.

"Beautiful," he whispered.

Her eyes were wild with need. He could see she wasn't thinking clearly. She was lust-drunk.

Good!

Cyclone was done for. There was no one else for him. She was it. His Angie.

He slid into her using just one finger. Nice and easy.

He needed to keep her there. From the noises she was making and the way her hips were rocking, he knew she wasn't going to last. Cyclone eased two fingers inside. Damn, but she was still tight as fuck. Tiny vagina was right. He eased his fingers in and out, crooking them just a little to catch her sweet spot.

Angie mewled. He glanced up at her face. Her mouth was open, her eyes at half-mast. Her dark hair was wild about her shoulders—her ponytail had come loose. Her cheeks were deeply flushed. So goddamn beautiful, it almost took his breath away. When he pushed a third finger home, her eyes widened up, and her hips jerked forward. Cyclone eased off before she could come.

"I'm going to fuck you now, Angie," he murmured. "We need this. It's been too fucking long."

"Yes," she whispered as he gently rubbed her clit.

His balls were so tight. Cyclone knew he wouldn't last. Couldn't! Not with her, his female. Not with Angie. They didn't need protection since she would have to be on birth control to be on dragon territory.

He lined up with her opening and nudged his way in.

"So big… Oh… oh god!" she moaned as he pushed deeper.

"Nearly," he murmured. A few more careful thrusts, and he was in. Flush!

They both groaned. He pulled her a little more off the table so that her ass was in the air. Her legs still firmly over his shoulders. He began thrusting into her using quick, punchy strokes.

Her eyes widened, and she groaned as his grip on her hips tightened. Hard, deep, but slow and easy.

"Holy shit," she groaned.

"Good," he ground out. "I missed this pussy. Missed *you*."

"No!" she groaned.

"No! Should I stop?" He would fucking die.

"More!" she yelled.

Cyclone started up again, picking up the pace. Angie made this strange noise at the back of her throat, her mouth opening.

"Yes!" Her pussy fluttered around him. His balls were in his throat.

Her tits bounced with every thrust. Her face was flushed. So fucking beautiful. So his!

Please! Fuck! She had to see it. Had to.

This had to work.

"Do you want to come?" His voice was so guttural, he could barely understand himself.

"Yes! Oh, god! Oh, yes…" Her eyes focused on him, but barely. "Please. Have to…" Her head fell back, and her tits kept jerking up and down. One of the sexiest things he had ever seen.

Oh, fuck!

He was about to come. About to… He continued to thrust into her, only he picked up the pace slightly, the pad of his thumb finding her clit just as he began to shoot off. Luckily, he had been keeping her right there for a while, so one little touch was all it took. Her pussy clamped down around him like a silken vise, her body milking him for all he was worth and maybe just a bit more. He couldn't help the grunt that escaped. It was just that fucking good.

Her mouth opened in a silent scream. Her back bowed, and then she groaned, long and deep. It was his name that she groaned, which made him shoot off even harder… if that was even possible.

It felt like his dick was exploding. He might have internal damage to his balls, he came so damned hard. Cyclone snarled, his hips jerking roughly.

Angie gripped the back lip of the table and yelled as her pussy kept spasming around him. All too soon, they were coming down, and her eyes were filling with horror. Then anger.

"Angie," he murmured. "Spice," he added as he took her legs off his shoulders. "Don't look at me like that." He cupped her face.

"Don't!" She pushed his hand away. "Get off me."

"You don't mean that."

"What just happened was a mistake," she said, her eyes burning.

Truth.

Shit!

"Off me!" she growled.

He pulled out of her, feeling instantly bereft. "Can we talk about it?" It seemed like a stupid thing to say as he watched his seed drip down her inner thighs.

"No! There is nothing to talk about. That was a mistake. We've always been good in bed. That doesn't mean we belong together. Shit!" She bent over, picking up what was left of her workout clothes. "Thanks! I only brought the one set." She chucked a piece of Lycra at him. "Go! Leave me alone. That isn't going to happen again. We are over. I was horny. I haven't had sex in a long time. Thanks, you scratched an itch, and now you can get yourself gone." She shoved him towards the door.

Cyclone pulled his pants up. They were around his thighs. He allowed himself to be reluctantly pushed towards the door.

"We belong together," he gave it one last try.

"We don't!" She closed the door in his face.

Angie had been telling the truth. She thought what had happened was a mistake. His plan was to get between her thighs. To make her come… hard, and then talk some sense into her. It was supposed to be foolproof. It was supposed to have worked.

What now?

Angie had left because he had kept her on the line. He'd kept her hanging. It hadn't been fair. He had been wrong. Things were different now. They could be together. Why was she being so damned stubborn?

Being inside her again had only bolstered his belief in them. They worked. Angie was the only female for him. She was all he wanted. All he needed. How did he get her to see it? To believe it? Good thing he was stubborn too. He'd find a way, so fucking help him.

CHAPTER 6

The next day…

ANGIE GROANED WHEN HER ALARM clock went off. She groaned even louder as she put her feet over the side of the bed, feeling a slight ache between her thighs. A good ache… What the heck was she thinking? Not a good ache at all. It was a terrible, horrible ache. An ache that should not be there.

What had she done?

No!

Angie was supposed to be strong. Scrap that! She *was* strong. Strong when it came to everyone on the planet… except for him. *Cyclone!* When it came to him, she was weak. So, so weak. She should not have come here. It was too late to leave. She walked into the bathroom and yawned.

There was only one thing for it. She needed to stick to her original plan and stay away from him outside of work. Avoid him like the plague that he was. They didn't belong together. There was no future for them. Lots had changed. Almost every damned thing, but not the one most important thing of all. Not that! Angie needed to get these guys trained, and then she needed to hightail it out of there. Like her ass was on fire.

Angie groaned as she stepped under the hot spray of water in her shower, trying to wash her shame away. What she'd done was wrong, wrong, wrong. So freaking wrong.

Arghhhhh!

Twenty minutes later, she stifled a groan as she walked outside her apartment.

"Morning," she muttered.

Equinox's eyes widened, and his mouth fell open.

Angie looked down at herself. She was half afraid that maybe she'd put her bra over her shirt. Or maybe her pants were inside out or something. Neither of those was the case.

"Um…" Her guard licked his lips. "Morning." He gave her a half-smile.

"Everything okay?" she asked, frowning. He looked like he had just seen a ghost.

"Great." He nodded a couple of times, almost looking like he meant it.

They didn't really chat much on a regular day. She hardly even noticed him there anymore. Equinox shadowed her to and from work. Angie had his number for when she wanted to go on an unscheduled excursion, which hadn't happened yet on account of hiding from Cyclone.

"Okay, then," she mumbled since he was still looking at her strangely.

Whatever!

Angie might have explored this further on a different day. Right now, she didn't feel much like talking. She made her way down the long hallway. Equinox followed her. She wasn't sure why she needed a babysitter. It was unnecessary. Angie touched her hand to the firearm strapped to her chest, feeling the weight of the smaller caliber weapon at her ankle. Both firearms were armed with silver ammo. If those goblins tried their luck, they'd be sorry.

Angie thought for a moment about going to the restaurant to grab some breakfast, but her stomach still churned at the thought. Good god, she'd had sex with Cyclone. Not just sex, but great sex. Amazing sex. Since when was sex with Cyclone anything other than amazing? Never, that's when. He'd ruined her all those years ago. Now he was ruining her all over again.

It had taken her the better part of two years to get over him. Get over him? Hah! More like learn to live without him. Two years before she slept with another man. *Letdown of the freaking century.* She'd tried again about a year later. Really, really tried. Both men had been super-sweet, but she'd felt nothing. Absolutely nothing. Nothing outside the bedroom and even less in it. Sure, she'd orgasmed. But there were orgasms, and then there were *orgasms.* The difference between the two was like comparing a firecracker to a fucking atom bomb. Both go off, but with very different results.

There was only one thing that would make her feel even marginally better. Angie headed straight for the shooting range. It was new and top of the range. The guards who flanked the door to the range both stepped to the side as she arrived. She keyed in the code, and the light went green as the door unlocked with a click.

Angie entered. She quickly donned a bulletproof vest and some safety goggles. Then she keyed in the code to the gun room, which she entered. Angie inhaled the scent of gun oil and hints of cordite. Her mind calmed, feeling instantly less chaotic. Angie walked down the line of weapons mounted on both sides.

"Eeny, meeny, miny, moe," she said, trying to pick her poison. She finally settled on a Remington R-25. This gun was highly accurate and useful against big game, AKA a goblin or two. This little baby would even work against the cave dragons. Although they had a whole arsenal of heavy artillery as backup should they need it. Hopefully, it would never come to that.

Locked and loaded, Angie made her way to the firing range. She glanced at Equinox, who was typing frantically on his phone. He looked her way for a second, then quickly back down at his device. Like he didn't want to maintain eye contact. The guy was acting weird this morning. Must have gotten out of the bed on the wrong side or something.

Again, it wasn't her problem. She pulled on some earmuffs and went to her happy place. It felt good to squeeze the trigger. To feel the recoil of the weapon. To smell the gunpowder. So good! Amazing. Better than sex. Unfortunately, she needed to rephrase that… almost better than sex with Cyclone.

Almost!

Arghhhhh!

He was not going to ruin this.

Happy place! Happy place!

Dammit!

Nope, it wasn't working. She groaned softly as she lowered her weapon and yanked off the earmuffs.

"Coffee?" someone said from behind her. Someone female. Someone who was smiling. Angie could hear it in her voice.

Angie forced herself to loosen her grip on the gun. Then she engaged the safety and turned around. Sure enough, a very happy-looking lady with a huge grin stood a few feet from her with a tray of takeout coffee in one hand and earmuffs in the other. She wore a business pantsuit and steel toe boots. Interesting combination. One Angie liked.

"I'm Amy." she smiled. "I'm head of security here at the lair. I would shake your hand, but I don't have one free right at this second." She looked down briefly before locking eyes with Angie again.

"Hi, I'm Angie."

"My apologies for not meeting with you sooner. I've been tied up with installations. Namely, with access control on the two rear entrances to the lair. They were identified as the weakest entry points to the lair. My company—soon-to-be ex-company—is responsible for… Oh my gosh! I'm rattling on. I'm sorry."

"No, that's absolutely fine," Angie said. "Sounds interesting."

"Nah! It's mostly boring. Putting up cameras is the biggest aspect of the project. So, you're Angela Stanger, the arms expert. You were with special forces and did a couple of tours of Afghanistan. Now you're…" She huffed out a breath. "I'm doing it again. I'm so sorry." She shook her head. "Shall we sit for a few minutes?" She glanced at a nearby table. "I brought donuts as an apology for not getting around to meeting you sooner." There was a box on the table. Amy's stomach grumbled loudly, and her eyes widened. "Oh… sorry… I haven't eaten yet today. I get hungry easily. So, do you have five minutes?" She lifted her brows.

And she was having so much fun. Oh well, Amy seemed nice enough. She was head of security, so this meeting was important.

"Yes… sure… let's sit. Let me take care of this first." She lifted the weapon about an inch.

"Of course. Go ahead," Amy said as she walked to the table.

Angie watched Amy set the coffee down. Equinox had left. He was probably outside, waiting for her to finish.

Angie spent a few minutes packing the firearm away where it belonged and locking the walk-in gun vault.

When she got back to the table, the box was open. The donuts were chocolate and vanilla glazed. They looked puffy and light. They looked pretty good.

"You have to have one," Angie said around a mouthful of food. "It's sugary goodness at its best. Worth every calorie, I swear." She took another big bite, groaning loudly.

"I have to admit, they do look amazing." Angie grabbed a napkin and started tucking into one of the treats. She groaned as well. "Yep." She licked some of the glaze off of her lips. "Good." Almost better than sex… with Cyclone.

Arghhhhh!

She needed to stop thinking about it already.

It was done.

Over!

Finished!

Not happening again. Ever!

"I hope you like cream." Amy pushed one of the takeout cups towards her. "I was trying to be healthy, so no sugar." She sniggered at her own joke, taking another bite of her donut.

Angie choked out a laugh as well. "Thanks." She took a sip of the coffee. "It's good."

"My fiancé, Vortex, is in your class. He's one of the Overlords."

"Oh, yes," Angie said. This felt awkward. She couldn't really relate to women in general.

"We're newly engaged."

"Congratulations." What now? Did she ask to look at the ring or talk about the wedding? No! Not her thing at all. Angie didn't have many girlfriends. Make that, she had no girlfriends. She liked guns and shooting. She'd been to war. To freaking hell and back. Talking about nails and diapers wasn't her thing. Although, the woman across from her wore steel-toed boots, had almost no makeup on, and had a couple of chipped nails, so perhaps there was common ground.

"Sorry about sneaking up on you before your day began, but it was now or never." Amy flapped a hand, still holding half a donut in the other one. "I knew you were here when you keyed in your code at the door, so I rushed over. I had twenty minutes to burn before my day starts. It's jam-packed. I'm on a tight schedule. You've been here for a couple of days, and I thought it was rude of me for not meeting you already. Cyclone is directly overseeing your aspect of the portfolio even though I'm head of security, or I would have found a way to meet you sooner. Anyway, getting the rear access control in place was my top priority. I had hoped it would be sooner. I read your file, and I have to say that I'm a little in awe of you, actually."

"Oh! Thanks. That's sweet. You shouldn't be. I was doing my job… that's all. Nothing to be in awe of, I swear." Angie took a sip of the coffee. A half-eaten donut sat on a napkin in front of her. So maybe she was hungry after all.

"I'm not just talking about the silver star you won. That's amazing, by the way, and you should not talk that down… ever."

"Does everyone know about my tours?" Angie was proud of her achievements, but she didn't like everyone knowing things about her. She was a private person.

"No." Amy shook her head. "It's in your file. Only the royals, the Overlords, and I have access, so don't worry. It's privileged information."

Angie huffed out a breath, taking another sip of her coffee. "Oh! Good."

"When I talked about being in awe of you, I was talking about how you stood up to Cyclone when you first met him." Amy held her lips together, trying to stifle a grin. "Most humans… make that people in general, non-humans too, are afraid of him. He's big, moody, and intimidating, just until you get to know him… but still. Most people are scared."

Crap! Amy was talking about how she kicked Cyclone in the nuts. It seemed like word had gotten around.

"Actually, that was probably wrong of me since, essentially, he is my client. He was being rude… but it shouldn't have happened."

"Cyclone can be… difficult at the best of times. I'm sure whatever it was he said to you warranted your reaction. I must say, when I first met him, before I got to know him and to understand him better, there were a couple of times I felt like kicking him myself."

Okay, she was a bit of a strange one. Angie nodded.

"That took some serious guts," Amy continued. "Some serious lady balls, and I admire that." Then she turned serious. "You should also know that although Cyclone can be a little gruff and a lot rude, he's actually an okay guy underneath all of that." She got this look. "Although he has been in a much better mood since you knocked some sense into him, so maybe it worked." Amy smiled briefly and then took a sip of her coffee. "I came mainly to introduce myself, but I also wanted to meet the woman who brought Cyclone to his knees." Amy's watch vibrated and lit up, but she ignored it. "I also wanted to make sure you knew the part about him being a good guy… deep… deep down. Like way deep. I'm hoping that you are cutting him some slack. Storm mentioned that you put a complaint in against Cyclone. That you were thinking of leaving."

"It's fine. We've sorted things out. I'm staying." Sorted things out. Ha. Not hardly.

"That's good to hear," Amy said. Perhaps Storm had put her up to this. Maybe this was a fishing expedition.

Either way, this was a discussion she really did not want to have, so she made a noise to show she was interested, while secretly hoping that Amy would move on to another topic. If the other woman didn't do it soon, then Angie would find something else to talk about. Like security at the lair. Or paint drying. Anything.

"I'm not sure how it all escalated to the point where things got physical between you two," Amy went on.

"How did you hear about it?" Shit! Did Amy know they had slept together last night? How could she? Had Cyclone said something? Surely not.

"One of the guards saw you boot Cyclone. The guard mentioned that Cyclone seemed a little over-familiar with you. Like he might know you or something, but that's crazy." She laughed, sounding unsure.

Oh! Shew! Amy was talking about the kick to the nethers. "Oh, yes. There was a guard there. I don't really want to talk about the incident. It was a misunderstanding that is firmly behind us."

"Good to know. I'm not here to pry, so let's leave it at that. The only thing I have to say on the subject really quickly is that I hope you will give him a real chance going forward. That's all. I'm glad you've worked through whatever it was that had you start off on the wrong foot. I also wanted you to know that I'm here should you need to talk about anything."

"That's good to know. Thank you!" Angie said. There was no way she was talking to Amy, or anyone else, for that matter. There was nothing to talk about. The sex had been a mistake. It wouldn't happen again. The end!

"I'm so glad I finally got to meet you." Amy's watch vibrated and lit up. "I wanted…" Amy looked at her watch, her eyes widening. Then she looked at her watch again and then back at Angie. Her mouth fell open. "Um… I have to ask, are you and Cyclone dating?"

What?

Angie sat back in her chair. "How is that an appropriate question?"

Did Amy know about last night?

Had someone seen Cyclone leave her apartment?

Shit!

"Why would you even ask me something like that? It's ridiculous," Angie went on, sounding out of sorts, which she was.

"Thing is, he's technically your direct superior. Even though you're only here for two weeks, a relationship would be frowned upon. It's only just recently that the royals started allowing single women contractors on site. Between you and me, I think it's great. Cyclone is a honey underneath that gruff exterior. Still, though, you could get some flak for this. I would set up a meeting with Storm ASAP if I were you."

"We're not dating. No meeting is required, thanks." She shook her head.

"Even if you're not dating, you guys had sex. It's a fact."

How could she know? Unless...

"HR is going to want to speak to you about it, too. Even if it was just a one-time thing. I understand that this is personal. I'm just conveying to you—"

"It *is* personal. Not something I want to talk about with you or anyone else, including HR. It happened once. It won't happen again. I can't believe Cyclone is blabbing about this," Angie muttered the last to herself. He was normally such a private person. They both were.

"Wait a minute," Amy said. Angie could see the other woman's mind working. Could almost smell the smoke as the cogs turned. "Angela… Angie… You're her," she whispered. "You're Cyclone's ex, aren't you?"

"No!" Angie said, almost too quickly. "Her who? What are you talking about?" She picked up Amy's coffee cup and made a show of sniffing it. "Did you slip a little something into your morning coffee? Drinking on the job must be against a whole lot of rules. HR would have a few things to say about that." It wasn't appropriate of her to speak like this to Amy, but right then, she didn't give a flying fig if she was asked to leave the lair. If she was fired for being rude to the Security Manager. Where did this woman get off? Although Angie had a healthy respect for authority, she didn't take shit from anyone, ever. Even well-intended shit.

Amy's eyes narrowed. "You had sex with Cyclone last night? You kicked him where the sun don't shine right after meeting him. After he became over-familiar with you, which isn't like him at all. Your name is Angela. His ex's name was Angela. You're her! You're his ex. The one who broke his heart." She gasped, holding a hand over her mouth. "I can't believe it," she said through her fingers.

"I'm not her," Angie deadpanned. "I would rather settle this with HR, thanks."

Amy rolled her eyes. "Please! I know that you are his ex. I think it's great. Are you guys getting back together? I know we don't know each other well, but my fiancé and I are friends with Cyclone. It would be a big deal if you were getting back together. You're probably playing it down because you work together. I understand that more than most."

"No, we are not getting back together!" *Crap!* She just gave herself away. "I mean… I'm not her."

Amy leveled her with a hard stare. "Nonsense! Don't even try to deny it. I think it's great." She smiled broadly. "Cyclone is a sweetie… deep down. I see through all his growling and blood-shedding… bone-breaking… assholery. I know he was in love with someone who broke his heart. That person is you. Now you're back."

"How can you know all of this? Did he tell you we slept together?" Since when was Cyclone such a blabbermouth? Since never. This didn't sound like him at all. "I'm going to freaking kill him. I'm going to shoot him in the head. No… I'll start with his legs. Then his groin area and then his head."

"You have anger issues. I'm not judging or anything, but you do."

"I like my anger issues, thank you very much," she blurted.

The other woman stopped smiling. "I'm sorry for overstepping. It's just that I know how serious Cyclone was… *is* about you. I know how it works with shifters. Once they decide—"

"I said that there was nothing between us. Sex one time does not make a relationship." Angie shook her head. "I would prefer it if we dropped this entire conversation. I like my privacy. It's a word. An important word that needs to be respected. It's a word I clearly need to teach Cyclone since he has such loose lips all of a sudden."

Amy chuckled. "Wait a minute. Do you think Cyclone told everyone you guys slept together? Because he didn't. Well, he sort of did, but without saying anything." She made a face.

"I'm not too sure what you are talking about." Angie leaned forward a little. "He had to have told people, otherwise, how would they know? How do *you* know about it?"

"You really have no idea." Amy cocked her head and looked at her strangely. "It's just that I thought you were with him before. Like *with him* with him. An item. Surely you should know about dragons if you two dated for a while?" Amy widened her eyes like she was letting her in on a big secret. Pity Angie had no idea what this woman was going on about.

Zero!

"Know what?" Angie threw her hands up. "Please spell it out for me." This was getting really annoying.

"Fine." Amy sat back in her chair. "Privacy. That's the thing. It *is* just a word around these parts. It doesn't really exist. You do know that everyone can smell him on you? At least everyone shifter, which is most of this lair."

"Smell him?" Angie sniffed at herself. "Smell... him... as in Cyclone? Smell what?"

"Wow, you really are clueless. You guys did the deed. You had sex. Did the two-backed monkey dance. You fed the kitty. Slimed the banana. You—"

"Stop that! Maybe you *should* be drinking laced freaking coffee. I know I shouldn't say this, but since you're being so personal, I'm going to get real as well. You're being highly annoying right now."

"When shifters know, they know. When they want someone, they normally get them. We need to face facts. You're going to have to get used to me being annoying because we're probably going to be besties when you and Cyclone finally get it together." The crazy woman smiled. "You must know that dragons have superhuman senses? This includes their sense of smell."

"I know that." Angie snorted. "Of course, I know…" Then realization hit her like a dead fish in the face. "Holy shit… Crap! Smell him on me." She gasped. "Are you saying that everyone can tell that Cyclone and I had sex just by smelling me?"

Amy winced and nodded. "Didn't he tell you any of this? How could you not know?"

"That asshole!" She was going to kill him. "He only ever saw me on human territory. I knew his sense of smell was amazing, but… *that* good? Really? Everyone will know we bumped uglies? Equinox knows?" She glanced at the door. That would explain his weird behavior.

"Yep. He texted Vortex, who knew I was here and texted me. It'll be going around the lair like wildfire. It won't be long before everyone knows."

"I hate that! I'm a private person."

"You mean you *were* a private person," Amy said.

"That asshole!"

"I know where he is," Amy offered. "He's been so happy over the last few days. I'm sure you guys can talk this out."

"Talk is cheap. I'm going to kill him," Angie growled.

Amy's eyes grew comically wide. "No. You can't! I can't tell you where he is if—"

Angie rolled her eyes. "I'm not going to actually kill him. Just hurt him a little." She clenched her jaw.

"In that case, he's practicing hand-to-hand combat behind the lair. I'll draw you a map on how to get there." Amy scrunched up her nose. "Wish I could watch. I'd bring popcorn."

"You're a strange one," Angie said with an unexpected

laugh. Strange but annoying. Different from most women she knew.

"I know. It's my secret charm." Amy bobbed her brows. "Now, talking about drinking…" she went on.

"We weren't talking about drinking."

"You accused me more than once of lacing my coffee. I didn't, but I am meeting the girls tonight for a glass of wine. Why don't you join us?" She put up both hands. "Don't answer now. I know you have other things on your mind. You go whip your man into shape. I want to hear all about it later."

"He's not my man," she threw over her shoulder as she walked away. Drinks with the girls. Um… hard pass!

CHAPTER 7

From happy and content to pissed off in zero point five seconds.

That's how long it took this morning when Cyclone woke up with her scent on him to go from happy to feeling his blood boiling. For a single blissful moment, he thought that they were together. Then he reached over to touch her. To pull her closer… and was met with an empty bed.

Cold and fucking empty. Like he felt right now.

He'd never been so happy about having a scheduled sparring practice first thing in the morning. Cyclone only prayed that one of the bigger males was there so that he could go at it hard.

Cyclone marched outside to the open field where they often practiced.

He growled low when he spotted Avalanche standing

in the middle of the crowd. There were other large males, but all he could see was the massive shifter.

Good!

Fucking great!

The male would work nicely. Avalanche was big and agile.

"You!" He pointed at him. "We're sparring," he snarled.

"Good morning, right back, Cyclone. It's good to—" The male's nostrils flared, and his eyes widened.

Cyclone's eyes narrowed on the male, daring him to say something… anything. Avalanche gave a tight nod and left it at that.

"You rutted the human," one of the males next to Cyclone said, grinning.

Cyclone turned and punched the asshole in the face. A bone cracked. Only one, so he got off lightly. The dickwad staggered back, blood spurting from between his fingers, eyes wide with shock.

"It was nice chatting to you about my personal life," Cyclone said. "Would anyone else like to have a conversation? I'm feeling particularly chatty this morning." He cracked his knuckles, looking around him.

The others shook their heads. Lowering their eyes and making sounds to the negative as they went back to doing whatever they had been doing before.

Good!

Fucking excellent.

"Let's go!" he told Avalanche. "Blades or fists?"

The male shrugged and pulled his sword from a sheath at his back. Avalanche was good with a sword, which suited him just fine.

"How about both?"

"Fine by me," Cyclone growled, unsheathing his own sword.

"Try not to kill your opponents," he shouted to the males before taking a swing at Avalanche.

The male brought up his sword, and there was a loud clang as the two blades collided. Cyclone went straight back in on the attack. This time, Avalanche wasn't quick enough to deflect the blow. The blade sank into his chest. It would take at least an hour or two to heal. The male grunted as Cyclone pulled the blade free.

"Too slow," Cyclone snarled, going at him again. He growled, his lip curling away from his teeth. He already felt marginally better. "Try harder!"

"That bad, huh?" Avalanche laughed, blood gushing from the wound. Cyclone went at him again. Avalanche blocked, pushing Cyclone off him, using his blade against the other male's sword.

"More fighting and less talking." Cyclone knew he was being a prick. He didn't care.

Their swords clanged as they came together again hard, causing vibrations to radiate up his whole arm. So much so that he gritted his teeth.

Good!

This was exactly what he needed.

They went at it until the sweat poured off both of them. Avalanche nicked him a couple of times. Cyclone got a couple of decent slashes and thrusts in. He had to work not to go too hard. Not to kill the male. Anger, frustration, and irritation rolled through him.

"Easy!" Avalanche growled when Cyclone sank his sword into him a fourth time. This time, getting him on the hip, his blade finding bone.

"Sorry!" Cyclone said, meaning it. "Let's lose the swords. I'm in a fucking bad mood," he stated the obvious.

"Understatement of the century. Female troubles?" Avalanche sheathed his sword, and Cyclone followed suit.

The urge to let his baser instincts run loose and to pummel Avalanche rode him hard. This was a sparring session. He didn't want to break the male. In his dark mood, he might accidentally do it.

"Yes." There was no use denying it. "Hit me!" he yelled, gesturing towards himself with both hands.

"You should meditate," Avalanche said.

"Medi… what?" Cyclone frowned.

"Meditate." Avalanche smiled. "I could show you. Give you a few tips. It's good for calming a person down. Better than fighting, at any rate."

"I would prefer to hit you a couple of times, maybe take a few hits myself. That would calm me right fucking down," he countered, still holding his fists up.

Avalanche laughed. "No, it wouldn't. Meditation is designed to lower stress and anxiety. It can even decrease blood pressure. No offense, but it looks like you might need that last one."

"Where the fuck did you hear about meditation?" Cyclone snarled.

"My female taught me how to do it. I meditate daily. You use breathing techniques."

"Breathing techniques!" he spat out the words like they were a cuss. "No wonder I'm kicking your ass. Meditation doesn't sound like my thing. Try to hit me!" He took a step towards Avalanche. "I dare you!"

Avalanche rolled his shoulders. "Are you sure you don't want to learn some breathing techniques? Maybe put your feet in the long grass? Look up at the sky and—"

"Feet in the… What the fuck, dude? I'm sure I want to fight." He was tempted just to hit Avalanche, but there was no fun in it if your opponent wasn't trying.

"Cyclone!" he heard a very familiar voice shout his name. It was Angie. And she sounded pissed.

"Looks like you're going to get that fight you wanted after all." Avalanche chuckled, wiping his brow with the back of his arm. "Maybe you could both learn to meditate."

Cyclone turned, looking into her narrowed stare. Her eyes were blazing. Her hands were on her hips.

"We need to talk right now," she growled.

The males whispered and sniggered.

"Shut the fuck up!" he snarled, looking around him. "Get back to work. I want blood and sweat by the end of this session, or I will beat all of you into a bloody pulp. Am I clear?"

"Yes, Overlord." They all inclined their heads and got back to fighting. There were grunts and the sounds of swords clanging.

That was so damned hot. Everyone jumped into line, obeying him immediately. Angie knew he meant it, that he would kick each of their asses if they didn't do as he said. Goosebumps rose on her arms.

What was she thinking?

No! No! No!

She wasn't noticing any hotness at all. Cyclone turned, striding to her.

Holy freaking hell!

He was so damned gorgeous with his body glistening with sweat, bloody gashes on his arms and chest. His muscles were pumped, and his eyes were a bright blue. He took long, graceful strides towards her.

She was there to kick his ass. To break his balls. To hurt him! Not to damn well admire him.

Head out of the gutter, Angie!

"I take it you want to talk this out somewhere private?" he asked.

"Unless you want your ass handed to you in public?"

He gave her a half-grin. *Not sexy. Not sexy at all!* Cyclone was an asshole. He hadn't warned her about everyone being able to tell they had sex. Hadn't said a damned thing.

"This way, then." He walked fast.

Angie almost had to jog to keep up.

They walked in silence for a few minutes, heading for a forest a couple of hundred yards away. The sun was already blazing. The ass-kicking would probably be easier in the shade anyway, so she kept walking.

They made it to the canopy, but Cyclone kept walking.

"That's far enough," she said, looking up. The canopy was nice and thick. The shade was cool.

"No, it isn't." He shook his head.

"It really is. No one will hear us from here," Angie said.

"They will if there's screaming involved."

"I don't care if they hear me kick your ass," she deadpanned. It was cooler under the trees. This had been a good idea. She started to loosen her shoulders. Gave her knuckles a crack.

"I was talking about the screams you're going to make when I suck on your clit."

Her body reacted. Her little nub did a happy dance, and her pussy got in on the excitement as it lubed itself up to receive his cock. She had to bite back a gasp and squeeze her thighs together to stop the ache.

No!

"That's not going to happen." Her voice was husky, so she cleared her throat. "It's not!" She wagged a finger. "Take it right out of your mind."

He smirked. "You take it out of *your* mind."

Holy shit!

Now she was picturing him between her legs. Cyclone had a great tongue. Long and thick and—

He gave her a sexy half-smile and winked. "It's happening, Spice. My tongue and your pussy have a date that starts in a few minutes. Should I start unbuttoning those fatigues now or once we're done fighting?" His eyes dipped down her body in a way that did things to her. *Damn him!* "They're super fucking sexy on you, by the way."

She swallowed thickly. "I said no," she half-whispered. "I'm angry at you. You're not sucking on my clit." Just saying the word "clit" made her cheeks hot and her panties wet.

"Not yet, I'm not. First, I want to hear what's got you so upset. Then I'm apologizing with my tongue deep inside your pussy."

"Stop talking like that. It's not going to happen, Cyclone. We can't have sex."

"You're needy. I could scent your arousal the moment I turned to you out there." He pointed to where they had been standing, where the men were still training. "Fucking delicious."

"Oh, my god!" This was so bad. "So, everyone there knows I was aroused?" she said, closing her eyes. Why even deny it? It was no use.

He nodded once. "They would have scented my arousal as well. There's no shame in it. We're attracted to each other. We're highly compatible." She'd forgotten how weirdly he spoke. How straight he was.

"Everyone knows we had sex last night." Her voice sounded horrified. Then again, she was mortified, so it made sense.

"Yes." He shrugged. "We have superior senses." He frowned.

"I didn't know your senses were that good. They knew!" She groaned, putting her hand over her face. "This is terrible. I'm a private person, Cyclone."

"People have sex, Angie. It's normal. Avalanche fucked his female this morning. The male I hit in the face jerked off. I don't think he even washed his hands." Cyclone made a face.

"Ewwww!" She wrinkled her nose and then sighed. "Everyone knows about us, though. You should have told me about this." Now that she was here, she suddenly wasn't so angry anymore. His explanation was logical. The forest was cool and quiet. His eyes were... they were beautiful. She needed to leave before she did something stupid. "Forget about it. You're right. I should have known. I'm overreacting." She started to turn to leave, but he took her hand.

"I'm sorry. I thought you remembered. I swear. Back when we were together, I used to tell you what you had eaten. Where you'd been. Who you'd been with. Our seed has a strong scent marker. I thought you were aware… that's all. It was kind of obvious. Although I guess it's been years since we were together. Maybe you forgot some of the little things." He looked a little sad as he said it. His eyes clouded up a little.

He was right. Cyclone had been able to smell the gunpowder if she'd been at the range. Or her mother's perfume if she'd been home. He knew things, like what she'd had for lunch. Angie was the idiot. She wasn't sure why she had been so angry. Maybe because it had happened in the first place. Maybe because she wanted it to happen again. Yep, that was probably it. She wanted it again.

Maybe because she missed him. Missed *them,* and she shouldn't… couldn't. They couldn't be together. It was as simple as that.

"Now about sucking on your clit…" He reached for her, but she pulled away.

Angie shook her head. "Bad idea, since we're not getting back together."

"I'm talking about sex, Angie, not a candle-lit fucking dinner. I mean, while our scent is on each other, we might as well take advantage. It hasn't been that long since we fucked. This could count as round number two, since you made me leave early last night."

"It's a bad idea if you still have feelings for me."

"Whether we fuck or not won't change my feelings. I want you in my life. It's a simple fact. Not just for a short while, but for always. I'll settle for your pussy on my mouth right now, though. I'll take whatever I can get."

How did he make dirty-talk sound romantic?

"Everything you just said is why this would be a bad idea." She started to pull away. Hating the look of affection in his gaze.

"But… I'm a grown male. I know you don't feel the same way, so I'll take whatever you can give me. Anything at all. Then you can leave. It shouldn't matter to you either way. Unless, of course, *you* still care. Unless you still have feelings for me. Then I would completely understand why you would want to be careful and not fool around."

"I don't have feelings for you."

"Well, then… We're two people who are attracted to each other. You might not want me in the long term, but your body sure as fuck does. And right now. Why fight our attraction?"

Everything he had just said made sense. "You won't come after me?" This was a bad idea. The worst. But she could feel herself caving in. Having sex with him a few times wouldn't change things, would it?

"No, I won't come after you." He shook his head, putting his hand on her hip and squeezing. "It's been so long since I made you come with my mouth. Since I tasted you. Fuck, Angie… just one more time. One last time."

"After this, we're done?" *Shit!* She shouldn't do this. It was stupid. She still had feelings for Cyclone. Having sex would make things worse. Then again, they'd already done it.

Arghhh!

This might just put her right back to square one. She'd hurt for a long time after leaving him the last time. This wasn't the same, though. It wasn't!

"Yes, after you finish training us, we're done. We fuck between now and when you leave," he said.

"No dinners! No cuddling! No kissing!" she warned.

His eyes darkened. "Kissing and fucking go hand-in-hand."

"Bullshit!" she pushed out. "This is sex. It needs to be clear. No tenderness. No kissing, Cyclone."

He narrowed his eyes in thought. "No kissing on the lips. Everywhere else is fair game?" He lifted his brows. "Like your pussy. I'd like to kiss those lips."

She choked out a laugh and rolled her eyes. "That kind of kissing would be okay."

Angie could do this. She could keep telling herself that she was leaving. She and Cyclone were good together. It would be a shame to let the opportunity for good sex pass her by. That's all this was; good sex. Then she was leaving.

"Okay, then." She shrugged.

"Okay?"

She nodded.

Cyclone picked her up and threw her over his shoulder.

Neanderthal!

"What the hell are you doing?" she yelled. She was also smiling.

"Taking you to where they won't hear your screams. I'm going to make you come so fucking hard."

"We have training in half an hour," she warned.

"We might be a few minutes late."

"No!" she yelled.

"Ummm… yes."

"You're insufferable," she growled.

"That's how you like me."

"I don't like you. This is just sex, remember?" Her voice sounded jerky since she was being jostled… hard.

He chuckled as he put her down. His face was taut, and he had this feral look to him. "Absolutely! Take your clothes off."

"Just the bottoms," Angie said as she unbuckled her belt. "We don't have time."

"There's always time for jiggling tits."

Angie gasped and chuckled. "You're a pig," she said as she toed off her boots, pulling her pants down with her panties.

"I'm honest, and honesty is the best policy."

"I'm opening my shirt and unhooking my bra. The gun holster stays, and I'm not taking it all off. You'll be able to see my jiggling tits. The ankle holster stays too." She pointed at the weapon there.

Cyclone groaned like he was in pain. "Holy fucking hotness. I might come zero point three seconds after thrusting into your snug pussy. What you just said is like foreplay to me. A gun digging into my back during sex… it's a fantasy of mine." His eyes darkened and his nostrils flared.

Angie had a sassy remark ready, but she forgot what it was, unbuttoning her shirt instead. Her bra had a front hook, and her breasts spilled out.

"Make that zero point one second… Shiiiiiit, Angie." His throat worked. He gripped his hard erection, which tented his pants and squeezed.

His reaction to her had always turned her on even more, and today was no exception. The way he looked at her like she was the most beautiful woman in all of the world… It warmed her inside.

"We don't have much time," she whispered.

"We'll be done in ten minutes."

"Why did you say we'd be late?" she asked.

His eyes turned feral. "You'll need a while to recover."

She laughed. "Arrogant much?"

"Remember that time we had sex in the bathroom at that restaurant? I can't remember its name…" He lifted his eyes in thought. "Something to do with sugar…" He clicked his fingers.

"The Sugar and Rum." Her cheeks started to burn. "It was the wine." She pushed her lips together to keep from smiling. Holy crap, she'd forgotten all about that night.

He smirked. "I had to carry you out of there. I told *them* it was the wine. You only had two glasses, so it could not have been the alcohol."

"I'm a cheap date." She grinned.

"No, you're not."

"Okay, fine! We'd better get started already so that I'll have enough time to recover. No pressure when it comes to delivering, Cyclone. You're not as young as you once were, and I've changed too."

He chuckled low, the sound settling in her lower belly. "First of all, females come easier as they get older. Secondly, I've gotten better with age."

"Really now?" She snort-laughed.

"Oh, yes." He took her pants and spread them on a grassy patch to the left of them. Then he took off his own and put them down next to hers to mimic a blanket. "Lie down, Spice," he instructed, his eyes locked with hers.

"You shouldn't call me that."

"Lie down, Angela." He licked his lips. "Better?"

It wasn't. It didn't matter what he called her. When he looked at her like that, he made her feel things. Want things.

Sex.

Sex.

Sex.

That was all this was!

And the sooner they got to it, the better. She did as he said, lying down where he'd made a bed for her.

"Open your legs for me, Angela." He stepped forward so that he was standing right in front of her. His cock jutted out from his body. He was a thing of utter beauty. Handsome, sexy… everything a woman could want.

Angie did as he said. Again, the sooner they got started, the better.

"Wider, Ange. I want to look at you before I fuck you with my tongue."

Holy fruit bats, this man was driving her mad!

Hearing him say the words sent shivers racing up and down her spine. It had her clit throbbing and other placing turning even wetter.

She sucked in a ragged breath. "Okay," she whispered, spreading her thighs.

Cyclone stared down at her. His nostrils flared. His muscles bunched. He looked like he was doing everything in his power to keep from pouncing on her.

"Fucking sexy," he growled as he knelt between her thighs. "And so damned wet for me already." It was all the warning she got. One moment he was staring at her, and the next, he had his tongue buried deep inside of her.

Tongue-fucking.

Now there was a concept. One she had forgotten. Cyclone was well-versed in the art. If there was a diploma for tongue-fucking, Cyclone could wallpaper his whole damned apartment with the things. He was that good. He knew where her sweet spot was and laid into it like this was his last supper. Her back came off the ground, and her eyes opened wide before she closed them tight. It took everything in her not to scream from the start. It would feed his huge ego, so she kept quiet. Panting like a crazy person didn't count as giving in. Especially since it was intense from the word go.

Cyclone knew exactly what he was doing. Of course he did; he was Cyclone. From the sounds he was making, he was enjoying himself, too. His tongue made lapping, sucking noises. Low little growls seemed to escape every so often as well. Then he slipped his tongue out of her and laved her entire slit. Even licked her inner thigh.

"Fuck, you taste so good. Amazing… I could live here…" His glowing eyes flashed to her. His gaze stayed on her for a few beats. Then he smiled. "Scream for me, Angela."

Then he was back between her legs, where he zeroed in on her clit. Using circular motions with his tongue, he kept at the bundle of nerves until she had to throw her head back. Biting back a moan, she grabbed his head, pulling him in closer as she felt the build, felt the tightening of the many coils deep inside her. Everything felt interconnected. Her muscles began to tense. Everything freaking tensed.

Cyclone was firm yet gentle. She's been with guys who treated her like she might break and others who treated her too roughly. This was just right. Cyclone gave a soft nip at her flesh and then sucked her clit hard. She clenched her teeth as her orgasm rushed through her. She wanted to scream with sheer pleasure but held back, groaning hard instead. Her legs vibrated with the sensations that tore through her from the inside out. Or at least, that's what it felt like. When she finally came down, she realized that she had his head squeezed between her thighs, that her nails were digging into his scalp. Angie knew he could take it, so she didn't apologize. She let him go instead. It took her a few seconds to catch her breath.

"That was an okay start," she lied through her teeth.

Okay?

That was spectacular.

Amazing!

The best!

Her mind was blown.

"Okay?" He licked his lips and chuckled. "You're such a fucking liar. I can tell, remember?"

How the hell did he do that?

"I can do better, though." He palmed his cock from the root to the tip. "Game on, Angela. Game fucking on."

Soooooo darned gorgeous. Damn him! She was already halfway to another orgasm, just imagining him inside of her.

"I think you should sit on my dick. Since I can't kiss your sweet lips, I'll have to suck on your titties instead." He winked at her.

"Wait just one minute. I get to ride you?" That would be a first.

"I told you, I've improved with age. I've since come to realize that being in charge of everything all the time is not necessarily the way to go. That includes rutting."

"You've obviously tried it with someone else. How could you?" It just slipped out. She sounded like a jealous girlfriend when she was neither.

Cyclone's mouth twitched. "For someone who doesn't care, you look and sound jealous right now, Angela."

"Stop calling me that. I'm Angie, and I'm not jealous. I'm merely making an observation. You wouldn't let me be on top. Not once, and yet you just let someone else? It just doesn't seem right. Even talking about sex with other people isn't right. How would you like it if I told you about—"

Cyclone growled low and deep, looking like he wanted to kill someone with his bare hands.

"Don't go there! And for the record, you will be the only female who ever sits on this dick." His voice was so low and deep, it caused goosebumps to pop up on her arms.

Was he talking about *forever,* ever? Because that would be sad. He had a really great cock. Then again, she hated the idea of him having sex with anyone other than her, which was something she didn't want to think about right now. Perhaps he was just talking about the position itself. In which case, back to her being upset about the thought of him with someone else, regardless of the position.

Arghhh!

She was stopping those thoughts right there. "I can ride you," she said. "Although you're supposed to be the one who makes it hard for me to walk later, which means you should do the work."

"You being on top is part of my evil plan. You'll use more energy that way." He winked, and she giggled.

Angie never giggled.

What the hell?

Cyclone sat his ass down and put his hands behind him.

"I'm all yours, babycakes." His cock stood up like a pole, which made her mouth water.

"Firstly, stop with all the endearments. Secondly, when you say 'I'm all yours,' you are just talking about sex, right?" she checked. Cyclone needed reminding at every turn.

"Absolutely." His eyes were dark, his jaw clenched. His biceps bulged. His abs popped.

Ride him? Angie could do that. No problem! She was seriously wet after coming so hard. So turned on. Despite having come so darned hard, it was a joke.

Angie straddled him and then bit down on her lower lip as she rose over him. He hissed as she took hold of his cock. Her fingers couldn't close all the way around. Not even close.

She rubbed herself up and down his long length until she was all-out panting, and his massive dick was well coated in her juices. There was no other way he would fit. She knew this from experience.

Cyclone looked like he was in agony. That or really angry. His traps were like ropes on either side of his neck, and his jaw was tight. In short, he looked freaking good enough to eat.

The eating would have to wait for another day. Angie positioned his cock at her entrance. She had to sit up and forward on his body, taking just his tip inside her.

Cyclone gripped her waist with one hand. "Holy fuck, but you feel good."

"You're not inside me yet," she moaned, agreeing with him anyway.

They both groaned as she pushed down on him. She moved up and down… up and down, slowly taking more and more of him. Both of them were already making obscene noises.

Sweat beaded on his forehead. His fingers dug into her hip.

Angie whimpered as he slid in a whole lot. Not quite there, but nearly. No one else would make her feel this full, this stretched, so utterly fucked. And she loved every second of it. She'd savor it because it wouldn't be long before she was headed home.

Instead of thinking about it, Angie pushed down some more. By now, the sweat was dripping off of Cyclone, and his lips were a thin white line.

"Are you okay?" She was panting hard herself.

He nodded once. "You feel so fucking good." He licked his lips. "All I want to do is to flip you over and fuck the hell out of you. It's tough being submissive. I kinda like it, too." He gave her a toothy grin; his teeth were a little sharp.

Holy shit, but he was sexy as freaking sin.

"We're almost there." She eased off of him and dropped back down. He threw his head back and growled low and deep. The vibrations running through her.

"Just a little more." Her voice sounded strained as she eased back up and let herself drop. "I love your big cock."

"I know you do." He grinned. His skin was so taut. Desire shone in his eyes, which had lightened up. He helped her lift up and down. Up and down.

His breathing was labored and rasping. "You're going to struggle to walk after this."

She arched her back as he slid home. "Oh, good lord… oh!" she groaned. "I did it."

"Yes, you did. Now for the good part." He parted her shirt, groaning when he saw her breasts, and then leaned back on both hands. "Take me… I'm yours." He winked at her. "Yes, I'm talking about sex."

Angie would've laughed if not for the sensations inside her. She nodded once, which was all she could manage under the circumstances. Then she started moving, still up and down. Up and down. They both groaned loudly. Her eyes fluttered closed.

"Oh… oh, wow!" she whimpered.

"I feel good, don't I?" Cyclone was rotating his hips a little.

"Uhhh… Uhhhh… Oh!" She could only make silly noises.

"I'll take that as a yes," he growled. "Your titties are bouncing." He grabbed the back of her shirt and held it open. "I love that you're armed. Badass as fuck," he grunted, fucking her a little harder from below.

No one could talk dirty like this man.

"Do you like riding me?" he asked.

"Yes," she ground out.

"We have one problem here." His voice was strained. "A big one."

She made a noise that told him she was listening, then groaned.

"If you keep riding me like that, I'm going to come before you. Fuck, Ange… fuuuuck!" He gritted his teeth.

"Come! I… dare… you," she groaned again.

"Not a chance!" He shook his head. "This needs to be the best sex you've ever had."

She giggled between her panting.

"It does!" he added, face taut. "By the time I'm done with you, Angela, you won't be able to forget me… ever. You might even call my name regardless of who's on top of you." His jaw clenched, and a look of fury crossed his face.

"I have to forget you," she whispered. It would be for her own sanity. She stopped moving, even though she was desperate for more.

"Not a fuck!" He flipped her onto her back in a move that left her breathless. His cock slid in even deeper, making her gasp. As if on instinct, Angie hooked her legs around him, feeling his solid ass beneath her heels. His hips undulated; his breath was hot and heavy against her throat.

"Holy shit! I still might come before you."

His admission was sexy. Everything about this was sexy. He was killing her one stroke at a time.

He pushed her legs a little higher on himself, seating himself more firmly inside her. They both groaned.

"Fuck! Fuck! Fuck! Fuck!" Cyclone growled in quick succession. He sounded frustrated.

He pulled out, and, in one quick move, had her on her knees. He splayed his hands on her belly and yanked her up, entering her in one hard thrust. Cyclone snarled like an animal as his hips hit her ass, as his balls slapped against her.

Angie cried out as he entered her again.

Shit!

Shit!

Holy crap!

She could feel that he meant business. Everything started coiling and tightening, and all at once. She was groaning and panting, her mouth open wide. There wasn't enough oxygen. Had the air thinned? It sure felt like it.

Cyclone kept pummeling into her. "Fuuuuuck," he rasped. Even the way he said it made her want more. It made her skin feel tight. Her eyes grow wide. Her breasts were bouncing like mad. Pity she didn't have a workout bra on her now. She needed a new one.

Angie mewled. She pushed back against him with her ass. Her hands were flat on the ground. She was having to brace hard. Good thing she worked out.

"Say my name," he groaned, his finger finding her clit. He rubbed ever so softly.

She was getting close. "No!" *Holy shit!* She was about to come. "Too intimate," she added, her voice shrill.

"Bullshit! My cock deep inside you is intimate. Fucking say it."

"Bossy!" she pushed out, whimpering.

"You're so wet and so tight… losing my mind," he rasped. He groaned as he pulled out and then plunged back in.

His balls were slapping against her ass. His grunts were loud. His cock was hitting places that had her making crazy-sounding noises.

The finger on her clit rubbed that tiny bit harder as she felt him come inside her. Angie lost it. She definitely screamed something, probably his name because... old habits. *Dammit!*

Then her back was bowing, her eyes squeezing shut as the most exquisite rush hit her hard. It went on and on. Cyclone had stamina that was second to none. Even when he began easing off, his cock was still hard. Even when he stopped moving, it was still ramrod straight and throbbing inside her. He leaned over her, his face between her shoulder blades, his breath hot and rasping as he tried to catch his breath.

"A pussy doesn't get tighter than that. I fit perfectly inside you," he ground the words out.

"Firstly, that's a little rude, and secondly, you're actually a little big for me."

"Firstly, you love it when I'm rude, and secondly, snug is perfect. Thirdly..."

She had to bite back a smile.

"Bareback is fucking amazing," he said in that deep baritone of his. The one that sent shivers up and down her spine.

Angie pulled away from him. "We should get to work. We're officially about to be late." Wet warmth dripped down her inner thighs, making her wince. "And I probably need to shower now first."

"No showering."

"I'm sticky, and I'll reek of you."

"Exactly. My scent will tell every red-blooded male in this lair to back the fuck off, or I'll kill them. Better to send a clear signal than to have me kill someone, wouldn't you say?"

Warmth blossomed in her chest, which was bad, so bad.

"Um... I'm not yours, remember?"

"You're mine while you're on dragon soil. It's better if our males see it that way… or back to me killing someone." He gave a one-shouldered shrug, like it was no biggie.

"Mmmmmmm…" She smiled. "Death would be a step too far."

"Beating and maiming would be okay with you, then?" He grinned. "You're a female after my own heart." He touched a hand to his massive chest.

"I should say 'no' to your question, but… as it turns out, I'm a sicko." She smiled sweetly.

Cyclone growled. "You're making me hard again."

"You never got soft." She laughed. "We really need to go." She glanced at her watch, panicking when she saw the time. The lesson was starting in three minutes.

Crap!

"Here." He handed her some moss. "For your inner thighs."

Angie cleaned herself up as best she could. Then she pulled on her pants. Cyclone handed her boots to her, which she quickly donned as well.

He pulled his own pants back on, waiting for her. Then she rose to her feet, staggering a step or two.

Double crap!

Cyclone grabbed her arm, grinning. He winked at her. "You're welcome."

Angie rolled her eyes but didn't say anything. It was no use. He would know that she was lying if she tried to deny how good that had been. How, even now, her legs were shaking.

"I've got you," he said, picking her up. Instead of cradling her to his chest, he threw her over his shoulder like she was a sack of potatoes and started walking.

She laughed, even though it was better that he wasn't getting all romantic on her.

"I feel really bad for your mate one day if you carry her over the threshold like this." Angie was going to keep reminding him that woman wouldn't be her. If she was honest with herself, she needed reminding as well.

Cyclone stopped walking and carefully slid her back off his shoulder. She slowly slipped down his body until she was on her feet. Her chest against his. His hands on her hips. Her hands on his shoulders.

"What happened, Angie?" he asked. "You never said anything. You just left."

"Nothing happened. The relationship wasn't working, that's all." She prayed he would leave it at that.

"It was working just fine, and you know it. We were together for a year. That's a long time and a lot to throw away without talking first." His eyes shone with something that looked too much like pain for her liking.

"We hardly saw each other during that year, though, Cyclone. It sounds like a long time, but it really wasn't."

"I don't get it, that's all." He shook his head. "I feel like there's more to this. That you're not being completely open with me about it. We spoke about mating. About having a wedding. Do you remember?"

She swallowed thickly instead of answering because she did. Angie remembered altogether too well.

"You wanted sunflowers instead of roses. You said that depending on the season, you were either going to wear boots or wellingtons under your gown because heels weren't your thing."

"They still aren't."

"We spoke about serious things." He took a step

towards her. "Do you remember how many kids we said we would have?"

She shook her head, not wanting to lie. "I'd rather not talk about it."

"Well, tough shit! Four. We said we wanted four kids. Two boys and two girls. We're both only children, and so we wanted a big family. We didn't want an odd number of children, so we settled on four since six seemed too many."

"I remember," she whispered when his eyes stayed locked on hers, searching.

"Well, then? We spoke about forever, and then you were gone. I don't get it. From talking about marriage and kids to you up and leaving. Why didn't you tell me that the long-distance thing was getting to you?" He cupped her jaw. The hurt shone in his eyes. "I would've done anything for you. Anything to make you happy. I knew it was selfish of me to ask you to wait. I knew it! I just wish you would have told me. Given me a chance."

"It wasn't the long-distance thing…" she blurted out. "I mean, it wasn't *just* the long-distance relationship part that was a factor." She bit down on her bottom lip.

"You're lying again." He let her go, even taking a step away from her. "That last part wasn't true, which means that there *is* something else. Something you didn't tell me then. Something you're still not telling me now." He shook his head, raking his hand through his hair. "Are you saying that it wasn't me or something I did?"

Angie owed him this much. "It was me… okay. I'm flawed. I don't want to talk about it. What's done is done. It won't change anything, so what's the point in hashing it out?"

"What's the point?" He gave a humorless laugh.

"What's the…" He sighed. "All this time, you had me believing that I was to blame. That I was a selfish bastard. I beat myself up. Tore myself down. I've lived in misery thinking I let you slip through my fingers when, in reality, there was nothing I could have done to keep you."

There was no use denying it. Angie shook her head. She didn't trust her voice.

"Even if I'd left my job? Moved onto human territory? Fucking worn a pink tutu, it still wouldn't have helped? Is that what you are saying?" His eyes were blazing.

Angie shook her head again. "No," she whispered. "I'm sorry. I'm truly, truly sorry."

"You should have told me why. You owed me an explanation. You still do."

"I can't." She shook her head.

"Actually, you can!" He sounded pissed. There was a gruff edge to his voice. Cyclone used a tone he had never used on her.

This was for his own good, even if he didn't realize it.

"No. Sorry, but I can't say anything more on the subject. We need to get to work. We're late… very late," she added as she looked at her watch.

"I loved you. I would've done anything for you. Anything. You stomped on what we had and left without a backward glance. You didn't even leave a goddamn note. You still can't be honest with me. Looks like I might have dodged a bullet." He turned and walked away.

Angie had to grab hold of a nearby tree to keep her knees from buckling out from under her. Cyclone would have done anything for her, but at what cost? That was the question. That was why she had stayed silent then and why she would keep her mouth shut now. Even if it killed her.

CHAPTER 8

That evening…

IT HURT. HER CHEST STILL felt tight. Her eyes stung, and her throat felt clogged. That's how she'd felt in varying degrees the whole day. Cyclone hadn't come back to class. She hadn't seen him the whole day.

All she wanted to do was go and find him so that she could…

Could what? Then what? What would she tell him? Nothing.

This outcome was for the best. The sex had been a mistake. She'd said it after the first time they had done it, and she meant it. It was a mistake. Look at where it had gotten them. Both of them felt like utter shit. Both of them were hurt. Cyclone most of all, and it was her doing all over again.

If she'd known back then that Cyclone was going to beat himself up, she would've left a note. She would've made something up to make him hate her, and he could've moved on. At least one of them would have been in a position to move on. Well, that sorry situation had been rectified. Cyclone hated her now. He would hurt for a while, and then he would... carry on with his life.

God, but it hurt to even think about it. If she was honest with herself, as much as she'd been hoping Cyclone was going to be with someone else, she'd also hoped just as much that he would end up being her Cyclone.

Not yours, Angie!

Not anymore.

"Thank you," she told Equinox as they reached her apartment. There was a box standing outside her door. She frowned, taking a closer look. The label had her name on it. It looked like it had been shipped from New York. There was a priority stamp on the side.

"What is this?" she muttered.

"Did you order something?" Equinox asked.

She shook her head.

"Shall I carry it inside for you?" he asked.

Angie tested the weight of the box. It was medium-sized but not too heavy.

"That's okay. I got it." She opened her front door, picked up the box, and carried it inside. "Thanks again," she told Equinox before closing the door behind her using her foot. "What on earth?" she asked herself as she set the box down on the coffee table.

Angie grabbed a knife from the kitchen and went to

work opening the box. It had been taped closed. Once she was done, she put the knife on the table and pulled the panels open.

"What the…?" There was a mountain of workout gear filling the box. All Lycra and in various colors. She couldn't help but smile, even though she was dying inside.

This had to be from Cyclone. It was thoughtful and just like him. There was a large black box on top of the clothing. She opened the box and pulled out a huge, neon-yellow dildo. The thing was massive. There were several vibration settings. There was a card as well, which she opened. The note was typed.

Dear Angela,

Sorry I ruined your workout gear—even though it was worth it, and I'd do it again. I'm sure this will make up for it. The dildo is for when you go back home. I know you're going to miss me and my huge cock.

Yours,
Cyclone

P.S. The dildo glows in the dark. You're welcome!

She pushed out a laugh that sounded too much like a sob for her liking. Cyclone had obviously organized this last night or first thing this morning. Before she'd hurt him. Angie dropped the note into the box. She was trying hard not to cry. This was shitty, but it was for the best. She needed to stick to the plan, focus on work, and then leave.

There was a knock at the door.

For half a second, she thought it might be Cyclone. Maybe he was here to talk things out with her. Angie knew him, though. Not that they'd had any major fights during the year they were together, but there had been one or two misunderstandings. He was the first one to come to her to apologize if he had been to blame. If she was the one who caused the shit, then she had to go to him. A man had his pride, and Cyclone was no exception.

It wasn't him at the door.

She heard a giggle. *What in the world?* It was followed by another giggle. Definitely not Cyclone, then.

Then there was another knock.

"Angie," a woman said. It was a voice she recognized.
No!

She couldn't deal with this now. She wanted to take a shower and crawl into bed with a tub full of ice cream.

"Angie, let us in." More giggling.
Us?
Shit!
Please, no!

"Angie!" Louder this time. "We have wine." Another voice this time.
Wine?

That changed things. Maybe a glass of wine would do her good. Then she'd kick them out, shower, and jump in bed with a gallon of Rocky Road. Yes! Sounded like a solid plan.

Angie opened the door to five women. Five!
Oh, hell no!
They all beamed at her. Two of them waved at her.

One using just two fingers. Who did that? One was heavily pregnant, as in, "where-is-the-ambulance?" pregnant. They all giggled and seemed to talk at once as they poured into the small apartment.

Crap!

On second thoughts, she'd drink fast and chuck them out. Five women! She could barely cope with one.

"What the heck is this?" she whispered to Amy as she walked inside.

"Where are the glasses?" a curly-haired blonde asked before Amy could respond. She'd been the one to wave with two perfectly manicured fingers. "I'm Melina, by the way. It's my wedding in a couple of weeks."

"Don't mind her." Amy laughed. "She's been doing that for months."

"Over a year!" someone shouted from the other side of the room.

"I'm fine… totally fine." Melina flapped a hand. "You have to come," she said to Angie.

"I'll be long gone," Angie said. "Um… what are you all doing in my apartment?" She tried not to sound too bitchy and probably failed.

"I invited you this morning, remember?" Amy said. "I didn't want you to miss out, so we decided to pop in. I told the ladies you wouldn't mind."

What?

Before she could answer, the bubbly blonde went on, "Oh, but will you really be gone in a few weeks? I mean, really?" Again, there was no waiting for a response from Angie. "It's so good to meet you. I hear that you and Cyclone are together." Thankfully, she didn't wait for an answer as she walked straight into the open-plan kitchen and started rummaging through the cupboards. "That's so awesome," she threw out over her shoulder. "You two… together, I mean." She opened yet another cupboard.

"It's good to see you again," Amy said, smiling broadly. "I'll introduce you to the other ladies, and then I want to hear all about how it went this morning." She lifted her eyebrows. "I heard a couple of rumors," she said in a sing-song voice. "About how you were very late for class. How you had taken a shower—that didn't help, by the way."

"Here we go!" Melina shouted, holding up two wine glasses. "Now to find a corkscrew. I hope you like a good full-bodied red?"

"Sounds delicious!" one of the women shouted back. She had fiery red hair and was gorgeous.

"I'll take an orange juice," the pregnant lady yelled.

"I know *you* like a full-bodied red, Ash." The curly blonde laughed. "I was talking to Angie, you dimwit."

"Okay," Amy chuckled, tossing a strand of dark hair over her shoulder. "So, I'll introduce you to the dimwit first. Her name is—"

"Hey!" The redhead pretended to be upset but ended up laughing.

Amy giggled. "Her name is Ashlyn. She's mated to Avalanche. Then there's Riley, who is mated to Fog. Both of their mates are taking your class."

"Yes, I know them. Fog has an excellent aim, and Avalanche is a natural with the semi-automatic rifle. They were allowed to shoot today for the first time." Cyclone should have been there.

"It's good to meet you," Ashlyn said. "Avalanche says that you are badass."

"I try." Angie gave a shrug.

Ashlyn laughed like Angie had just said the funniest thing. She really wasn't good with people, least of all women. Why was that so funny?

"You seem really nice," Riley added.

"Don't forget about me," that same someone shouted from the other side of the room. It was the pregnant lady. She had the most striking eyes. A flawless beauty, even in her heavily pregnant state.

"That lovely lady over there is Azure. She's a she-dragon. One of the few at the lair. She's preggers with Ice's baby. He's her mate," Amy said.

"Hi." Angie forced a smile. She gave a little wave, mimicking the earlier behavior. Only she used her whole hand, because two fingers…? No! Just no.

Azure laughed. "You look afraid, which I completely understand. We're a lot to take in. Especially me, since yes, in answer to your question, I'm due any day now. Do you mind?" She put her feet up on the coffee table and leaned back, huffing out a breath. "That's so much better. This little one is taking after his father." She rubbed her belly. "He's big."

"Could be a she," Amy remarked.

"Doubtful. The healer reckons that the baby is more than likely a boy due to his size."

"It might be amniotic fluid," Angie said. All the eyes in the room turned to her. "Not that I know much about these things, because I don't. It's just that the wife of one of my teammates was pregnant. She was huge as well." *Crap!* She looked at Azure. "No offense." *Shit!* She was really bad at this. Women took offense to things easily.

The pregnant lady smiled. "None taken. I *am* huge. I've been calling myself a whale shifter of late."

Angie smiled because it was kind of funny.

"Go on with the story," Azure told her.

"It's not much of a story. Ivan—that's his name—showed us pictures of his heavily pregnant wife. They FaceTimed almost every day. Anyway, the baby was tiny when he was born. Doctors said that she just had excessive amniotic fluid." She shrugged. "Maybe that's the case with you. I do need to add that I'm not qualified in the least to give advice on this subject since I know nothing about it."

True story. Pregnancy and babies were not her thing.

"That's interesting." Azure rubbed on her belly some more. "I'm glad you shared the story. I have no idea what's going on in there." She looked down at her belly. "Ultrasound doesn't work on us."

"That's interesting," Angie remarked. "Not that I know much about ultrasound, either. Another guy at work showed us his baby's sonogram. His wife was three or four months along. I didn't know what I was looking at." She shook her head. "Elliot had to point out the body parts. Turned out it was a boy. Clear as day, once you knew what you were looking at."

All the women laughed.

Why?

"I wish I could see inside myself. I wish I could see my little one," Azure said, sounding whimsical.

"It won't be long before we know for sure." Melina held out a glass of wine to Angie. It was pretty darned full. She took it, anyway, taking a big gulp. Angie had a feeling she was going to need it.

"You should know in a couple of days," Riley added.

"Don't jinx me," Azure said. "Pregnancies can

sometimes go on past their due date. I really can't go for much longer. I'll burst if I get much bigger. Then there's the 'having to push him out' problem I face." She groaned. "I'm scared… so, so, so scared."

"Oh, hon'…" Melina went and knelt next to her friend. "You'll do great. I don't know anyone who's stronger than you."

"Thank you, Mel." They hugged tightly. Melina had to work to get her arms around Azure's belly.

"You'll be fine," Angie said. "I'm going to assume you have all the facilities you need here? A hospital, or clinic, at the very least?"

"Yes." Azure nodded. "We have state-of-the-art facilities, and both dragon healers and human doctors."

"I once helped a woman give birth in the middle of nowhere. In the dirt, with bombs going off around us. The child came to this world to the sound of gunfire and dying screams. Both mom and baby made it through just fine," she said to Azure.

"Badass," Ashlyn said with wide eyes.

"Not really," Angie said. "It's a case of doing what you have to do with what you have to do it with. We're well trained to deal with anything that comes our way… even childbirth."

"Now that's totally badass," Riley agreed.

Why? Angie didn't get it. All the women were looking at her like she had lit the sun.

"Cheers." Amy held up her glass.

"What are we toasting to?" Angie asked. It had better not be to her.

"To friendship." Everyone held up their glass and said cheers, and then everyone drank, including her. Azure had her orange juice, and the wine was actually pretty good.

Amy turned to her and clinked glasses. "To new friendships." She smiled. "Melina and Azure are besties." Amy looked over at Riley and Ashlyn. "Riles and Ash are also besties. They've known each other all their lives. I'm really hoping we can be friends, too."

Besties? Um… wasn't going to happen.

"I'm leaving in just over a week," Angie said. "Otherwise, I'm sure we would have been friends." Amy seemed pretty nice.

"What's that about leaving?" Melina asked, taking a sip of her wine.

"I'm here for two weeks to give arms training. I was just saying that I'll be going soon. We can stay in touch," Angie said to Amy, knowing it probably wouldn't happen. She didn't want to be unkind to the other woman. Amy seemed nice enough, but facts were facts. Perhaps they could have been friends if things had been different.

"I thought that you and Cyclone were together, though?" Melina said. "I heard that you guys were old flames who reconnected."

"Did you tell everyone?" Angie narrowed her eyes on Amy, who put her hands up.

"I didn't tell anyone anything. I told you, keeping secrets around shifters is almost impossible."

"We were together once… years ago. It's over now. The end. Can we please not talk about it anymore?" She took another sip of her wine.

"You guys had sex, though," Melina said.

"Twice," Azure said from the sofa.

Angie covered her face with a hand and sighed. "I'm a private person. Can't people pretend not to know my business?"

"No!" all the women said in unison.

"Look, sex and a relationship are *not* intertwined," Angie added. "We had sex *twice,* but that doesn't mean that we're getting back together."

"Vortex said that Cyclone was pretty cut up today," Amy said. "That's why I suggested we come and see you. I figured something had happened between the two of you."

"You smell sad," Azure told Angie. "I think you might be cut up as well. That's more than just sex."

"Back to the part where I want my privacy respected. Where I don't want to talk about this!" Angie blurted. *Sheesh!* This was too much.

"Yeah… there isn't any privacy in the lair, and talking helps," Melina said.

Angie took a huge swig of the wine. Lord, give her strength! "Ahhhh… there's nothing much to talk about. I hurt Cyclone really badly. He's upset with me. The end!" she tried to end the conversation.

"And angry with you," Amy said. "Vortex mentioned a fair bit of anger, as well as being hurt. He was extra salty, which is saying something since we are talking about Cyclone here."

"Thanks. That's good to know," she mumbled. Not that she was going to be able to do much about it. "And don't call Cyclone salty. He's one of the nicest people I know. I hurt him. He's upset. I am sad about the whole thing. I wish I could take it back, but it's better this way."

"Why is it better?" Melina asked.

"Surely you're going to go and see him?" Amy asked. "To straighten things out?"

"No." She shook her head. "I'm leaving at the end of next week, so there's no point."

"You plan on leaving things unfinished?" Amy asked, eyes wide.

"We were finished years ago," Angie said. "We're still finished now. There's nothing to say."

"You're getting all of this unsolicited advice, and for that, I'm sorry," Melina said, not looking sorry at all. "Doesn't mean I'm going to keep quiet, though, because it doesn't look finished from where we're standing."

"Not even close," Ashlyn added.

"You should talk to him," Amy said. "He cares a lot for you. I've never seen Cyclone like this."

Angie was on the verge of kicking them all out. In fact, she was pulling in a breath and getting ready to do just that when Amy said, "Change of subject!" in a rather loud voice. "Vortex and I are going ring-shopping in a couple of weeks. I have to go home to wrap things up. To pack. That kind of thing, and we're making a trip out of it." She turned to Melina and gave a quick wink. "And don't worry, it's the week before your wedding. We wouldn't miss the big day."

"That's great… on both counts," Melina said. "Any idea of what kind of a ring you want?"

"Not at all. I mean, do I go straight diamond? Maybe a ruby or emerald in a diamond setting would work. I need to choose my stones and then go to a jeweler to do my setting."

Riley leaned forward. "Ooooooh! I think a solitaire would be perfect for you. Maybe in a teardrop shape."

Just like that, the pressure was off of her. Angie felt like she could breathe again. Well, sort of. Friends sure got into each other's business. Angie didn't like it at all. And yet, she wasn't feeling quite as miserable as she had been earlier. There were pros and cons to this friendship thing. It looked like Amy had her back, changing the subject like that, which was something she rated highly.

Unfortunately, their advice stank. It wasn't advice Angie actually planned on taking because, although these women meant well, they didn't have all the facts. It would do neither of them any good if Angie came clean to Cyclone. In fact, it would make things worse.

CHAPTER 9

H E'D ALMOST BITTEN HER.
Holy fuck!

Cyclone knew he was in deep, but he didn't know quite how fucked he was until that very moment. His mouth was near Angie's neck while he was rutting her. He'd been so damned close to sinking his teeth into her. No holds barred. He wanted to make her his. That's why he'd turned her onto her knees instead and finished like that with his eyes glowing and his teeth sharp, and a grimace on his face that would rival most MMA fighters in battle. At least he'd been away from her neck.

Thank fuck he'd held back. Mating behavior would only fuck with his head even more. Fuck with his dragon a whole hell of a lot.

Then she'd dropped the bomb, and he'd been even more grateful for holding back.

Their breakup had never been his fault. He'd carried that with him for years. For fucking years, he'd blamed himself. He'd felt like a selfish bastard, and it wasn't him after all. There was something else. It was something big. Something that had torn a hole right through them, and she didn't have the decency to tell him then. Even more infuriatingly, she wouldn't tell him now. It irritated the fuck out of him. Cyclone was all bristling energy as he landed on his balcony and shifted back into his human form.

Normally, being in his scales made him baser in his thoughts and feelings. It gave him breathing room to just be. Not tonight. He'd flown hard and thought harder. He'd fatigued quicker than normal. Probably on account of pushing himself so hard. And yet, he couldn't switch his brain off. He couldn't stop his thoughts from going to her. Always to her.

Fuck!

Nothing was helping. Cyclone growled as he stepped under the shower, letting the warm water cascade over him. His muscles stayed tense. All he wanted to do was to go to her. Then what? It wasn't like Angie was going to tell him anything. She'd kept him in the dark for years now. *Fucking years.* What could it be? What was so bad that they couldn't be together? It wasn't another male. It wasn't that there was no attraction between them. That part of the equation was alive and well. He'd bet good money that she still had feelings for him, too.

What then?

Once he finished showering, he stepped out of the

stall and toweled down, getting the worst of the wet off of him. Cyclone felt tired, exhausted even, but he also felt keyed up, and in a big way.

Perhaps he should have listened to Avalanche when the male tried to teach him meditation this morning. He needed something to calm himself the fuck down, or he'd never sleep tonight. Hell, he might not sleep again this week.

Tea!

Yes!

He'd bought some a few months ago when all of the shit with the cave dwellers had started. There had been no sleeping for him then, either. It was always like this with him. Whenever he was stressed, sleep eluded him. Cyclone opened the cupboard to the right, grabbing the half-finished chamomile tea.

"Fucking pussy," he grunted to himself. This was what his life had become. A fucking shitshow of epic proportions.

Chamomile tea and meditation.

Once the kettle boiled, Cyclone seeped the herbal brew, making it strong. Then he took himself to bed, where he sipped slowly.

He checked his phone. There was a message from Gust.

> I think I ate something bad. I can't stop vomiting. I might not make it in tomorrow.

Poor schmuck. Cyclone sent a thumbs-up. At least he wasn't the only pussy in the lair. He set his alarm, even though it wasn't necessary since he woke up at five every morning like clockwork. Then he put his phone on silent and turned his sidelight off.

Cyclone was asleep in less than five minutes.

The next morning…

Her alarm was going off.

Angie felt for her phone on the side table and frowned. It wasn't her alarm. She had five missed calls from a number she didn't recognize, all within the last few minutes.

Crap!

She touched her hand to her head and squeezed her eyes shut for a moment. Her head thudded with the start of a dull headache. That would serve her right for drinking wine on a work night. She'd ended up having two glasses. Two *big* glasses, too. The list of regrets was growing longer.

The ringing continued. Angie sat up in her bed. What the heck was making the noise?

Following the sound, she turned backward. Looking at the wall behind her. There was a phone mounted there. One she hadn't noticed before. It was ringing… loudly.

She slid out of bed, arriving at the phone just as the ringing stopped.

"Typical!" she mumbled, rubbing her face. She would grab some painkillers, and then she'd call that number back since it seemed to be urgent.

If this was a sign of her day ahead, she was in big trouble.

Angie was halfway to the kitchen when the phone started ringing again.

"Argh!" The painkillers would have to wait. She turned and headed back. Yep, it had to be something important.

Then again, what was so crucial at five to five in the morning?

"Yes?" she snapped into the receiver.

"Angie." It was a female voice she recognized but couldn't quite place on account of it being so freaking early and her still having brain fog and a headache.

"Yes. Don't you have a clock?" She couldn't help being snippy as she suddenly realized who the person was. If her new BFF wanted to go for an early morning jog or something along those lines, Angie was going to have kittens. An entire litter of the things.

"It's Amy. I'm sorry to call you so early. I think we're under attack."

"What?" For a moment, Angie was sure she had heard wrong. "What makes you think that?" The other woman had probably had a bad dream or something.

"I'm serious. I think we're under— Wait a sec… Are you sure you're okay, babe?" Amy's voice was softer, like she'd removed the phone from her ear. There was a murmur as someone male spoke in the background. Angie couldn't make out what he said. Amy continued, "Sorry about that. My fiancé isn't feeling well. Maybe it's something you ate, Vortex? Can't be, though, since we had the same thing for dinner." She sounded confused.

Again, there was a response Angie couldn't hear.

"What makes you think we're under attack? And if we *are* under attack, time is of the essence here. You need to tell me what the heck is going on."

"Yes, you're right!" Amy breathed out hard. "Shit! Of course. I got an alarm about ten minutes ago that the north-eastern Cave-3 forest camera had been activated. It happens sometimes. It's mostly a deer, or a—"

"Yes! Yes!" Angie didn't mean to be a bitch about this, but hell.

"It was… them… the goblins." Angie could hear genuine fear in the other woman's voice. "Lots of them," Amy continued. "A group streamed past."

"I thought groups of goblins have been seen regularly. That although it's a big deal, it's not truly a big deal. Why is this any different?"

"Smaller bands were seen on the regular. Then the goblin queen made an example and had the last vigilante group of goblins put to death. There have been no goblins sighted for weeks."

"So, they started up again. Inform security—"

"That's just it. Security should have informed me. They didn't, hence the backup alarm going off on my phone. I tried calling the control room, and there was no answer. No, babe!" the infuriating woman began talking to her boyfriend again. "You're not going. You're sick. It's probably a false alarm or something. I'll go. Angie is a decorated war veteran; she says she'll go with me… to the control room, please. I can be at your place in five minutes," and suddenly Amy was talking to her.

"Um… yes… sure."

"Great!" Amy still sounded freaked out. "Five minutes." And the line went dead.

Angie headed straight for the kitchen. Her purse was on the counter. She reached in and snagged a couple of painkillers, drinking straight out of the faucet to swallow them down.

Then she pulled on some clothes, which included jeans and a long-sleeve t-shirt. She was almost done brushing her teeth when a knock sounded at the door.

"Coming," she shouted.

Angie rinsed her mouth, pulled her hair into a messy bun on the top of her head, and went to the door, opening it.

Amy was pale, with wide eyes. "There's something wrong. I can feel it."

"Let's go to the control room. There has to be a reasonable explanation for all of this." Angie was sure that this would be the case.

They walked through the hallways at almost a jog speed.

"It's too quiet," Amy said, gnawing on her bottom lip.

"It's just past five in the morning," Angie countered, even though she was getting a strange feeling.

"It doesn't matter. The lair operates twenty-four hours a day in shifts. It's normally quiet in the morning, but not like this…" She shook her head. "This is dead."

Angie didn't say anything. Amy was already freaked out enough for the both of them.

"Those goblins are terrifying. They're huge, and… the reason they're doing what they're doing is for human women. They want to take us because apparently, we have open holes." She got this disgusted look.

"Open what?" Angie slowed for a step or two before picking up the pace again.

"Goblin women look just like the men, including *down there*."

Angie frowned. "That can't be right. How does that even work?"

"The females are bigger and stronger than the males. They rule over the male goblins and with an iron fist, from what I've heard. The way it works…" she was breathing quite heavily, "is that the females are the ones who are the aggressors in bed. They have a working penis that can retract into relatively normal female anatomy but only if they want to procreate or if they feel like it, which isn't very often."

Angie didn't like where this was going.

"They know that the dragons have taken females to mate with. They know that there are humans here. They know that we are weak, and…" Angie swallowed thickly; her eyes were trained ahead.

"They know we have open holes. That's disgusting."

"It's—" Amy's phone beeped with an incoming message, and she checked it immediately. "Shit!"

"What?"

"Vortex said that five of his team members have called in sick with vomiting and diarrhea. This is bad."

"I don't like it," Angie said. Her gut felt hollow.

"That door leads to the control room," Amy said. A CCTV camera blinked above them. The other woman keyed a code into the pad next to the door, which turned green. The door clicked open. Amy gasped, stopping dead.

"No! Oh no!" She ran into the room.

CHAPTER 10

THE ALARM BLARED.

It was loud, obnoxious, and hurt his head instantly.

Cyclone sat up in his bed. Something was wrong! Something— He leaped up. Although, "leaped" wasn't quite the right word since he was moving too slowly to use that verb. More like *staggered* out of bed. He staggered out of bed, and staggered to the bathroom, trying hard not to gag.

Then he threw himself over the toilet bowl and heaved a few times before last night's dinner made a big appearance in the form of projectile vomit. Even after his stomach had been emptied, he still continued to dry-heave, eventually throwing up bile.

Fun times!

All the while, his alarm continued to blare in the background, adding to his already throbbing headache.

Fuck!

Something was not right! It wasn't just his stomach, or how weak he felt, or the nausea that still rolled through him. It wasn't the message Gust had sent him last night, complaining of being ill. This was no coincidence! There was a feeling he had in his gut.

Fuck!

Still heaving, he forced himself to his feet, staggering to the basin so that he could wash his mouth out. Cyclone stopped, staring at his reflection in the mirror.

Double fuck!

He looked like utter shit. His skin was flushed. There were welts on his right cheek and around his hairline. There were more on his chest and back. Nausea, vomiting, weakness, his body felt sore, the welts.

Cyclone looked down at the faucet and backed away. He went to his refrigerator and grabbed a bottle of half-finished orange juice he'd opened a couple of days ago. He used that to rinse out his mouth. This was followed by more gagging. Once the nausea and dizziness eased enough for him to move, he walked back to his bed, sitting heavily. *Shit!* More dizziness had him squeezing his eyes shut for a second before he silenced the blaring cellphone alarm. He had numerous messages from males on his team. Two had come after Gust's message last night. There were a couple more that had just come in, including one from Vortex.

Call me as soon as you read this.

Cyclone didn't like what his gut was telling him.

"I'm sick," Vortex said as soon as he answered. His voice sounded weak.

"Me too," Cyclone croaked. His throat hurt.

"Amy got an alarm."

"They're coming!" Cyclone said.

"Yep, they're coming. It was a large group of goblins north… ahh… north-east at Cave-3." The male was breathing heavily. "I had three rounds of desensitization, and I'm fucked."

Cyclone growled. "I only had two. I'm beyond fucked." He growled even louder. It was partially because of another bout of nausea that rolled through him, and partly because of the goblins. "I think they put silver in our water supply. I feel… I feel… like shit," he repeated. "This is seriously bad."

"Fuck!" Vortex cussed. "Bastards. More of my males are sick, so I think you might be right. I have red skin… I showered last night."

"Same here. My skin is red with welts. I also took a shower last night. This feels like silver. I feel like fucking death." All he wanted to do was to lie back in his bed. To sleep this off. But he couldn't.

The goblins were coming.

"I had extensive desensitization, and I feel weak as a day-old fucking lamb," said Vortex. Most of the males had only had one round of desensitization. They would be absolutely fucked right now. Incapacitated.

"We need to spread the word about the water," Cyclone said.

"Not just in the taps. It could be in the food. In the bottled water."

"Anything delivered within the last few days should be considered contaminated," Cyclone added.

"Exactly!" Vortex growled.

"Fuck! I'll broadcast this on the intercom system." He'd go via Angie's apartment. If he didn't see his female, he wouldn't be able to function.

"I'll… Fuuuuck… my head…" Vortex grunted. "We need to close the rear entrances to the cave. Have all individuals still capable of fighting meet at the shooting range. Your female can give all of us a quick lesson. We'll be down on our numbers, which means that everyone will need to be armed against these fuckers."

"I'll fetch her," Cyclone said.

"No need. She's with Amy. They went to check on the males in the security room. After you make the announcement, you can head to the shooting range. That's where they'll go. We can get a better idea of what we're up against."

"I have a bad feeling."

"Me, too. I never saw this coming," Vortex said.

Chemical warfare. That's what this was.

"Cowards!" Cyclone spat. He was already moving. It took everything in him to put one foot in front of the other with any purpose. They were in deep trouble, he thought to himself as he felt the sweat pouring off him, and he had only just reached the hallway.

CHAPTER 11

THE TWO SHIFTERS WERE SLUMPED over the desk. The place stank of vomit and excrement. For a second, Angie was sure that the men were dead. Then one moaned. That was it, the tiniest noise.

The other guy looked worse. His chest was barely moving. His face looked puffed up and swollen. As did his hands. His fingers looked blistered and red, like he had been burned.

"What the hell?" Angie muttered. "This looks like they've been exposed to something they're allergic to."

"Silver," Amy said. "It can only be silver. It would explain why the dragons are sick. It's not just these two. Vortex, too. And the males from his team who messaged him to say they were sick." She looked up at the screens and made a little sobbing noise.

Angie did the same, and what she saw chilled her to

her bones. Goblins. A whole band of the things. There had to be at least a hundred.

"Charlie Foxtrot!" she whispered.

"Charlie what now?" Amy asked.

"It's military slang for cluster fuck."

"You can say that again. It's Charlie Foxtrot of note. A hundred goblins are actually not that many," Amy said. "The goblin queen might not even notice that they're gone until it's too late. I suspect that most of the dragon shifters will be incapacitated." She looked down at the two slumped before them, covered in their own excrement. "We're in trouble here. We'll have a handful of sick dragons. Maybe one or two who didn't ingest or bathe in whatever has made everyone sick. There won't be anyone to fight them off. They planned this. Oh, my god! How did this happen?" Amy scrubbed a hand over her face. She looked like she was on the verge of tears.

"They've spent months planning this. The silver could be in the air, the food, or the water… or all of the above. Classic chemical warfare."

"It's definitely silver. The only people who won't be affected are a handful of us humans. There are only thirty-two of us. Less, when you take into account the women who are pregnant. We can't fight them. We're sitting ducks."

"How long do we have before they get here?" Angie asked, looking up at the marching goblins. They were an ugly bunch. They looked like they had been made for war.

"We have less than an hour before they get here." Amy pulled a Perspex cover open and pushed down on a green button. An alarm sounded, and the button went from green to red. She did the same with a second button. "Thank god we installed access control to the two rear entrances, or there would have been no hope for us. We may as well have given up." Her eyes were wide.

"Don't talk like that."

"I know what they are capable of. Trust me when I tell you that they are much bigger in real life." Her eyes were wide, and her chest was heaving. Amy pushed a few keys on her phone. "Thank god you answered," she said, her voice shrill. "The goblins are coming. There are at least a hundred of them. I sealed the two rear exits." She listened for a moment. "Okay." She listened again. "Understood. We'll head over there." Amy listened again. "Be careful! I love you."

Her fiancé said something back, and she ended the call.

"Vortex is going to make sure that the back of the lair is secure. That side of the mountain is a fairly easy climb. The goblins would have easy access. Once he's done, he'll meet us at the shooting range in the south wing. Cyclone is on his way there now."

Angie pushed out a breath she hadn't even known she was holding and put a hand to her chest since her heart was racing.

"I'm glad he's okay. I take it he's okay?" Angie asked.

"Sick but mobile. As an Overlord, Cyclone has had the desensitizing and probably more than once. He's on his way to—"

"Attention, Air dragons. This is not a drill. I repeat, this is not a drill." It was Cyclone talking over the loudspeaker. She'd recognize his deep baritone anywhere. They walked outside the control room to hear better. It felt good to get some fresh air. "Dragons, we have been poisoned. Do not drink the water out of the taps. It has been contaminated." He must know something more than they did. "All cooked food should be seen as poisoned. Any products delivered within the last three days should not be consumed. I repeat, our water is contaminated with silver. If you are sick, it is silver poisoning. Those of you who are able to do so should make your way to the newly built south wing of the lair. If you are able to get there on your own steam, you are deemed sufficiently fit, even if you are very sick. The goblins are coming. I repeat, a horde of goblins is making their way here now. This is not a drill! War is upon us. In less than an hour, they will attempt to make an ascent of the cliff face to gain access to our lair. We have to stop them. All humans, make your way to the south wing. Those of us who can stand on two feet need to stop them. I repeat, if the goblins gain access to our lair, we are fucked!" He ended the broadcast on that note.

"He doesn't mince his words," Amy said. Her bottom lip trembled.

"Cyclone is right."

"I know." She sniffed. Angie could see that the other woman was trying hard to hold it together.

"Let's go," Angie said. "The gun safe is in the south wing. The plan must be to arm all abled-bodied individuals and then to blow those pricks to hell and gone. They think we're a bunch of weak women and sick dragons. I say fuck them. We'll show them!"

"I can't shoot. I've never fired a gun." Amy's eyes were wide.

"I'll teach you the basics."

"They're going to reach us in less than an hour. How can we learn—?"

"That's more than enough time to learn how to shoot a gun. I was informed of your incident with that goblin at the mines. I was told how brave you were. You can do it again. Think about what will happen should they make it up here."

A tear tracked down Amy's cheek. She wiped it away quickly.

"Think about what that fucker wanted to do to you," Angie went on.

"This isn't helping," Amy said. Another tear ran down her cheek.

"We all get scared. I get scared. I'm afraid right now." It was true. Angie's gut churned, but she pushed down her fears.

"You don't look afraid."

"I've learned how to hide it. How to use it, even. It's what we do with the fear that counts. Use it to pull up the rage. Hold on to that. Let it fuel you. We can do this. Thirty-two armed women can easily take out a hundred goblins." It wouldn't just be human women; there would be a couple of dragons as well. Surely some of them would be unaffected?

"Do you think so?" There was a touch of hope in Amy's voice.

Angie tilted her chin up. "I do." She touched the side of Amy's arm. "Let's get to the south wing."

CHAPTER 12

"**F**UCK!" CYCLONE GROWLED AND GRABBED the wall for support. He was out of breath and wheezing slightly. His chest felt tight. Sweat continued to pour off him. He swiped the back of his forearm across his forehead as he looked down at the guards who had been positioned at the door to the royal chamber. Just like every other dragon he had passed along the way, they were both on the floor, lying in their own vomit.

One was out cold. The other opened his eyes, making a god-awful groaning noise. His face was a bright red.

"Overlord," he pushed out. "Help."

Cyclone wasn't sure if the male was asking for help for himself or for the royals.

"You've been poisoned," he told the male. "Do not consume the water from the faucets or any recently prepared food. It's more than likely contaminated. We'll get help to you soon," he reassured the male, unsure of how true it was. They might be overrun by goblins soon.

The male nodded once and then passed out cold.

Cyclone banged on the door to the chamber using his fist. He banged a second time, then entered.

Thunder was holding onto the jamb. His king's skin was badly blistered. The male looked like he might pass out at any second.

"You need to lie back down." The queen was gently tugging on his arm. "Oh!" Her eyes widened when she saw Cyclone. "We heard your broadcast."

"Yes, it's silver. You should go back to bed, Sire."

Thunder shook his head, swallowing thickly. Beneath the welts, he'd taken on a sickly gray coloring.

"I need to get word to the rest of the lairs," he choked out.

"I already tried to contact them, but all I get is a busy signal," Cyclone said. It was the first thing he'd done after talking to Vortex.

"Fuck!" Thunder growled. "Are they also under attack?"

"I'm sorry, Sire, but we have no way of knowing." He shook his head.

"Are the goblins really less than an hour out? Surely that was an exaggeration," Thunder asked; his bloodshot eyes were clouded with pain.

"It's not an exaggeration, Sire," Cyclone said.

The queen gasped, clasping a hand over her mouth.

"It'll be alright, love," Thunder assured his mate.

"A horde at least a hundred-strong are approaching from the north-eastern side. They're marching for our lair as we speak," said Cyclone.

The king stood tall for a moment, taking a step towards Cyclone before falling to one knee.

"My phone. We must send word to the goblin queen," he croaked, reaching his hand forward.

That made sense. It wasn't something Cyclone had thought of. If the goblin queen had orchestrated this, she would know the horde was on their way. If not, and this was a group of her vigilante males, she would more than likely send help. She'd dealt with the last group harshly.

The queen ran back into the bedroom, returning with a cellphone.

"How many of the Air dragons are down?" Thunder asked.

"I'm not sure. It doesn't look good, Sire." He briefly told Thunder of their very rough plan. "We are at an advantage due to being above the goblins. We'll blow them away. Make them eat silver in bullet form." His lips curled away from his teeth as he snarled. "Fuckers will be sorry they messed with us."

"You look like shit, Cyclone," Thunder said, groaning. His king grabbed his middle, looking like he might throw up.

"With all due respect, you're one to talk, Sire. I'm not as bad as I look." It wasn't true, but he wasn't going to take this lying down. If he went down, he would go down fighting.

"I feel worse than I look. Here goes nothing…" Thunder dialed out. "Fuck!" he choked out. "It's a busy signal."

"I suspect that our external lines have been cut. That, and that the cellphone towers are down. We're on our own," Cyclone said. "Vortex and I will take care of it."

There would be a handful of males still standing. He only prayed that it would be enough to keep those bastards at bay.

"Thank fuck," Storm growled from the doorway. He swayed, grabbing the doorjamb in much the same way the king had done. His mate and children stood wide-eyed in the hall behind him. "Are you able to walk?" he asked Thunder. "Tammy, you need to get the children."

Thunder looked up at him.

Cyclone offered the male a hand, pulling him to his feet. His legs were shaky.

"Will you make it to the bunker?" It was essentially a saferoom on steroids. There were sufficient supplies to last a month. It was fully kitted out. It was also very small. It would be cramped with just the royals inside it. There were plans to make it bigger and to add an escape tunnel. Right now, Cyclone wished they had put that at the top of the list.

"Yes." Thunder nodded once. "You need to secure the lair. Keep the humans safe." He was having trouble talking.

"You need to get to the bunker, Sire. My prince." He looked to Storm.

"We will be fine." Storm grit his teeth. "I wish I could help you. That some of the human females—"

"We need to follow protocol. All royals need to lock themselves in the bunker. I will handle the goblins. You don't have long. Please hurry!" He added extra growl to his voice, striding from the chamber. Then he headed down the hallway, falling against the wall to catch his breath once he was out of view of the royals.

Fuck!

They were in real trouble.

CHAPTER 13

THEY WALKED QUICKLY, FINDING TWO unconscious dragon shifters along the way. Otherwise, the lair was quiet. They arrived at the south wing and headed for the shooting range.

"Melina!" Amy shouted, running over to the blonde, whose hair was a mass of messy curls. The one side was flat against her head. She wore jeans and a sweater that had clearly been thrown on in a rush because the sweater was inside out.

"I can't believe this is happening." Amy hugged the other woman, who hugged her back.

"They're really coming." Melina sounded like she was on the verge of tears.

Amy nodded against her. It was like she couldn't trust her own voice.

"I can't believe it. Freeze is sick." Melina broke down into tears. "I didn't want to leave him."

"I'm sorry," Amy said. "I'm glad you came. There seem to be only a few of us."

The other woman was right. It was too quiet. The shooting range was only big enough to hold a relatively small group of people, and there was no one outside.

"Let's go in," Angie said, gesturing to the entrance of the shooting range. "We can't wait too much longer. We'll need to start soon."

Amy nodded.

They started walking. "When I said goodbye to Freeze, I felt like it might be the last time I ever saw him." Melina broke down again, tears streaming down her cheeks, even though it looked like she was trying to hold them back.

"Don't talk like that!" Angie warned. "We have a whole arsenal of weapons."

"I can't shoot." Melina's throat worked, and another tear tracked down her wet cheek. "I've never even held a gun."

"That doesn't matter, because I will teach you everything you need to know. You'll do just fine. Please join the others, and no more negative talk. It's up to us to protect this lair. Talk like that will cause panic, which isn't beneficial at all," she told Melina.

"Yes, but—" Melina started, getting on Angie's last nerve.

"Listen carefully; do exactly what I tell you, and you'll get to walk down the aisle in a couple of weeks. Amy, you said you were going to get yourself an engagement ring. Listen to me, and you will get the chance," Angie said, trying hard to sound like she meant every word.

"Oh, my god." Melina clapped a hand over her mouth. "Is this it?" She looked from Angie to the small band of people waiting and then back at Angie. "There is only a handful of us. Where's everyone else?"

"More will join us shortly. Vortex is on his way to make another announcement to the lair. Cyclone will be here soon as well." Angie glanced at her watch. They had roughly half an hour left before the goblins arrived. Time was slipping away fast.

"Still," Melina sniffed, "there are only three dragon shifters. Two of them look very sick."

"Five, including the other two," Amy corrected. "Heat is one hundred percent fine. He drank soda and ate day-old pizza for dinner. He didn't shower, so he wasn't affected. The others are sick but functional."

"Five!" Melina scrubbed a hand over her face. "Holy shit! That's it? Out of the whole lair. What—"

"Don't say it if it's negative," Angie warned.

"I'm sorry. I'm normally upbeat. It's just that everyone is sick. Azure too. I'm worried about her. Ice is unconscious. She's all alone and heavily pregnant. Thankfully, she had desensitizing treatments due to being pregnant, so she's not too bad and hanging in there. I can't even go to her." She squeezed her eyes shut, but a few more tears escaped.

"No, you can't, but you can fight for her and her unborn child," Angie said. "We need to focus on the things we can manifest instead of the things that we can't."

"Yes, I can do that." Melina nodded, as if trying to convince herself.

"Mel!" It was the redhead, Riley. "You made it. How's Freeze?" They hugged.

"Not great!" Melina said as she pulled away. Her lip wobbled, but she didn't cry again. "He was completely out of it, with burns all over his skin. I feel bad leaving him."

"Avalanche isn't great, but at least he's here." Riley glanced over at her mate. They exchanged a look. The poor guy was covered in welts. He looked like his face was slightly puffy. His eyes were bloodshot. The big shifter turned his gaze to her and nodded once.

It had to be costing him to be here. She nodded back. Hopefully, more shifters would recover enough to help out.

The speaker system crackled. "All able-bodied individuals, please make your way to the southern wing," Vortex said over the loudspeaker. "We need you. The goblins will be here soon. This is not a drill. Human females with young, we urge you to pick one or two females to oversee the children and for the rest of you to join us. We need hands. This is urgent!"

"We can't expect mothers to abandon their children," one of the women said. It was someone Angie didn't recognize.

"The best way to protect their children would be to fight," Angie said. So far, there were only six human women, including herself, out of the thirty-odd who were staying at the lair. They needed more.

"You're clearly not a mother." The woman looked upset. She waved a hand. "I'm sorry. That's unfair. I lost my daughter three years ago. I know all about motherly instincts. If she'd still been alive, I wouldn't leave my daughter for anything."

"I take it that most of the human women will have

children?" Angie directed her question at Amy, who nodded.

"Yep, that's correct. We're the newbies. Everyone else is pregnant, or they have babies or young children, or all of the above."

Angie held back a curse. She'd been hoping for a bigger turn-out. She was sure to school her reaction. In situations like this, the individuals looked to the leaders for support.

"You don't look worried, which worries me," Amy said.

Clever lady! She didn't miss much.

"How do you figure?" Angie lifted her brows. "You have nothing to worry about. We're the ones who are armed to the teeth. I'll be back in a second."

Angie keyed her code into the pad next to the door that led into the housing facility for the weapons. The door slid open. She walked inside and grabbed a 9mm Ruger off the wall. There were another fifty of its kind all lined up. She removed the magazine and then checked that the chamber was empty. It was. Angie pocketed the magazine and turned, walking straight into a wall of muscle.

"Cyclone," she whispered as she looked up into his eyes.

He gripped her in a bear hug that almost had the air pushed out of her it was so tight. Just as quickly as he snatched her up, he let her go.

"We're unable to communicate outside of this lair. We suspect the goblins cut us off," he rasped.

"Makes sense that they would do that." She nodded once.

"It doesn't matter." Cyclone shrugged. "We're going to bag us a horde of goblins, and then you and I are talking. I won't take no for an answer."

"You look like you could do with a nap." His eyes were red-rimmed. His face was creased with fatigue, and… underneath the red tinge of his skin was a green hue. Cyclone was sick.

He barked out a laugh that held zero humor. "I'll sleep when I'm dead."

"That's the spirit. I need to teach some civilians how to shoot, and then I'm giving you a five-minute lesson on how to handle an automatic weapon. You missed class yesterday."

"Five minutes is all I need, and it's your fault I missed class. You're the most stubborn female I—"

"Not now." She pushed past him.

"Later, then. You're telling me why you left." He was being all gruff. In his weakened state, she was having a hard time telling him no.

Angie turned back, and they held each other's gaze for a few long moments. There was a pleading look in his eyes.

"Fine," she pushed out.

"I'm holding you to it."

"Sure thing." What the hell was she promising? Then again, there was a distinct possibility they wouldn't make it out of this alive. So, whatever.

Sick from the poison, his stomach rolling with nausea, his skin on fire… and yet his dick still took note when he was anywhere near this female. Her scent filled his nostrils, and his balls pulled tight. Cyclone couldn't help but look her over as she strode away. Her ass was tight in those jeans. Her hair had been pulled into a messy bun.

Fucking hell!

She was beautiful and maddening. A lethal combination. An inspired one too.

He'd meant every word; he was going to kill those green bastards, and then she was coming clean. Whatever the issue was, they'd work through it together.

"Can I have everyone's attention," Angie said, using an elevated voice.

The group stopped their chatter and moved closer to her, turning their attention to Angie. Vortex was with his soon-to-be mate. He had his arm around her and was whispering something into her ear.

"Who has fired a gun before?" A couple of the shifters from her class started to put their hands up. "Not my students. The rest of you."

A female put up her hand. "My father taught me how to shoot. He's a hunter. I know how to shoot a gun, but… um…" she bit her lip, "I'm not sure I'll be able to kill anything. Much to Daddy's disgust, I never took to hunting. I just… I can't pull the trigger." She shook her head, her eyes wide. "I'm not sure how much help I'm going to be today, either."

"What is your name?" Angie asked.

"Robin."

"Please, can the shifters move to one side? Robin, I want you to stand with them, please."

"Um… okay." The female licked her lips, looking unsure.

Cyclone joined the shifters. He clasped wrists with

Typhoon, who had since joined them. The male was sick but standing. Hopefully, more would arrive soon. They were a sorry group. Vortex was the only male who had done the desensitizing three times. There were a few who had done it twice, and he was looking at them. Most of the lair had done the treatment only once. At least he hoped they had, or this level of silver might just kill a dragon. Thankfully, all the young had been through desensitizing. Most of them while in their mother's bellies. Most were completely immune. Or only slightly allergic. Still, it was a fuck-up! This whole thing stank.

Those goblin fuckers had planned this all along. It made him feel better about using human weapons. About using silver. It was fortunate that Storm had been so proactive in this regard. His statement about being over-prepared had never rung truer. It would be fighting fire with fire. Fuckers deserved what was coming their way.

It wasn't like they could shift and fight them that way. Shifting with all this silver in his system would be near impossible. Flying? Forget about it. They were going to have to take up arms and fight. It was the only way to even up the odds. The best part was that the goblins weren't expecting it. If they hit hard, it might scare the bastards off.

"Okay," Angie said, addressing the women. "This is a Ruger 9mm. It is a decent caliber weapon, especially considering it will be loaded with hollow-tipped silver bullets." She held the weapon up so that everyone could see, paying particular attention to the human females. "The nice thing about this gun is that it doesn't have a major recoil, and it's easy to reload and to shoot."

Melina put up her hand. "I'm not sure I'm the right person for the job."

"Do you have two hands?" Angie asked.

Melina nodded.

"A pair of working eyeballs?"

"Um… yes. Are these trick questions?"

"No. Not at all," Angie said. "If you answered all of those questions with a yes, you will be more than capable of firing and reloading a weapon. You'll therefore be able to defend this lair. We are all the people this community has. We're it. Look around. We might be few, but we're enough." She pulled in a breath. "Do you love your mates? Your fiancés? Your friends? Your colleagues?" Angie took her time looking from one member of the team to the next. "Do you love waking up every morning? Smelling the roses? Do you want to see another sunset? Maybe hugging puppies is your thing. Perhaps you're desperate to hold a child in your arms someday." She addressed Robin, whose eyes filled with tears. "We're all this lair has right now. We are enough, though. We can do this! Do you know why?" she mainly addressed the humans who had never seen battle. "We can do it because we have to. There is no other choice. Those goblins think they can poison our men and then come in here and cart us off. That we'll go willingly. Well, I say let's give them a run for their money. I say let's tell them 'No' by putting a couple of bullets into them." She held up the gun again. "We're stronger than those goblins think. No more negativity. You need to pay attention. It's easier than you think."

Pride burned bright in Cyclone.

What a female!

His female. Or she would be soon.

Everyone in the room was focused on Angie. A new

determination shone in their eyes. He felt it too. Cyclone felt stronger.

"First of all, a couple of basic rules," Angie went on. "Never aim your weapon at a team member. Aim at the goblins. Easy, right?"

Melina nodded.

Riley and Ashlyn giggled.

"This is the safety lever." She pointed at the lever on the side of the weapon. "It's within easy reach of your thumb. When the safety is engaged, you will see the letter S and a white dot." Angie flicked the lever with her thumb and showed everyone what the weapon looked like with the safety engaged. "I recommend that the safety be in place when you reload your gun. You should still point the weapon to the ground and away from one another. I once saw a guy shoot his own foot while reloading a weapon. He was lucky he didn't lose it. You might not be quite so lucky. Even in the heat of battle, you need to remain vigilant. This is probably the most important rule of all."

"What if we forget? What if—" It was the redhead.

"You'll do just fine. If you only ever point this gun at the enemy, it won't matter. That's really the most important thing to remember."

"Point at the enemy and nothing else," Riley said.

"You got it." Angie winked at the human.

"Now, I'm going to teach you how to load your weapon." She pulled a magazine from her pocket. "This takes ten bullets when fully loaded. The good news is that we have plenty of pre-loaded mags ready and waiting. I will teach you how to fill a magazine just in case we blow through all of them."

"O-okay," Ashlyn said, nodding wildly.

"Inserting the magazine is easy; just slide it into the well of the handgrip like so…" The magazine clipped into place easily with a loud click. "Removing it is just as easy. Press this…" Angie went through the motions. Showing the group how to insert the magazine again. "Once your mag is in place, you load the gun by gripping the slider and pulling all the way back. You will hear the bullet enter the chamber. That means the gun is loaded, with a round in the chamber and the hammer cocked. It's ready to fire at this point." She looked at each of them in turn. "Keep your finger off the trigger unless you're ready to shoot."

"And remember the rule about only pointing your gun at the enemy," Melina said.

"Correct." Angie nodded, looking at Melina. "When you are ready to start firing, unclick the safety lever. You will now see a red dot." She did it as she said it. Then she turned to the firing range. "This is how you stand, knees slightly bent and apart. You use both hands in this position on your weapon. Your arms should be extended outward, like this. Don't worry too much; the recoil on a Ruger won't be too harsh." She demonstrated by shooting off a few rounds.

There were one or two squeals, and two of the humans put their hands over their ears.

"It's as easy as that," Angie said as she clicked the safety back on, pointing the weapon at the ground.

"That doesn't seem too difficult," Amy said, looking nervous.

"It isn't. From there, point at the enemy and squeeze the trigger to fire." Angie gave a one-shouldered shrug.

"Aren't you supposed to breathe out as you shoot?" Robin asked. "My dad said it helps with accuracy."

"Don't worry about any of that stuff. Be careful where you point your weapon. Hold the gun with both hands, arms out in front of you, and fire at the enemy. You have ten rounds before you need to reload. Do so quickly. Kill as many goblins as you can. The end!"

"Do we get to practice?" Melina asked.

"No need. It's simple. You can practice when those bastards start climbing the cliff face. You must wait for my command before you start shooting. We need to wait until they are in range. This is also important." Angie kept her eyes on the group.

"I'm not sure I can take a life." Robin shook her head.

"I can!" Amy said in a stern voice. "Those goblins are foul creatures. They're on their way here to kill our men and to steal us to use as sex slaves. I can't wait to shoot the shit out of them." She gritted her teeth, breathing heavily.

"Everything Amy just said is true." It was better if they understood what they were up against. "These are not cute, cuddly individuals popping in for a cup of coffee. They're intent on murder and rape with a side of pillaging."

"Don't make jokes!" Ashlyn sobbed, looking anguished.

"I'm not joking! This is war." Angie's eyes were blazing. "Aim and squeeze, ladies. You've got this." She licked her lips. "All of you need to follow Vortex. He'll make sure that you each have a weapon and a backup. As well as plenty of replacement magazines and bullets. He'll show you how to refill a magazine, as well, for when you run out of loaded mags." Hopefully, it didn't get to that.

Vortex nodded once. "Follow me."

"Not you, Robin. I want to show you how to use a machine gun. You're going to need to pay close attention. That goes for all of you." She looked at her students.

"A what?" Robin's mouth fell open. "I just told you that I'm not sure about killing anyone, and you want me to use a machine gun?"

"Yes. I'm convinced that once you see them coming for us, you might change your mind. If not, I'll have to cover for you. I have two minutes to show you how to use this weapon." She touched her hand to the gun to the right of her. It was standing on a tripod. "Then we all need to get into position. Between the seven shifters and the two of us, we'll need to cover the entire cliff face. They shouldn't come from above since the drop is too high. They'd end up with too many injuries and deaths. We'll put the women between each of us to help with the faster goblins who slip through. If need be, we can put the other women onto machine guns as well. We'll be spread very thin. It's important that we all pull our weight to prevent any of them from reaching us. You should all have one or two handguns in case this happens. Be aware of who is behind your target if shooting from the balcony. Let's try to avoid shooting each other."

"That's good advice," Heat sniggered.

Robin swallowed thickly, but nodded once. The human looked pale.

"Cyclone, since you weren't at the training yesterday, I'll need you front and center as well." Her eyes locked with his. They softened for half a second before she turned to Heat. "You're the only healthy shifter, Heat. Since I also found you to be proficient in training yesterday, I'm going to need you to go and fetch the weapons. Don't forget about extra barrels and belts. We're going to need tons of ammo."

"I could shift and—" Heat started.

"You would run the risk of being overrun," Cyclone told the male.

"I think you can do more damage with silver bullets and a weapon capable of shooting up to 1,000 rounds in a minute," Angie told Heat.

"Got it." Heat nodded once. "Man my station," he told Angie, who nodded.

Cyclone was one hell of a sick fuck. They were about to stop an assault on the lair. War was upon them, and all he could think of was this female. How sexy Angie was, especially when she took charge like this. How brave and capable. How all this talk of weapons and bullets made him hard for her.

Yep, they were going to have it out once those goblin fucks were all worm food. Then he was keeping her. Angie was his mate. His dragon had decided it a long time ago. It was time to make it a reality.

CHAPTER 14

IT LOOKED LIKE IT WAS going to be a beautiful day. The sun was rising steadily under a crimson sky. An eagle called in the distance. A warm breeze blew across the balcony.

"Holy fucking shit!" Melina whispered. The weapon in her hand shook. Her eyes were on the ground below them. "Amy said they were big and mean, but… shit! Look at them." She shook her head slowly. "I can't believe they're actually here!"

There were more than a hundred, but not by much. Big, burly goblins preparing to climb the cliff walls, which were sheer and rocky. There was the odd bush or small tree that jutted from the unforgiving rock. Gnarly roots hanging on for dear life on an otherwise barren surface.

"They bleed just like anybody else," Angie reminded the others.

Melina nodded, looking down at the pile of magazines at her feet. "I'm ready." She unclicked her safety. Her finger stayed where it was on the weapon.

Good student!

Angie leaned over the railing, looking to the left along the multitude of balconies. Vortex and Typhoon were still setting up. Heat was ready. Cyclone and the others, too; he lifted a hand in acknowledgment. Her heart beat faster. Her throat felt dry, even though there was a full bottle of water at her feet, along with half a dozen spare barrels. There was enough ammo to drop a small army on her own. She was going to do her damnedest to make it happen, too.

Robin was on the far right of the main balcony, and Angie was on the far left. The other woman stood behind a machine gun set on a tripod. Although her hands were steady, she looked like she might just throw up at any second. It wasn't uncommon for the most well-trained individuals to feel sick with fear leading up to their first skirmish. The ladies were doing well, considering.

Her own machine gun was on a tripod as well, set up at the part of the balcony without a railing. It was already aimed down at where the attack would take place.

Let them come!

Almost as soon as the thought had run through her head, the goblins gave a loud battle cry. The closest to the cliffs leaped up with surprising agility and speed. Once the first of their line was up and climbing, more jumped up behind them and again and again. They had lined themselves up all along the bottom of the cliff. A blanket of green muscle and testosterone.

"Oh, god!" Melina said. "They're fast." She looked over at Angie, terror in her eyes.

It was true. The bastards climbed like they had been doing it their whole lives. They'd give Olympic rock climbers a run for their money.

"Bullets are faster," she told Melina. "Hold!" Angie shouted. "Not yet," she added when Heat started stepping from one foot to the other. They needed to wait until the green bastards were in range.

Nearly.

Nearly.

She gripped her weapon. "Aim and fire!" Angie shouted. "Now!" she added, doing as she instructed and opening fire on the first line of goblins.

They went down in a spray of blood and shock.

Good!

Assholes!

Angie took a second to look to her right, where Robin still stood frozen.

"Aim and shoot!" she screamed at the other woman.

The goblins were getting closer. She could see the expressions of hatred on their faces. Angie let loose again, trying to cover for Robin. The goblins on their end were gaining ground. If Robin didn't unfreeze and soon, she would need to swap Melina with Robin. In the meantime, she worked hard to keep the goblins from advancing enough to reach them.

Then she heard it. The goblins were chanting. Her blood turned cold.

"Cunt! Cunt! Cunt! Cunt!"

Robin must have heard it, too, because she gave a cry of outrage and opened fire. A whole group of goblins fell from the cliff. Those who fell toppled the goblins below them. The goblins didn't seem to care about the gunfire or blood or about their comrades falling around them. They continued to climb and continued to chant that awful word. "Foul creatures" was an apt description.

Melina changed her magazine like a fucking pro. She aimed and fired. Aimed and fired.

"Keep going!" she shouted encouragement.

The goblins gained ground as she reloaded a new belt.

"Fuck you!" she snarled, taking down a particularly big goblin as she opened fire again.

Amelia screamed as one of those bastards hoisted himself over the railing.

Where the hell had he come from?

Angie pulled a handgun from her chest holster and shot the fucker twice between the eyes. He dropped hard. Angie grabbed the machine gun and loosed a spray of bullets into the fuckers who were still left. Many had fallen.

A harsh, guttural shouting sounded from below in a language she didn't understand. As quickly as those assholes climbed up, they began retreating. Angie kept firing, as did the others. There had to be at least thirty of them left.

There were plenty dead and gravely wounded, but some of the injured were hobbling to their feet, joining the others.

Melina flicked her safety on and lowered the weapon. The other woman was grinning.

"We did it!"

"Careful! The muzzle will be hot," she shouted to the ladies and to whomever else could hear. She'd forgotten to mention that part. "They're regrouping." Angie hated to be the one to give bad news, but it was true. "I think they'll try again soon."

They would look for a hole in their defenses. It was that or add to the numbers. Right now, they could take a deep breath and replenish ammo and refreshments.

Angie looked to her left of the balcony. Cyclone staggered back, falling on his ass. Avalanche didn't even try to stay on his feet. He collapsed into a pile. It looked like he was gagging, possibly even throwing up. She couldn't tell from her position.

"Help me!" a woman shouted from behind them.

Angie turned. It was the pregnant lady from last night. She clutched her heavily distended belly. She lurched a few steps towards them, almost looking like she might fall.

"Azure!" Melina shouted.

"Help!" the she-dragon croaked. She looked sickly. Her hair was plastered to her blistered forehead. Her lips were cracked.

The thing that had Angie reeling back was her wet cotton pants. They clung to her inner thighs. Her eyes were wide and bloodshot. Her breath came in rasps.

"He's coming," she croaked before falling hard on her knees. "My baby."

"Azure!" Melina shouted, running over to her.

CHAPTER 15

ANGIE LOOKED DOWN. THE GOBLINS were regrouping. They weren't leaving. They were strategizing.

Shit!

This was bad. Seriously fucking terrible.

Melina had gone down on her knees. "What must I do? What do you need?" she asked her friend. It was clear that she was panicking.

Azure was trying to clamber up, which was a bad idea. Her pants were torn, and her knees were bleeding. Her belly was enormous. It was a wonder she'd made it this long. Of course, Murphy had decided to rear his asshole head during a goblin attack. That's how these things normally worked.

"Don't!" she told Melina when the woman tried to move her friend. "Let's make her more comfortable right there."

"But—" Melina started.

"She's weak. Needs to save her strength for the labor." They would also be able to help between fighting if she was close by.

Melina nodded once, getting up and grabbing a couple of pairs of cotton pants from a nearby shelf. The shifters left them there for when they shifted back into their human form. They would come in handy now.

"Please tell me that there are doctors in the lair," Angie said, looking down at the stricken woman. Azure clutched her belly, groaning loudly through clenched teeth.

"The healers are all sick, I'm sure, or they'd be here," Melina said. "What about the gynecologist—the human doctor? I can't remember her name." She placed a couple of pairs of pants behind Azure's head while she talked.

Azure was panting through her mouth. Sweat beaded her brow. She eventually relaxed back, working to catch her breath.

"It's bad. Oh, god! No… um… the human doctor is on leave, visiting her family. She only gets back tomorrow. I would have been fine with a healer, so I wasn't concerned about her going. There isn't much a human doctor can do for a dragon shifter."

"So, there are no other doctors on-site?" Angie asked, keeping her voice and her expression even. At least, she hoped she was keeping them even. It looked like they might be on their own.

Crap!

This was bad. Worse than freaking bad.

Azure shook her head. "Not that I know of. There aren't that many of us yet. There are plans to expand but—" She groaned, clutching her belly.

"What about the specialist giving the desensitizing treatments?" Angie asked. He or she had to be a trained doctor. Perhaps they'd worked in the ER or something.

"Monique is at the Fire lair. I had my desensitizing already. My last treatment was a few weeks ago. Dr. Oliver moves from lair to lair." She licked her chapped lips. Her eyes were glassy. Sweat dripped off of her.

Angie fetched a bottle of water from a nearby table. "Is this your first child?" She handed the bottle to Melina. "You need to keep hydrated."

"No... I... I can't risk it." Azure looked at the water like it was a five-headed serpent.

Angie couldn't blame her. "It's safe. Tried and tested. It's from the storeroom. This batch of water was delivered a week ago."

"You're sure? I'm still feeling sick. I can't afford to get worse." She pursed her lips together, as if saying the word "sick" made her feel worse.

"I'm very sure. It's safe. I'm sure you're dehydrated. You'll feel better once you get your fluid levels up."

Azure nodded, then her eyes widened, and she started panting again. "It's another one."

Melina put the bottle to her lips. "Drink. Before the pain gets too bad."

Azure took a sip or two before shaking her head. "Enough. And yes... this baby is our first." Tears leaked down her cheeks. "Ice is unconscious. I couldn't wake him. I tried!" She groaned. "I didn't want to leave him... Oh, god! Nooo!" she cried. "This can't be happening now. Please!"

"Breathe." Melina grabbed her hand and squeezed. "I'm here. Ice will get better soon."

"It wasn't supposed to happen like this." Azure tossed her head from side to side; her eyes were tightly shut. "I need my mate. I need a healer. I can't have this baby right now."

"The good news is that first-time pregnancies normally take a while to progress. At least, I hope that's the case with dragon shifters, too." Angie lifted her brows.

Azure was still clutching her belly but clearly coming down from a big contraction.

She nodded. "Yes… I was told that the average is eleven to sixteen hours from the onset of the pains." She was a little out of breath.

"How long have you been in labor?"

"It's hard to tell. I've been sick for two hours with stomach cramps and nausea. My waters came about a half-hour ago."

"So, it's safe to say that you are probably in the earlier stages," Angie said, giving Azure a reassuring smile she didn't feel inside. It was a bit of a white lie since the membranes rupturing normally caused the contractions to become more severe, thus progressing the labor more quickly. For now, she wanted Azure as calm as possible. Melina, too. If telling a white lie helped make that happen, then she'd do it. "It's going to be a while before this baby comes."

"We hope," Melina said. Her eyes were wide. Her face was pale.

Angie gave the other woman a hard stare, trying to shut her the hell up.

"How is it looking?" she asked Robin, who was standing by the railing. "What are the goblins up to?"

"They're talking in groups. They're seriously barbaric. Their wounded are having to tend to themselves."

"Good. That means fewer will recover." Something was up. This wasn't over.

Melina was coaxing Azure into taking in more water. The she-dragon was clearly still feeling the effects of the silver. She gagged a couple of times. It was a minute or two before the next contraction started up.

"We should time these," Angie said. "Time how far apart they are."

"I can do that," Melina said, fiddling with her watch. If nothing else, it would give her something to do. "You've done this before, right?" Melina asked Angie, clutching Azure's hand while she breathed through a contraction. "You said so last night. You helped a woman give birth."

"I've done advanced first aid training. We mainly handled injuries in the field. I did help with a birth once, yes. I caught the baby. My male teammates decided that since I'm a woman, I was the best qualified. I was pissed at the time, but I'm happy about that now." She was babbling. "In answer to your question," she cleared her throat, "yes, I've done this before." Not that she was qualified or anything, because she really wasn't. In fact, she was probably the least qualified person around.

Someone cleared their throat behind her. Angie glanced over her shoulder, straight into Cyclone's eyes.

"You'll let me know if anything changes?" she told Melina, taking a step back.

"Like changes how?" Melina asked, sounding panicked.

"If Azure's contractions get much closer together. If

she gets the sudden urge to push. That kind of thing." They were in so much shit!

Melina's eyes grew wider, and that panicked expression got even worse. She gasped. "A sudden urge to——?"

"It's a long way off. This is Azure's first baby. It's all going to be fine."

Melina pulled in a deep breath, which she slowly released. "Okay… okay… fine. I've got this."

"Time the contractions. Try to keep Azure comfortable."

"I can do that." Melina nodded too quickly.

"I'll be back in a few minutes," Angie said. "Robin, you're my eyes. Let me know if they try anything."

"I will." Robin nodded, keeping her eyes trained on what was happening at the base of the cliff.

Angie turned and strode to Cyclone. Even with dark smudges under his eyes and welts on his chest and forehead, the man was still as gorgeous as they came. That she even noticed in the midst of everything was just plain crazy.

"What are you doing here? Those goblins could start climbing again at any second. We have no idea what they are planning. They might have something up their sleeves."

CHAPTER 16

ANGIE PUT HER HANDS ON her hips and cocked her head. She was right to question him. "It's fine. I have Fog covering my section. He woke up about ten or fifteen minutes ago when the shooting started. I put him on my balcony. I came over because it looked like you could do with an extra set of hands." He glanced at Azure.

Melina was whispering words of encouragement to the female.

"Even more reason to finish the goblins," Cyclone muttered to himself. Bastards needed to be put down. Every last one of them. He gave a small shake of the head, forcing himself to focus. "Hail woke up as well. Vortex sent him to the gun room to fetch more supplies. I'm putting him between Avalanche and Typhoon. We had three goblins make it over the railings on that side. The area could use extra reinforcements. I'm hoping you agree?" He lifted his brows.

"I do. What do you think they're up to?" She nodded in the direction of the railing.

"No idea! I don't like it. I don't like waiting it out. Not my style." He grit his teeth. "I wish I could shift and tear them to pieces. Heat offered, but one dragon on that many goblins would be suicide. If only Air dragons could breathe fire. That would change things. We can't! And we use up too much energy making lightning."

Angie rubbed her shoulder. She rolled it a few times. "Agreed. One dragon isn't nearly enough if they come at us again. We handled them just fine before. It seems like more and more shifters will be able to join us soon."

"There will be more." Cyclone nodded. "But whether they'll get here in time is anyone's guess. I knew goblins were crazy sons of bitches; I didn't realize that they had no fear of death. I had plenty of them look straight up into the barrel of my machine gun and keep on coming. Blew their heads off, only to be met with the next set of eyes. Fighting an enemy like that is disconcerting."

"Fear is important for survival. It's easier to kill your opponent when they're fearless. I think that they're more brawn than brains." She pulled a couple of wayward strands behind her ear.

"Don't underestimate them. They came up with this plan. It's a good one. I, for one, never saw this coming."

She gave him a half-smile. "All it would have taken was one goblin to come up with the plan. I won't underestimate them, though. That would be foolish."

"And your feelings on that situation?" He glanced at Azure, who was in the middle of a contraction. She looked like she was in a shitload of pain. "I noticed you used your tell."

"I wish you would tell me what my 'tell' is already."

She pushed out a breath. "I think it's going to happen sooner rather than later," she whispered.

"So, when you said that she was in her early stages…?" Cyclone mouthed, even though Azure was groaning and panting loudly. He didn't elaborate. Didn't have to.

Angie shrugged. "I have no idea. Her contractions are strong and coming frequently."

Fuck!

"Okay, well, I'm staying here to cover for you in case you're needed elsewhere."

"I'm fighting. Protecting this lair is number one on—"

"Holy shit!" Robin yelled. Her hands were over her forehead, shielding her eyes.

The dragons further up the balcony began gesturing and shouting.

"What is it?" Angie asked as she strode to the railing.

"The backup just arrived," Cyclone growled. "We kind of figured more were coming." They'd hoped it wouldn't be the case.

It was another horde. This time, there had to be at least two hundred goblins. All for a handful of human females. Desperation did strange things to a male. Still, it didn't make much sense to him.

Hail walked out onto the balcony, carrying a machine gun with a bag of supplies.

"Looks like I woke up just in time." He staggered a few steps, almost falling.

They were a sorry bunch. How had this happened? How had they not realized that the water supply was contaminated? The shower had felt scorching hot, even though the faucet was set to a more normal setting. He'd felt weak and tired, but he'd thought it was just him. The day. His life. The silver had slowly infiltrated their systems while they slept. It was fucking ingenious.

"Leave that there and then get back to your position between Typhoon and Avalanche." Cyclone gestured to the open section where Melina had been.

Hail nodded once, dropping the supplies. He held onto the railing, breathing heavily. When his gaze moved to the approaching horde, his shoulders went back, and a look of steely determination appeared on his face.

"I'm gonna bag me a whole bunch of those goblin fucks. I'll be wearing green leather boots until the day I fucking die."

"You don't wear boots." Cyclone laughed, setting up his tripod.

"It might be a good time to start," Hail said. "Since we'll have us a ton or two of green leather after this."

"I hear that green bags are all the rage in Paris," Melina shouted, still holding Azure's hand. "I wouldn't mind matching boots myself."

"A green leather bag sounds amaaaazing. I'll take a pair of those boots as well," the she-dragon chimed in weakly. Her hands gripping her belly.

"Coming right up," Hail said as he walked to the doors. "I'll see you all a little later."

Cyclone hoisted his machine gun into place, feeding a strip of bullets into the slot. He tried hard not to touch the silver bullets.

"They're chanting in a big group," Robin shouted. The human had her hands on her weapon. "This is what happened last time, right before they attacked." Cyclone could scent her fear.

He could hear the goblin's chanting in their strange

guttural language. The gold they wore, on their ears and wrists, glinted in the sun. He could make out their sharp teeth and beady eyes. Eyes that were almost pitch-black but somehow glinted in the light as well.

Let them come!

He was eager to get this over with. Inaction wasn't his thing. Cyclone glanced to his left. Angie was in position as well, her eyes trained on what was unfolding below. She must have sensed him looking because she glanced over at him.

They shared a look for a few seconds. His chest clenched. He felt better now that he was closer to her. He was still weak.

Fucking silver.

Then Cyclone looked up the line. Everyone was ready and waiting. All except Angie, and Hail, who was still setting up.

"Same as before," Angie shouted, knowing full well that even the farthest dragon would hear her. "We hold until they're within range. There may be more of them, but there is only so much cliff face to navigate. Don't let their greater numbers scare you."

It was a short wait before their battle cry sounded, and the first line jumped up and onto the cliff. There were so many others to take their place. Green leather boots for life was probably right.

"Hold!" Angie shouted. "Not yet!" she added ten seconds later. "Nearly," she shouted. "Fire!" she screamed, and they let rip.

He watched the bullets pelt the first line of goblins. Blood flew. The back of the skull of one of the creatures flew into the face of a climbing male, knocking him loose. Goblins fell, screaming as they died.

Still. They. Came.

Twenty minutes later…

They kept coming. More and more and more. An endless volley. From time to time, a goblin made it to the railing but was quickly dispatched. The two extra sets of hands were proving helpful in filling in the gaps. Robin held her own. The pile of bodies at the bottom of her section of the cliff was impressive. The lady could shoot.

Angie's back ached, and her shoulder throbbed. Sweat dripped down her forehead. This was tedious. It also took serious concentration. A one-second lapse would cost them big time.

She felt a tap on her back. "Not now!" she shouted.

"They're getting closer together," Melina shouted. "Azure's contractions," she bellowed louder, trying to be heard over the rapid gunfire.

Angie kept shooting. She didn't stop until her ammo was all used up. She spoke while reloading. "Does Azure have the urge to push yet?" There was no way Angie could help the woman right then. Keeping everyone in the lair safe was her first priority.

"No!" Melina shook her head.

Thank god!

"But her contractions are becoming more painful and closer together. That means that the baby is coming, doesn't it?"

"It means that she's dilating, which is a good thing, but until she starts getting the urge to push, we're good. Keep monitoring the situation. You're doing a great job." Angie started firing at a group of advancing goblins. "Fuck!" she yelled as two reached the edge of the cliff.

She pulled her handgun and shot them both before

holstering the weapon and letting loose with a spray of bullets. Their numbers were diminishing, but it was taking so damned long. Angie hoped that the dragon shifters would hold on. If she was feeling the strain, then the guys would be too. They were still sick and weak. Fighting like this wouldn't be doing any of them any favors.

Azure screamed from the doorway behind them.

Angie had to focus on what was going on below. That was the thing with a defense like theirs. It was thin. One hole. One breach and they would fall. The goblins would overwhelm them. It would be over in minutes.

Angie felt something land on her head. She looked down. There were tiny loose stones at her feet that hadn't been there before. More clattered to the right of her.

Shit!

Angie turned in time to see two ropes come down off the overhang of the balcony. A handful of about thirty goblins were finishing their descent down the cliff to them. There was about a fifty-foot drop from the edge of the overhang to the balcony.

The goblins began their downward climb. They were quicker and more agile than expected for such a huge species. At least ten more ropes dropped down from the edge as Angie screamed a warning. She pulled her handgun and shot the first goblin, who landed a mere ten feet from where Azure was breathing through another contraction. Both women screamed as the goblin jumped back to his feet, bleeding from a stomach wound. She shot him again, hoping he would stay down. Another goblin jumped from his rope, breaking both his legs as he landed. She shot him as well. Then Angie looked up in horror as a whole bunch of goblins began their descent down ropes.

Angie shot two more before her bullets ran out. It took her precious seconds to reload. Four goblins landed on their balcony. More landed on the balconies further up the way. Some injured themselves when they landed. Not enough of them, though. By now, the others had realized what was happening. There were shouts of outrage. The shooting faltered, which meant that the goblins climbing would gain ground while they took care of the immediate problem, namely the goblins in their midst. They needed to get things under control and fast, or it was over for them.

Shit-shit-shit!

Angie had been sure they wouldn't come over the mountain. The sheer drop was too dangerous to navigate. What she hadn't factored into the equation was that these were goblins, not men. They were bigger, faster, stronger. They were able to land hard and keep going. They were fearless in the face of injury and death.

The one closest to her sniffed the air and smiled.

"Human," he said, just as Angie put a bullet between his eyes.

She put a bullet into two more when the fourth knocked her gun out of her hand, grabbing her tightly.

"Cunt!" he growled, sounding excited.

Did they have such a limited vocabulary? If so, being abducted by them was going to be fun, indeed.

Angie kicked him in the balls… hard. He squealed like a girl but didn't let her go. If anything, his grip tightened.

Cyclone barreled into him, freeing her just as a whole lot of goblins climbed over the balcony railing.

Nooooo!

They were well and truly fucked. Angie had

underestimated the goblins. She'd done the one thing she swore she wouldn't do. But Angie would go down fighting.

Fuck that!

She wasn't going to end up as some war trophy. She heard a dragon screech. Heat must have shifted. Cyclone was in half-shift and fighting four goblins. Everyone was fighting hard. Angie began firing. If she could free up her machine gun, she could do more damage and stop more of them from reaching the balcony. Several goblins dropped. Not nearly enough.

Once her bullets were finished, she pulled the gun from her ankle holster. This was her emergency weapon, and as far as she was concerned, this was a serious emergency.

A goblin grabbed her from behind just as she lined up a shot, making her miss.

"Fucker!" she yelled, doing the totally unexpected; she dropped her arms, shooting him in the foot.

He howled and let her go, freeing her up to shoot him in the head. They were ugly up close. For every goblin she shot, three more appeared. They were becoming overrun. This was it.

Her gun clicked loudly.

Fuuuuuuuck!

She was plumb out of bullets. There was no time to reload. Both Azure and Melina were screaming. There was roaring, snarling. The crack of lighting. Must be Heat, using his Air dragon powers. Crappy that they only had one healthy shifter among them. Time almost seemed to stand still. The goblins closest to her were grinning, hands reaching for her.

A bugle sounded. At least, it sounded like a bugle.

That, or a trumpet or… a wind instrument that made a godawful racket. It was so out of place that the fighting stopped. Everything stopped.

The goblin's eyes widened. They turned. All of them. In unison. They looked to the source of the trumpeting. The bugle sounded again, louder this time. The goblins began talking among themselves in the same strange language. Then the weirdest thing happened.

They left.

They jumped over the railings. The bugle sounded yet again. At this point, the goblins looked panicked. They clambered down. Clambering over each other. Goblins fell, crashing onto the piles of bodies below. Heat took to the sky, screeching, his great wings flapping.

She felt a presence next to her and turned. Cyclone was breathing heavily. One eye was swollen shut. His mouth was bleeding. There was a cut over his left cheek. He clasped a hand over his ribs on the right side of his chest, wincing.

The bugle sounded yet again.

"It's the goblin queen." He smiled, wincing when his lip pulled tight. "She's brought an army. I feel sorry for the goblin vigilantes who are still standing."

Sure enough, a sea of goblins appeared. A group of them carried a golden throne. They were still too far away for her to make out the features of the queen. From what she had been told, the queen looked like one of the goblin males, only much bigger.

"The queen's horde is here." Cyclone chuckled. "Those poor fucks!"

"Looks like the queen is going to be wearing green boots for the rest of her life, too," Robin piped up. It sounded like she was smiling.

"And then there are the bags. Don't forget the bags." Angie was on the verge of tears. She'd never been this emotional. "That was close," she managed to push out.

"Too fucking close for my liking." His voice sounded strange, so she turned to face him. Cyclone's eyes rolled in his skull, and he collapsed before she could do anything to help him.

"I need to push!" Azure shouted. "I feel pressure down there. The baby is coming."

CHAPTER 17

ANGIE GASPED AND WENT DOWN onto one knee. Cyclone's chest was still moving. There were dark smudges under his eyes. It was sheer exhaustion and possibly a broken rib or two. She touched his cheek for a moment to reassure herself that he was still breathing. That he was fine, despite being unconscious. He was a dragon shifter. He would be fine!

"Is everyone okay?" she yelled to whoever was nearby as she rose to her feet.

"No!" Melina shouted. "Help!"

"I'll be there in a sec," she reassured the woman.

Robin was still holding onto the machine gun; her knuckles were white against the gray of the metal. She looked shell-shocked as she watched the queen's horde giving chase after the vigilante goblins.

"I wouldn't watch that if I were you," Angie warned.

"They're evil," she whispered. "I want to watch." Her voice took on a hard edge. "They deserve what's coming to them." Her jaw tightened.

Angie made a mental note to ensure that everyone here today received counseling. Angie knew more than most how war could affect a person. She could also understand where Robin was coming from.

She cupped her hands over her mouth. "All good?" she yelled over Azure's screams to the others on the balconies further up.

Heat gave her the thumbs-up. Angie could see that, just like Cyclone, some of the shifters were down. Hopefully, from pure exhaustion and not because they were gravely injured. The women seemed shook up, but okay. Vortex looked like he had things under control. No one was panicking, so it must be fine.

"Angie!" Melina yelled. "We need you, now."

There were bigger fish to fry right now. Or, in this case, a baby. He was coming. Angie took a deep breath, hoping she would recall what she had been taught and that she would be able to draw from her one and only experience in birthing a child.

Angie rolled up her sleeves. "We'll need towels, boiling water, and a pair of scissors," she yelled.

Melina's jaw dropped. "Really?"

"Isn't that what you're supposed to say?" Angie asked.

Azure managed a weak chuckle.

"This isn't the time for jokes." Melina narrowed her eyes as Angie got down on her haunches next to Azure.

"It probably is," Azure backed her up. "I can do this," she added.

"You absolutely can!" Angie told her.

"Yes, you can." Melina still sounded panicked. "We can! I mean, you… you can."

"No, 'we' is right." Azure squeezed her friend's hand. "Thank you for being here." There was a sob in her voice. Then she gripped her belly. "It's another one." She started making these grunting noises. "I need to push. Please tell me I can push?"

"The one thing we were taught in advanced first aid is to listen to your body. Yes! Push!" She looked between Azure's splayed thighs. Her pants had been removed already. "You found a blanket?" she asked Melina as Azure began to push, placing her chin on her chest.

"Yes… I mean, no… It's a drape. I had to improvise. I found some cushions too."

Azure looked as comfortable as she was going to get, under the circumstances. Angie peered between the other woman's legs again. There wasn't much to see.

"Keep pushing!" she encouraged.

"You're doing great!" Melina murmured.

Azure grit her teeth while the last of her contraction caused her belly to remain tight. She finally fell back against the cushions, panting hard.

"Water," she whispered.

"Here." Melina held a bottle to her lips.

"Not too much," Angie advised. "Women can get nauseous in their final stages of labor."

"You're probably right," Azure said. "I still have silver in my system. I hate throwing up." She clutched her distended belly as it began to tighten with yet another contraction. The poor woman's face twisted in pain. A few seconds later, she started to push.

Cyclone cracked his eyes open. The sun was bright, and so he squinted, groaning.

"Are you okay?" the human asked. Robin, her name was Robin.

"Yeah," he groaned again, moving into a sitting position. He felt like crap. Not as bad as before, but still not great. All he wanted to do was to lie back down and catch a few more Z's. Wasn't going to happen. He glanced over the railing. Goblins were removing the bodies of the dead and injured. A whole procession of shackled males was being led away. He was sure that they were destined for the same fate as the vigilantes before them.

Death.

It would be deserved. A shudder ran through him as he thought of what could have happened. At the helplessness he had felt as he watched those males surround his female. He fought hard, but he knew he wasn't going to get to Angie in time. The goblins were going to get her.

Fuck!

He ran a hand through his hair, trying to shake the memory. It hadn't happened. Thank fuck the queen had arrived in time.

Azure's cries had him looking their way. She had her chin against her chest. Her legs were wide, knees bent. It looked like her hands were linked around the back of her thighs. He couldn't see properly because a blanket was over her lower body. The she-dragon was pushing like her life depended on it.

Angie knelt between Azure's thighs, under the blanket, peering between her legs.

"Okay, so something is happening," Angie said.

"Something? What does that mean? Is it good or bad?" Melina asked. It was clear that the human was in semi-panic mode. He couldn't blame her. This was serious. A whelp was on its way. A tiny little baby.

"Good! It's fantastic! I think he will start to crown soon. That means that I'll be able to see the top of his head. You're doing such an amazing job," Angie told Azure.

The she-dragon slumped back, panting heavily. When she turned her head, he noticed that her eyes were bloodshot. Her face was flushed and dripping with perspiration. Her lips looked chapped.

"That's good. Crowning is good," Azure repeated, nodding.

"Everything is going according to plan. I think I might even be able to see the top of his head on the next push."

"Oh, good… but…" Her eyes swam with tears. "What about Ice… my mate?"

"I'll get him," Cyclone interjected, getting to his feet. His side hurt like a bitch. Probably a broken rib. He ignored the pain. It would heal up soon enough.

"Oh… please… please, could you? It would mean so much," Azure said, her eyes brightening up. "He might even be awake by now."

"I'll carry him here if I have to," Cyclone promised.

"Thank you… thank you so much."

He touched his hand to the top of Angie's head for a second. His female looked up at him and gave him the sweetest smile.

Then the birthing pains started up again, and the moment was over.

"What was that about you guys being broken up?" Melina asked as he walked away. "Did almost dying change your mind about being in a relationship?"

Cyclone slowed a little, wanting to hear what she had to say. "We are still broken up. Nothing has changed," Angie said.

Those three words were like daggers to his chest.

Nothing.

Has.

Changed.

He couldn't see her, but he knew that she was telling the truth.

Fuck!

Something *had* changed, though, to make her feel this way. It had happened years ago. He wanted to damn well know what that something was.

Cyclone picked up a jog, running into Vortex.

"Good. I'm glad to see you," said Vortex. "More shifters are waking up. I'm going to organize a team to start helping the sick. We need to distribute uncontaminated food and water. I suggest—"

"Stop there. I need to fetch Ice. Azure is having the baby as we speak. Then I'll help with getting the lair back up on its feet. We also need to fix our comms. Stat."

"I've got my cellphone, and internal calls are still possible."

"I'll be in touch," he shouted over his shoulder, still jogging. He felt so fucking tired, but he pushed past it.

A few minutes later, he reached Ice and Azure's apartment, throwing the door open.

Ice was on the floor, trying to crawl to the door. The male looked fucking terrible.

"Oh, thank god," he croaked. "I can't find Azure… sick… I'm…"

"You were poisoned by silver. The whole lair was poisoned. The goblins attacked."

Ice pushed himself up. He was deathly pale behind the red welts. His eyes were sunken and bloodshot.

"Azure. Do they have my—?"

"No! Relax! She's fine. We're all safe. Your mate is about to have your whelp."

Ice tried to get up, but he was too weak.

"Allow me." Cyclone picked the male up, putting him over his shoulder. "If you need to toss your cookies, you need to tell me."

Ice grunted.

Cyclone wanted to run because Azure was close to birthing the whelp, but he didn't. Firstly, because he was still weak as fuck, and then secondly, because he was afraid the male would puke all over him. He walked fast. It was nice to see some movement in the hallways. Regular announcements were being made over the loudspeakers for the benefit of those who had been unconscious during the ordeal.

Cyclone passed a male who looked bewildered. Then two more, who were carrying a third.

Fucking goblins!

The lair was in shambles. Hopefully, no one had been seriously hurt or killed. It could have been so much worse. He squeezed his eyes shut for a second as cold rage flooded him. Goosebumps lifted on his arms. *Never again!* They needed to be more prepared. This couldn't happen again.

Thank fuck! Cyclone heard Azure's strangled cries. It sounded like she was still birthing the whelp.

"Are you ready to be a father?"

Ice grunted as he set him back on his feet. Then he slung an arm around the male to hold him there.

"Let's go."

Ice grunted again. They shuffled towards the balcony.

Cyclone wanted Ice to be on his feet when he saw his female. He would have wanted the same. Not that there was shame in being carried, but still.

They rounded the corner, and Ice made a noise deep in his throat.

Azure was hunched over as much as her heavily swollen belly would allow; she pushed hard. Then she drew in a deep breath and pushed again. The she-dragon growled, snarled, panted.

She didn't notice when Cyclone brought Ice next to her. The male went down onto his haunches. From the tense lines on his face, Cyclone could see that it took some effort to keep from collapsing. How much fucking silver had they been fed?

Ice brushed the wet strands of hair from his mate's face.

"You're so strong," he murmured.

"Ice!" Azure sobbed. She grabbed his hand and squeezed. "You made it. I can't believe it's you, my love."

"I'm here now. I'm sorry you had to go through this alone," he pushed out.

"I wasn't alone. I had my friends. You're here now. That's the most important part of all!"

Ice swallowed thickly and nodded. "And I'm not leaving either of you." He touched a hand to her belly. "I'm so fucking proud." Then he cupped her cheek with his hand, and they shared a look.

All Cyclone could think was that he wanted that. He wanted all of it. He wanted it with Angie.

He looked at her, his female. *His* dammit! Her eyes were glinting with what looked like tears. Angie licked her lips as she locked eyes with him. Then she looked away.

"Okie dokie, let's get this baby out," Angie said when the next birthing pain hit.

"I feel a lot of pressure down there," Azure choked out. The whole pushing process started up again. Azure strained and strained until her face turned red and sweat dripped from her forehead.

"I can see the top of your baby's head," Angie spoke calmly. She looked up; a smile was playing with her beautiful lips. "I need you to stop pushing now."

"My body says push," Azure argued. "You said to listen to my body."

"I don't want you to tear," Angie said. "We need to take it slow. The last lady I helped tore badly. I asked the surgeon back at base about it, and he said it was because the delivery went too fast. Pant through this contraction." Angie was under the blanket. Cyclone wasn't sure what she was doing. "Pant!" she instructed.

Azure did as she was told.

"That's it. The baby is still coming, only slowly. It's giving your body time to stretch."

"You're doing great, sweetheart," Ice said; sweat poured off the male. Cyclone knew exactly how he felt right then. Sick as anything. Probably running on adrenaline.

Azure made a growl of frustration, falling back against the pillows. Melina used a wet cloth to wipe her head.

"Your baby is right there. One more good push, and he or she will be born," Angie said. "And you can push on the next one."

Ice had a sip of water after Melina offered it to Azure. He gave his mate words of encouragement. This was one of the most amazing things that Cyclone had ever witnessed.

All too soon, her breathing hitched, and her body began to tense in preparation for the next contraction.

"Are you ready to hold your baby?" Angie smiled. Hair spilled out from her messy ponytail. She had a smudge of something on her left cheek. Cyclone had never seen her look more beautiful. His strong, capable female.

Azure nodded, growling low as she put her chin on her chest and clenched her teeth.

"Good." Angie went down between the she-dragon's thighs. "Push, Azure, push!"

Ice held onto his female. "You can do it, babe!" he whispered. "That's it."

His female's loud growl turned into a triumphant shout. Everyone held their breath.

Angie suddenly looked really busy under the blanket.

"Your baby's head is out!" she shouted, her voice laced with excitement. "I'm just checking that the nose and mouth are clear. There is no umbilical cord around the neck. All good."

Cyclone wasn't sure what an umbilical cord was. One day, when Angie was pregnant with their whelp, he'd read up on it. He'd make sure he knew everything there was to know about the subject. That he was fully prepared. They were meant to be together. He knew she loved him.

"He's nearly here," Azure whispered. "Very nearly."

"Yes. You're doing so damned well." Ice sounded slightly better. Again, it was probably the adrenaline of the moment.

"So well," Melina mirrored Ice.

"Everything is looking great," Angie said. "On the next contraction, we'll free his shoulders. Your baby is almost born."

"It's another one," Azure sounded excited. She growled, and seconds later, she let out a cry of happiness.

"Oh, my!" Angie yelled. "You guys were right." She glanced up at Ice and Azure. "It's a boy. You have a baby boy." Then she placed the whelp on Azure's chest. The little one squirmed. He let out a wail.

Both Azure and Ice were grinning. That, and crying. This had to be the best moment of their lives. Nothing could touch how they must be feeling. Cyclone could only imagine.

Azure clutched the baby to her chest, looking down at the tiny bundle. Ice was looking at Azure like she had hung the moon and all of the stars. He whispered his love for her and their child.

"Wow!" Cyclone looked back as he heard a voice behind him. It was Typhoon. The big male was wiping his eyes. "That was amazing." He sniffed. "Congratulations."

"Yes." Cyclone finally found his own voice, which was choked up. "Congrats to you both. Your boy is… he's perfect." He sniffed as well, barely holding it together. And if that made him a pussy, then so be it. He didn't care.

Ice grinned at him. His eyes were still bloodshot, but he looked much better than he had ten minutes ago.

"You're so freaking strong, Azure. He's adorable." Melina had tears running down her face.

"He's really very small, but other than that, he seems completely healthy," Angie said. The little one made fussing noises. "He's active. His skin is lovely and pink. He's breathing normally."

"He's beautiful," Azure murmured. She was looking down at her baby, still crying softly. Her lips were curved into a gentle smile.

Ice kissed her cheek, hugging her to him. "You did it, love."

"We need to cut the cord. I guess I wasn't joking about scissors," Angie told Melina, who laughed.

"You will start to feel mild contractions soon. Don't be alarmed; it's just the placenta," Angie said to Azure. "I'll go and see if I can find something to cut the cord with. It's not a rush."

"I'll go." Melina jumped up. "You should stay…" The human disappeared inside.

Azure opened her shirt, putting the whelp directly on her chest. "He's so small. Look at his little hands and feet. He looks just like you," she told Ice.

The little one had blond hair and vivid blue eyes, just like the male.

Azure moaned and clutched at her belly with one hand, holding the baby to her chest with the other.

"What is it?" Ice asked.

"Don't worry," Angie reassured him, repeating what she'd told Azure. "It's just the placenta. It'll be a little uncomfortable. Do you want to try to nurse him?"

"What is a placenta?" Ice asked.

It was a good question. Cyclone had no fucking clue.

"The feeding sac," Azure said through gritted teeth. "This is more than just uncomfortable, though." She winced. "This feels… it feels…" She groaned hard. Then her eyes opened in horror. "I have the urge to push again."

"I'm sure it's just the placenta," Angie said, positioning herself between Azure's legs again. "Everything looks fine. It should be out quickly and easily. Push, Azure."

"Do you want me to take our whelp?" Ice asked.

"I've got him," Azure pushed out before starting to bear down all over again.

Azure pushed hard, resting between contractions and pushing when the urge hit.

Angie was frowning heavily. *What was wrong?* "I'm sure this will be over in a minute," she reassured Azure.

"Is this abnormal?" Ice asked.

"It's fine."

A total lie. Fuck!

Then Azure was pushing again, and Angie disappeared under the blanket.

"Um… shit!" Angie sounded shocked.

"What is it?" Ice growled.

Angie came up from under the blanket. Her face was pale, and her eyes were wide. "I see the top of another head." Her eyes darted from Ice to Azure and back. "You're having twins. Twins!"

"What?" Melina shouted as she walked on the balcony. The human dropped the scissors.

Typhoon started clapping.

"Two whelps?" Ice looked shocked.

Cyclone barked out a laugh because… *fuck!* This was amazing.

"I can't believe it," Azure said between pants. "Are you sure? Maybe it's the feeding sac."

Angie laughed. "Placentas don't have hair. This time it's dark like yours, Azure. You're having twins. That's why you're carrying big." His female laughed some more. "Two or three pushes, and you'll have another baby."

"Twins!" Ice shouted. "I'm going to be a father to twins."

Cyclone had never seen the male this happy. He couldn't blame him.

Melina squealed.

Typhoon clapped again and gave a yell.

Cyclone looked at the happy expressions on Azure and Ice's faces. It made his heart clench with longing.

CHAPTER 18

That evening…

ANGIE KNOCKED SOFTLY ON THE bedroom door. "You can go on in," Ice said. The guy was beaming from ear to ear. He looked much better than he had earlier. The welts were gone. He still had dark circles under his eyes, which were bloodshot. Angie suspected that wouldn't change much going forward. Not with twins.

"Hi," Azure said as Angie walked into the room, sounding extremely chipper for someone who had given birth just a few hours earlier after a hard labor. With pillows propped up on either side of her, she was breastfeeding the babies. Both at once.

"You look like you're doing well." Angie smiled. "I'm sorry to bother you. I thought I would check in on you before going home."

Home.

Hah. Hardly.

Her home was back on human soil in Grand Rapids, Michigan, where she'd go back to helping her father run their hunting store. At least until she found something that inspired her. Something that made her heart beat faster. Her mind wandered straight to Cyclone, which was a problem.

"No bother at all." Azure was looking down at the bundles of joy in her arms. "I still can't quite believe it."

"You did so well."

"That's what everyone keeps telling me, but I could never have done it without you. You were amazing today. Thank you." Azure's whole expression softened.

"No need to—"

"No, really… thank you," the other woman insisted.

Ice came into the room. He had a big glass of what looked like apple juice in his hand.

"Have you told her?" he asked Azure, putting the glass on the table next to her.

"Not yet." Azure smiled broadly. "I was waiting for you." She pulled in a deep breath, looking over at Angie.

"Told me what?" Angie frowned, not sure where this was going.

"You don't know this, but my mother died giving birth to me."

Angie gasped. "I didn't. I'm so sorry. That can't have been easy."

"It wasn't. Mainly because I had to watch my father pine for her. He did his best. He named me after her because I have her eyes, but also as a tribute. I've always been grateful to have something of hers. I feel it connects me to her in a way." Azure licked her lips, which were still a little dry. "I was very afraid of how things would go with my own labor and childbirth. I had visions of… Well… they didn't end happily."

"I can imagine," Angie said.

"That's why I'm so grateful to you, Angie. You made me feel strong. Your presence was reassuring. You calmed me."

"I didn't do much." The truth was, she was fumbling along in the dark. "I did what anyone else would do."

"You were rock-solid, capable. A light in the dark. You kept me going. You made me believe in myself and my ability to birth this child… these children." She giggled. "I'm still trying to wrap my head around twins." She smiled. "We named our little boy after Ice's father, Glacier."

"That's a great name." Angie looked down at the little boy, who looked like he had fallen asleep on the breast.

"We didn't have a name for our little girl because she came as such a surprise." Azure got teary; she sniffed. "We thought Angela had a nice ring to it."

Angie grabbed her chest and gasped. "Oh, my god! Really? You're serious? I mean, you don't have to do that. You—"

Azure laughed.

"We want to name her Angela… with your permission, of course?" Ice lifted his brows. "We love the name, and we want to honor your role in bringing our daughter into this world."

Angie didn't mean for it to happen, but she burst into tears.

"Oh, no! Um… are you okay?" Azure asked. "Please tell me that these are tears of happiness."

"They are." Angie wiped her eyes, pulling herself together. She never cried. "Thank you so much! I'm honored."

"It looks like she's finished nursing," Azure said. "Do you want to hold her?"

"Um… no… Thanks, but…" She shook her head. "She's just so small. She needs her mom right—" Ice put the little girl in her arms. "Oh! Wow." She swallowed down a lump forming in her throat. Her namesake was too beautiful. She was sleeping deeply. She had little bow-shaped lips. Everything was in miniature, from her little button nose to her tiny ears and hands.

Her heart clenched so hard she made a tiny sobbing noise from the pain. *Shit!* Tears coursed down her cheeks.

"They're tears of joy, right?" Azure asked.

"Of course. She's so beautiful. Hi, Angela." The tears came faster.

⚜

"No." She shook her head as she drew closer to her apartment. "Not tonight."

Cyclone leaned back against the wall. He wore a pair of jeans and nothing else. He still looked freaking amazing in denim. Maybe even better than ever.

Cyclone stood tall as she got closer. His expression morphed into one of concern.

"Are you okay?" He cupped her jaw. Angie had to stop herself from pulling away. Not because she didn't like it, but because the opposite was true. She wanted to lean into him. To breathe him in. To feel his arms around her.

"I'm fine. It's been a long day. An emotional day. I really want to go to bed. I'm exhausted. Can we do this tomorrow, please?"

"Of course." He dropped his hand. "You were amazing today. I'm in awe of you. I don't think that there's anything you can't do."

"Thanks," she mumbled. "It wasn't that big of a deal."

"It was to me." He stood so close she could almost feel the heat coming off of him. She could smell his unique scent. It did things to her insides.

"Well, thanks." She nodded a couple of times, hoping he would leave. Hoping just as hard that he would stay a little longer.

"No, really. Azure giving birth was one of the most amazing things I've ever seen. It… it reminded me of why I want things to work out between us. Why I know we can find a way. Seeing that baby in your arms." The look in his eyes almost floored her.

"I handed them to their mother," she deadpanned, hoping he would leave. "I didn't actually hold them." Angie was not prepared to have this conversation. Not yet.

"Still. Seeing you. Seeing them. The love. Angie…" There was so much emotion in his gaze. He reached for her.

Angie backed away. "No! Everything you're saying right now… It's just bolstering my decision. I made the right choice. You've always wanted a family, Cyclone. You've always wanted kids."

"Not just *me*… *we*. What happened to *we?* We could have that." He pointed down the hall. "We could have all of it."

"Only we can't because I can't have children. Okay, there! I said it. It's out!" she yelled. Then she ran her hand through her hair, closing her eyes for a second.

Cyclone just stared at her. He blinked a couple of times. His jaw was tight. His eyes blazed.

"That can't be…" He shook his head. "You're young. You—"

"It *can* be. It is! I'm infertile. I have a condition called POI or primary ovarian insufficiency. I've had all the tests done. I've taken the drugs. I went from having a spotty menstruation cycle to no cycle. I had it checked out as a precaution… it was only supposed to be a precaution."

"This happened while we were still together?" He frowned deeply.

"Yes, I found out while you were away." She nodded.

"You didn't think to tell me? To involve me?" he asked.

"No! I didn't think it would turn out to be anything major. I was exercising more. I was trying to eat healthy. I wanted to look good for you. I lost weight, which can affect a woman's cycle. I didn't think it was anything major… until it was." She could hardly breathe. "Until I was given my diagnosis. You've always wanted kids. Don't you dare deny it. Kids and a family. At least two boys and two girls, remember? I was told that I have an acute form of the condition. Ovarian failure is the words they used."

Cyclone swallowed thickly. His eyes had darkened. His chest was heaving. He just stood there, looking at her.

"I made a decision back then. It was the right one. Now, if you'll excuse me." Cyclone didn't try to stop her.

He didn't say anything.

For a few moments after entering the apartment, she just stood there, waiting, but nothing.

Zip! Nada!

Good!

It was for the best. It made things simpler. Made them easier. Turned out that she'd made the right decision, after all. Of course, she'd known that. It still stung. Who was she kidding? It hurt!

Angie stripped out of her clothing as she headed for the bathroom. She made the shower water hot. Then she stood beneath the scorching spray and allowed herself to be weak one last time. She cried. She cried because things hadn't worked out with Cyclone. Cried because his rejection had stung far worse than him begging her to stay would have. She mostly cried because of how good that baby had felt in her arms. How right. Angie felt empty. She felt wrung out. More lonely than she'd ever felt in her life.

Tomorrow, she'd pick herself up. Tomorrow she'd be strong. Today... today was the day to let it all out. To just let herself be broken.

CHAPTER 19

Two days later…

ANGIE HOISTED THE LAST ASSAULT rifle up into its place on the rack. After packing away the left-over ammunition and earmuffs, she headed out of the gun room, closing the door behind her. A figure stood waiting.

Crap!

It was Cyclone. He was waiting at the firing range. She hadn't seen him since coming clean to him, and she'd hoped she wouldn't have to see him for her remaining time there. Certainly not like this. Alone.

Storm had asked her to sign on for more training programs in the near future, but she declined, even though she enjoyed this kind of work. It beat selling hunting gear by a mile. She couldn't bear the thought of future run-ins with Cyclone. He'd move on now; she was sure of it. Then she might have to see him with someone else. It would kill her.

Why was he here? Why?

They'd said everything there was to say to one another. At least, she had said what she needed to say… and then his silence had spoken volumes.

"I don't give after-hours training," she said. "You can come to class tomorrow, and I'll help you catch up."

Cyclone turned slowly, locking his gorgeous blue eyes with hers. "I thought I'd let you know that the goblins who raided our lair were put to death today."

"All of them?"

"Every last one, even the wounded." He nodded. "The queen was pissed off, to say the least. She had their heads removed from their shoulders. There was no mercy shown."

"Thanks for the information." She nodded once.

He looked down at the ground for a few seconds. "There were two elders who didn't make it. The silver poisoning was…" He looked down at the floor.

"Oh, no! I'm so sorry to hear."

"The silver poisoning was just too severe. We're lucky we didn't lose more lives in this senseless act."

She nodded absently. "I heard that the other three lairs were unaffected?"

"We were targeted because there is a stretch of land between our lair and the sea. The other lairs are built along cliffs right on the ocean. Also, our cliffs are not as high."

"We're easier to access?"

"Yep." He nodded. "All the lairs are working on bolstering security. It'll be our main focus for the foreseeable future." He gave a humorless chuckle. "They made an error in judgment since we are the first lair to carry arms and ammunition. Assholes didn't see that coming."

"I made an error in judgment. I didn't see them coming over the top of us since it's too dangerous. I didn't take into account that they aren't human."

"Coming over like that *was* dangerous. At least one in four goblins injured themselves. Two snapped their necks coming down that way further along the balcony. I would never risk my males in that way." Cyclone shook his head. "None of us anticipated them coming down and over that high lip. It was stupid."

"More like desperate."

"That too."

Argh!

Their conversation was stilted. This sucked so badly. Angie felt her cheeks heat.

"Um… well… Thanks for the feedback." She started backpedaling towards the door. Someone needed to put an end to this godawful discussion.

"Storm tells me that you turned down future training work with us."

She nodded. "Yes, it's not what I—"

"You love training the team. I've watched you in action. It's fantastic money. Why would you turn it down?" He folded his arms across his massive chest.

"It would be awkward, and you know it. This whole conversation is awkward. We're awkward. This lair is too small. The water under our bridge is about the size of a small ocean."

"It wouldn't be too small if we were together again."

Angie choked out a laugh. "Together?"

"Yes."

"I told you I couldn't have children, and you clammed up. You couldn't speak. That's fine… I get it."

"I was in shock. It was the last thing I expected you to say."

"Your reaction was true. You froze because you so desperately want a family. You told me more than once that it's how you guys are wired. We may not have seen each other often in that year we were together, but when we were with one another, we made it count. We talked for hours, foregoing sleep. Not going out."

His eyes darkened. "We did more than just talk."

Her stomach tightened. Her nipples, too. Damn her traitorous body. She nodded once.

"Yes, we did," she agreed.

"I clammed up because I was shocked. I needed time to process the whole thing. You should have told me back then, Ange." His eyes blazed.

"Why? You want a big family. I can't give you one. You would have talked me into staying."

"Damn straight! You're right; it doesn't change anything. It doesn't change how I feel about you. Not one bit. Not then, and not now."

Her heart felt lighter hearing him say it, even if he was two days too late.

"It will when you watch more of your friends become fathers. When you start to…" She swallowed thickly. "When you start to hate me because I can't give you what you need."

"I would never hate you." He took her hand and rubbed his thumb over the top of her knuckles. "It could never happen. This isn't your fault. It isn't something you did. We can get through this together. We can go and see doctors, and specialists. We can—"

"Don't you think I've done all of that? Because I have. I've gotten three other opinions from the best gynecologists in the country. I don't have viable eggs. I don't ovulate. I'm on hormone replacement therapy at the age of thirty-two... and have been for the last few years. I'm not even a good IVF candidate."

"IV... Sorry... what?"

"Fertility treatments. That's when they harvest the egg from the woman and the sperm from the guy and grow the start of a baby in a petri dish."

He frowned.

Angie continued, "They get the baby going outside the woman's body and then put it back inside her when conditions are one hundred percent. That wouldn't work with me because I don't have eggs in the first place." She gave a frustrated-sounding sigh. "Look, it doesn't matter. I was told that I would be lucky if I ovulated once or twice more in my lifetime. That the chances of becoming pregnant would be as likely as lightning striking me."

He let lightning crackle between his fingers. It was mesmerizing to watch. Little blue crackling streaks that went from finger to finger like webbing. Reminding her of those glass balls with lightning strands inside that you touched with your fingers.

"I could make the lightning strike happen, you know." He looked up at her.

Angie laughed. "Then I'd be dead. Not pregnant."

The laughter quickly died on her lips. "You'll meet someone else." God, it hurt her to say it. "You'll have a family someday, and you will be happy."

"That's not even remotely possible, because I wouldn't have you."

"No, but you'd be absolutely fine." She smiled through her pain.

"I love you. I know you don't want to hear it, but it's true. I fucking love you, Angie. I want to be with *you*. My dragon has already chosen you. There is no one else for me. I do want kids, but if that's not in the cards for us, I'll live. I'll feel shitty for a while, but I'll be fine because I'll have you. When my friends have whelps, I'll offer to babysit. I love you." His voice took on a desperate edge. "I can deal with everything else. I can't deal with losing you."

Cyclone loved her. She could see it in his eyes. Her heart sang and withered all in the same breath.

"When you hold a baby in your arms one day," she sniffed, working to keep all of her emotions tucked up inside of her, "you'll thank me. Your dragon will thank me even more. You're going to make an amazing dad."

Cyclone shook his head. He started saying something, but she interrupted him.

"I saw how you looked at them… Azure and Ice with their babies. Their little family. I saw. Your face was an open book. I saw the longing. The ache. Maybe there was this nagging doubt inside of me before. In fact, I know there was. That's why I didn't give you a chance to talk me out of it. I knew you'd be able to do it, but after seeing you the other day, I'm convinced I made the right decision now, more than ever."

"I would have liked to have had children, but it's not possible. I'm okay with that," he deadpanned.

"You're *not* okay with that. If you'd been okay, you would have spoken up sooner. It's not okay, Cyclone. You *can* have them. *I* can't. I will finish up with this training course. I will be leaving as soon as I'm done. I won't be back. You'll hurt for a while, and then you'll start to feel better. Then you'll move on."

"I won't! Don't do this." His eyes were pleading.

"You will. And I have to do this. It's the right thing to do. I'll meet someone who doesn't want kids. Or someone who already has them. I'll make a life for myself."

"You're lying," he choked out.

"I'm hurting right now too, and if that means I have to lie to myself to get through this, then so be it. My lie will become a truth someday." Angie tried hard to mean that.

His jaw tightened.

"This is for the best. Don't try to stop me. I've made up my mind," she told him.

"I don't get a say in this?" His voice was choked.

"No." He would thank her in a couple of years. He would! She knew it deep down inside. Angie loved this man with every fiber of her being. That's why she had to walk away.

She reached up and kissed him on the cheek.

"Stop beating yourself up. That's my only regret in all this; that you blamed yourself. It's me. I'm the problem. You're perfect. The world needs little Cyclones."

Then she walked away before she crumbled.

CHAPTER 20

Four days later…

HER EYES CLOUDED WHEN SHE caught sight of him. What did she think? That he was going to let her go without even saying goodbye?

Fuck that!

Cyclone had stayed out of Angie's way out of respect. She had made her decision. If he thought for even one second that he would be able to change her mind, he would climb fucking mountains to do it. This was a decision she'd made a long time ago. Time hadn't changed anything. There it was again. Those three stupid words.

Nothing has changed.

Only for him, they *had* changed. He was no longer angry with her. How could he be angry now that he knew her reasoning? He fucking couldn't. Not one bit. If anything, her selfless actions made him love her more. The fact that she thought she was doing the right thing for him made him love her a million times over.

Cyclone put his hands up as he closed the distance between them. "I came to say goodbye, not to try to make you stay."

She nodded once, relaxing just a smidgen. To the right of them, a formation prepared to shift to take her back to human territory. He glanced at the sky. The weather was good. No high winds or storms.

"So, are you going back to Grand Rapids?" he asked. "To your hometown?"

"Why? Are you going to stalk me if I do?" She winced. "Sorry, that was a stupid thing to say."

Actually, he had thought of doing just that. He'd racked his brain to think of ways to get her back.

"Stalking isn't my thing," he finally settled on.

Angie giggled, showing her nerves, which didn't happen often. She didn't often let herself show any emotions.

"You're less of a 'skulk in the shadows' and more of a 'throw a woman over your shoulder' kind of a guy," she told him.

"You got me there." He smiled, certain it didn't reach his eyes since he was hurting something fierce. "I just wanted you to know that I'm going to miss you."

Her beautiful eyes clouded up, and she looked at her shoes for a moment.

"I would say something back, but you would just tell me that I'm lying."

"Because you will miss me right back… you just don't

want to say it." Damn, he hadn't planned on attacking her. "But that's fine." He nodded. "It's fine if you can't say it because I know it. I know it in here." He touched his chest. Round about where his heart was. He watched the delicate column of her throat work.

"Take care of yourself, Cyclone. I hope you have the best life. You deserve it."

Motherfucker, but it hurt!

"I'll be here if you ever change your mind, and until then, you have my gift," he told her. It was a stupid joke in a situation like this, but he didn't like seeing her sad.

A hint of a smile lifted the corners of her mouth.

"Then, just so you know, you can stalk the fuck out of me anytime." He touched the side of her arm.

Fuck it!

Cyclone pulled her in and kissed her. A soft brush to her lips. A small, silly little kiss that meant everything, not just to him, but to her too. He could see it in her eyes. He could see it in the way she touched her fingers to her lips for a second when they pulled apart.

"Stubborn, female," he murmured.

Then he turned and walked away. It was the hardest damn thing he had ever done in his life.

Dang it all to hell!

Shit on a freaking stick.

She couldn't breathe. Angie just stood there, her mouth tingling. Every part of her angled towards the man walking away. The man who would carry her heart… always.

If she thought for even half a second that she was

wrong about all of this, she would call to him. She would be selfish and give in to her heart's desire. Namely him! Angie wasn't going to do that.

"You're really going?" Amy asked, giving her a fright.

"Shit! You snuck up on me." She pushed out a breath.

"Not really." Amy smiled. "You were so busy watching Cyclone walk away that a herd of elephants could've stampeded past, and you wouldn't have noticed."

"Not true," she grumbled. "I didn't sleep so well last night. I zoned out just then… that's all it was."

"Yeah, right." Amy rolled her eyes. "You're really and truly leaving?" she asked again.

"Yep." Angie nodded. "My work here is done."

"I can't believe it. It's just that you and Cyclone… The way you look at each other. The way he was when you were together."

"We weren't together." Angie shook her head slowly.

"Okay… when he thought he had a chance with you." Amy sighed. "I just witnessed two people who are very much in love saying goodbye to each other, and I think that's tragic. As your friend, it is my duty to convey that to you. That's all!"

"Well, you've done your duty." Angie turned to the shifters. They were waiting for her to give the signal that she was ready to leave. "I think the guys are waiting for me at this point."

"I really thought that you would stay. That we would eventually be besties. I was so sure." Her eyes were filled with concern.

"You were mistaken about Cyclone and me. Although we will always care for each other, and I will never forget him, we aren't meant for one another." Her voice wavered for a second, so she cleared her throat. "It's not meant to be, that's all."

"I don't see the 'not meant to be' part. I don't understand it." Amy shrugged. "But that's your business, I guess. If we had made it to besties status, I would've forced you to tell me more about this, just by the way." She lifted her brows.

Angie laughed. "You don't want to know; it's all quite depressing. But I'll be fine. So will Cyclone. Things will work out in the end. They always do."

"Vortex and I are on human soil in two weeks. Can I look you up? Maybe we could go for a drink?"

Angie frowned. "I thought you were going to New York. I'm all the way in Michigan. It's too far."

Amy shrugged. "We can make a trip of it. We might skip New York entirely. It's probably too busy for Vortex, anyways. I have the stones for my ring all picked out; I just need a jeweler to set them for me. I'm sure the jewelers in Michigan are just as good as the ones in New York. I'll give you a call when I'm in town, and we can have dinner."

"Sounds good," she said on autopilot. Angie doubted they would go that far out. If they did, it would be nice to get some news on Cyclone. Also, Amy had grown on her. They might not be besties, but they were definitely friends.

Amy nodded. "I'll do that." She pulled Angie into a hug. "Binge-watch a couple of horror series… or a couple of those murder mysteries or something. Eat plenty of chocolate and ice cream. I can see that you're sad about leaving."

"I will." Angie nodded. "If you think it will help?"

"It'll help, alright. Stay far away from romcoms. They'll just make you feel worse."

Angie laughed. "Got it. Thanks for making me feel so welcome here and for being so nice to me."

"Anytime." They hugged again. "Call me if you need to talk."

"I will."

Amy walked away, turning and waving once she reached the balcony doors. Angie waved back.

"Ready?" Typhoon asked her.

Angie nodded. "As ready as I'll ever be." Which wasn't very ready at all, if she was being honest with herself.

CHAPTER 21

Two weeks later…

HER PHONE DINGED FOR THE fifth time. And for the fifth time, she ignored it. Just like she'd ignored the three phone calls half an hour ago.

Angie put the cushion over her head and groaned. Was an afternoon nap too much to ask for?

It shouldn't be.

There was a stupid movie droning in the background. One she didn't want to watch. One she was being forced to watch being unable to sleep because of all the interruptions.

Then her doorbell rang.

"No! Come on now!" She kicked her legs in the air, using energy she didn't have. Feeling instantly drained. "Just one little nap. One nap, dammit."

Angie pulled herself up off the sofa and walked to the door. She wasn't changing, and she wasn't brushing her hair. Screw whoever was there. They could see her like this. Angie didn't care one bit.

She opened the door. "What?" she growled, expecting to see a delivery guy or… a neighbor. "Amy?"

"Um… Surprise?" Amy mumbled, taking a step back. Her eyes widened as she took Angie in. Then she turned to Vortex, who was standing a little way behind her.

"Hi, Angie!" Vortex said. "Yeah… um… I have to go do that thing." He pointed down the road while he backpedaled. "You know. That… um… thing we spoke about."

"Yes, you go. I'll call you when I need you to fetch me." Amy turned, and they kissed. It was quick, thank the lord. Angie didn't think she could stand watching them be all kissy-face with one another.

"This isn't really a good time for a visit," Angie said, realizing that Amy had come a long way to see her but not being able to give a shit. She needed a nap! Anyway, Angie was so freaking depressed, she would not be good company at all.

"Let's go inside." Amy ushered her in. "This is the perfect time for a visit. In fact, I got here just in time." She gasped loudly. "*Dirty Dancing?* Are you kidding me? You're watching *Dirty* freaking *Dancing?*"

"It isn't a romantic comedy."

"No! It's worse. Way worse! It's a romantic drama dance film, which is way, way, waaaaay worse. And what's this?" She picked up a plate containing five apple cores. "I said chocolate and ice cream. This is health food. I'm pretty sure apples don't even count as food after a breakup."

"I didn't feel like chocolate. They were the big, green juicy ones, and I couldn't resist." Her mouth had watered when she'd seen them at the grocery store. The chocolate hadn't called to her at all. After a couple of gallons of ice cream, it had lost its appeal. So, she'd grabbed the apples.

"You're doing this all wrong. No wonder you look so shitty." Amy looked her up and down. Her frown deepened. "What are those on your pajamas?"

"Flying pigs. Are you going to give me shit about my pajamas as well now?" That would be going a step too far.

"No! I actually like the pajamas. They're a great shade of purple. Makes the pink piggies pop. They're cute and look comfy."

"Oh." Angie smoothed a hand over her jammies. "They *are* comfy."

"My question to you is…" Amy looked at her watch, "why the hell are you wearing them at two-oh-three in the afternoon?"

"I wasn't feeling so great, so I took the afternoon off. I thought I would take a nap, catch up on my sleep. Then someone started texting me and calling me. Someone also decided to come over for a visit out of the blue."

"Well, if you answered your messages or picked up your damned phone, I wouldn't have to be a pest." Amy put her hands on her hips. "I popped by the store you said you worked at and met your dad, who was really happy to finally meet some friends of yours."

"Wait just a second. I never told you where I worked."

"Um… Oh, yeah…" Amy chewed on her lip. "I had Vortex pull your file. He got your basic information just in case you decided to ignore me. Back to your dad; he's very sweet, by the way. He's worried about you. Jack said that you were late for work yesterday. That you didn't go in on Monday and that you missed two days last week."

"I haven't been myself." Angie shrugged. "I'm not sleeping well. I'm tired all the time. I'm not eating properly. I'm… I'm…"

"Sad. You're sad and depressed and lonely."

Way to make her feel better. Angie nodded. "Yes, I guess I am." She chewed on her lip and tried hard to suck it up by blinking a few times. Weren't friends supposed to make you feel better, not worse?

"If it will help you feel any better, Cyclone is doing worse than you are."

"He is?" Her voice sounded light and bright. It made her feel better to know that he was just as miserable. In the next breath, she felt crappy about it. "I'm sorry to hear it. Do you want to sit down? Um… I can get you something to drink?" She wracked her brain, trying to think of what she had to offer. "I have water or coffee… no cream, so it would have to be black."

"I'm fine." They sat in the living room. "Yep." Amy sighed. "He took a few days' vacation after you left. Only, he didn't go anywhere. He stayed in his apartment. When he finally emerged, he looked like shit. He's grown a beard."

"What?" Angie shook her head. That couldn't be right. If anyone could rock a beard, it would be Cyclone, but… it wasn't him.

"Yes, you heard me right, a beard. It looks like something big and furry died on his face. He's grumpy as fuck. I mean, ten times worse than before. He speaks in grunts, adding a word in here or there just so we'll understand him… and then, not always. Nope… he's not coping at all."

"That *does* sound bad. It hasn't been that long, though. He should improve soon enough." She tried to sound positive and to sound like she meant it.

"Doubtful. He seems to be getting worse. Avalanche mentioned that he's taken up meditation." Amy made a face.

"That's good. It's something positive. It should help him."

"Yeah… no. He growls the entire time he's supposed to be meditating. He even snarled a few times the other day. He's spending more and more time in his dragon form."

"Oh… that's not great." Amy shook her head. "Look, he'll get over me again. He'll move on. I know it!"

"He didn't get over you the last time. Or should I say, he still isn't over you from back then." Amy shook her head; her eyes were filled with concern. "Sorry, it's just that, even if we're not going to be besties anymore, Vortex and Cyclone are BFFs, and that means that the big old lug is a good friend of mine, too. When Cyclone hurts… we hurt. I hate seeing him like this. I hate seeing you like this, too. You guys clearly belong together. As someone from the outside looking in, I can tell you that it's as clear as day. I had hoped that I was wrong when you left. But after seeing the two of you…" She lifted her brows. "I'm convinced."

"I can't have children," Angie blurted.

"I'm sorry to hear that." Amy's eyes filled with compassion, and she touched the side of Angie's arm.

"I've had time to work through it. I don't want to get into the details of my condition, but it is what it is. One of the gynecologists told me that my chances of conceiving are on par with getting struck by lightning. I had a look at those odds, and they're one in five hundred thousand. Not great odds at all. All of the specialists have told me to put it out of my mind. After I saw the third one, I enlisted. I couldn't tie Cyclone to me. Not after hearing how much he wanted to become a father. I saw one more specialist, just to be sure. They all told me the same thing. So, I put all of my energy into fighting for my country. Learning I'd never be a mother didn't break me. This won't break me either. Cyclone is far stronger. I know he'll be fine."

"The hand you've been dealt is tough. I can't imagine. I guess the only thing I can say is that maybe Cyclone has changed his mind about wanting kids after you told him you can't have them." Amy rested her hands on her legs and moved a little closer towards Angie.

"You don't change your mind about something like that. You just don't! Having kids is important to Cyclone. We spoke about it in depth. I could see the look he got when he talked about a family. We couldn't wait to officially be together. We planned on trying to get pregnant as soon as possible. We had so many hopes and dreams."

"You can still have hopes and dreams and a future without having children," Amy insisted.

"I can. He doesn't have to. I'm not tying him to me. I won't do that." She shook her head.

"You couldn't tie that man if you tried. All I'm going to say is that you might be making a mistake." Amy tucked some hair behind her ear, pulling in a breath. She seemed to be thinking her next words through. "Give it some thought. Again, this is from the outside looking in. Sometimes you see more from this angle… just saying… but think on it. Maybe he envisioned a family with you. If that's changed, then perhaps his thinking would change too. Stands to reason, doesn't it?"

No! It didn't stand to reason at all.

"Promise me you'll give it some thought," Amy went on when she didn't say anything.

That was an easy thing to promise since it was all she could think about, anyway. Angie wished she could *stop* freaking thinking about it already.

She nodded. "Sure, I can promise that." It didn't mean she'd change her mind.

Amy huffed out a breath. "Good. That's good." She squeezed Angie's arm. "Then, about dinner. Please tell me you'll join Vortex and me? We have reservations at a fancy restaurant here in town."

"It sounds like you have a romantic evening planned."

"Not at all. We would love it if you could join us." Amy clasped her hands together.

"Thanks for the invite, but I won't make a great dinner guest. I have some chocolate lying around here somewhere and a whole season of *American Horror Story* I haven't watched yet. I think I'll do that instead." Angie smiled. "Maybe next time you're in town…?" She lifted her brows. "I'm depressed and boring. I would rather pull out my nails than change out of these pajamas."

"I can understand that last part. It's a date, since I plan on coming back." Amy smiled. "Now, promise me you'll eat a whole damned slab of chocolate and that you'll stay away from anything with the word 'romantic' on it."

"I will," Angie said.

"Promise you'll think about what we spoke about as well?"

"I will," she repeated.

Thank goodness that seemed to satisfy Amy, who texted Vortex to fetch her. Angie wanted to be alone with her pitiful self. She'd give herself a little longer, and then she'd figure out what to do with her sorry life.

CHAPTER 22

Four days later…

BY THE TIME CYCLONE MADE it back to the lair, his wings shook with exhaustion. He felt weary from his snout right down to his tail tip. He landed on his balcony, yawned wide, stretched his great dragon back, and then shifted into his human form. It took a while to change back due to how fatigued he was right down to a cellular level.

Good!

He'd take a quick shower and then hopefully sleep. He'd better fucking sleep. After flying for all those miles, the Sandman had better bring a sack of his sleepy shit and do his goddamned job for a change. It was that, or Cyclone was going to rake his own eyeballs out. He was tired of being tired. Tired of—

Someone was in his apartment. His scales rubbed as he pushed the door open, eyes narrowed.

"Finally," Vortex said. The male lounged on his sofa. He held up an almost empty Budweiser. "I took your last one. It's your own fault for making me wait so damned long. It was also the only thing, other than sour milk and ketchup that you have inside that refrigerator." He pointed towards the kitchen with his thumb.

"You didn't tell me you were coming," Cyclone barked.

The male gave him a long stare. "I texted you three hours ago."

"I was flying." Cyclone shrugged.

"You've been flying for three hours?" Vortex lifted a brow; he didn't look impressed.

"Yes. What of it?" Cyclone shrugged.

"You worked a full shift today. If I'm not mistaken, you decided to do a check of our perimeters with one of the guard formations. That was after hand-to-hand combat early this morning. You took on three males, breaking several of their bones. Only to go flying for god knows how long after all that."

"And now I'm tired and want to be left alone. So, you can take what's left of my last beer and fuck off," he growled the last.

"Firstly, it's not healthy to push yourself this hard. Look at you! You look like shit."

"You're not an oil painting yourself," Cyclone threw back. Where did this asshole get off? "If you keep talking, I'll turn you into a fucking abstract. Those are paintings that look nothing like the thing they're supposed to represent. In other words, you'll look nothing like the male you once were. You'll be an abstract version of your current self."

"Secondly," Vortex ignored him flat, "being in your dragon scales for too long is not good for you. It dulls your human emotions and—"

"It doesn't dull shit!" Cyclone growled. If fucking only.

"Amy went to see Angie while we were on human soil."

Cyclone's chest tightened. "I see." He sat on a nearby sofa. "What did she say? How is she? No! Fuck! Don't tell me." He scrubbed a hand over his face. If she was looking great, it would fucking kill him, and if she wasn't, it would kill him even more.

"She looked like shit, too. Only, thankfully, females don't have facial hair, so you are worse by far because of that thing on your face." Vortex focused on his beard, making an expression of disgust.

Cyclone stroked it. "It's fashionable. All I need now is a man-bun, and I'm all set."

Vortex choked out a laugh. "It might be fashionable if you actually trimmed it. If that beard was an animal, it would be rabid. Then, concerning the man-bun… good thing you're not a man." Then he turned serious. "Now, shifter the fuck up!"

Say what now? Cyclone growled a warning. "I don't want to have to clean blood off my floors, and your female would cry if you died. I fucking hate crying females. Those are the only two things saving you right now. Careful, asshole!"

"Calm the fuck down! I'm here as a friend. You stopped me from making the biggest mistake of my life once, and I'm here to return the favor," Vortex said, his voice even.

"Make it quick because I'm tired. There's actually a small chance I might be able to sleep tonight if whatever you're about to say doesn't aggravate me too much."

"You love Angie," Vortex said.

Cyclone rolled his eyes because what the fuck? "I know that. Tell me something I don't know. You're wasting my time."

"She loves you. In fact, I'd go so far as to say that she's fucking crazy about you."

"I know that too." It made him feel slightly better hearing it, even if it would be infinitely better coming directly from her.

"You're both heartbroken." Vortex downed the last of the beer, plonking the bottle down.

"Not news." He yawned.

"You once told me that I needed to go after what I wanted. Or, more precisely, *who* I wanted. You said I needed to fight for Amy. That I needed to be willing to give up everything for her. That I would live with regret for the rest of my life if I didn't do it. Do you remember that?" The male lifted his brows.

"Of course I do. It wasn't that long ago." Cyclone hoped that the male would get to the point really soon because he was getting irritated. The only thing keeping him from lashing out was the fact that Vortex was trying to be nice. He wasn't a bad male. A little slow at times, but not bad. Also, he would hate it if Amy cried. She'd sob noisily. It would be messy and even more irritating. It would affect his sleep, which he needed.

"Are you listening to me?" the male growled.

"Yes!" Cyclone snarled.

"You're not. What did I just say?"

Cyclone folded his arms.

"That's what I thought. I was telling you that you would regret it if you let Angie slip through your fingers. She's your mate."

"I know that! Tell me something new. Angie doesn't want me, though. That's the difference between you and me. Between our situations. Amy wanted you. You fucked up when it came to her, but she wanted you. Angie doesn't want me. I tried hard, but it didn't work."

"Try harder! You're acting like a pussy," Vortex growled.

Cyclone jumped up off the sofa. Every scale rubbed. His teeth felt sharp. He fisted his hands.

"Say that again," he said through clenched teeth.

"You heard me." Vortex stayed where he was. He even leaned back to get a more comfortable position. "You need to try harder."

"Not that part. The other part. Say it again," Cyclone rasped, his fists clenched.

"No!" Vortex said. "You heard me the first time."

Clever asshole! He knew how far to push and when to back off.

"What should I do? What do you suggest, if you're so fucking smart?" Cyclone asked.

"Go to human soil. Go speak to her."

"It won't work. I talked plenty when she was here. She wouldn't listen. Not once," Cyclone said.

"Go to her! Pursue her. Don't take no for an answer. Don't give up on her. Show her that you mean it when you say you don't mind about her not being able to have a baby." Vortex's face softened. "Angie told Amy, and we don't keep secrets from one another. Moving on...

you need to make her believe that you're okay with it. Right now, she doesn't believe you. She thinks she's doing you a favor by cutting you loose."

"She isn't!" Cyclone insisted.

"I know, dammit! That's why I'm here. Don't give up. Go to her! Convince her." Vortex sounded animated. His eyes blazed.

"She won't listen." Cyclone realized that he did sound like a pussy. *Fuck!* It was true, though. Angie had been very clear. "Short of abducting her, tying her up, and then forcing her to listen to reason, I doubt anything would work."

"That sounds like a solid plan to me." Vortex smiled.

Cyclone fell back in his chair. His mind was working a mile a minute.

"Fuuuuuuck!" he finally pushed out.

"So, when are you leaving?" Vortex asked.

"First thing."

"Atta boy!" Vortex jumped to his feet. "This is the part where we hug it out." He walked towards Cyclone, his arms wide.

"Don't you fucking dare." He pointed a finger at Vortex. "Unless you want to bleed. And I happen to like this sofa."

"It's okay for males to hug," Vortex said. "There is such a thing as a man-hug."

"We're shifters," Cyclone deadpanned.

"You have a point. So," Vortex smiled, "tomorrow, then?"

"Yep." Cyclone nodded, a smile spreading across his face for the first time in a long fucking time, and it felt good. No, it felt great!

CHAPTER 23

The next day…

PACKING SHELVES WAS JUST ABOUT the worst job that there was at the store. That and selling camping gear. She hated it!

Right now, she was unpacking sniper gloves and hanging them on the display rack. From here, she got to unpack the new stock of fur hats. The ones with the ear flaps since winter wasn't far off. Lucky her! Life was wonderful. If she didn't find herself something better to do, she'd go stark raving mad. At the same time, she had a lot to be thankful for. At least she had a paying job and parents who loved her. There was that.

Working for her father wasn't what she wanted, though. Angie wanted to do something important with her life. She wanted to put down roots. If she was honest with herself, signing up with the military had been her way of running away from her problems. She didn't want to run anymore. She wanted to live her life. Really live it. Her mind went straight to a certain tall, gorgeous guy with the most striking blue eyes.

Stop!

Stop!

Stop!

Angie rolled her shoulder, which felt a little stiff today, then she picked up a box of gloves. Her father was helping a customer. There were two more men in the tent section. They'd said they didn't need any help. She hung a few gloves. There was a squeaking of boots on the polished tiles behind her, so she turned around. She'd missed this person coming into the store. As she locked eyes with him, her mouth fell open. Then she dropped the gloves with a bang. The box fell over, and a couple of pairs fell out.

Crap!

Angie took it back. She *did* want to run. Running was the right thing to do. Especially in a situation like this.

"Angela. Just the person I wanted to see." It was Cyclone. Holy shit, but he looked like a tall drink of something delicious. A piña colada with an extra hit of rum, perhaps. Or maybe something nonalcoholic instead, since she tried to drink her sorrows away the other night and ended up puking after the second glass. Her rug would never be the same. Now the thought of alcohol was offensive. A tall drink of something else, then.

No!

Stop it, Angie!

"What are you doing here? You shouldn't be here," she told him. "We had a talk about stalking."

A couple walked in, reminding her of where she was. There were customers around. She needed to play it cool and keep her voice down. *What was he doing here?*

"I'm not here to stalk you. You can relax. I'm going on a hunting trip. I decided I needed a break from… my side of town. Thought I would take the trip on *human*…" he mouthed the word since the tent guys had just walked into their aisle, "—soil." He said as he pushed his hands into the front of his jean pockets. Holy smokes, but that sweater fit him just so. It was emerald green. She was sure she could see his eight-pack through the knit.

Then his words registered. "Hunting trip? Why would you want to go on a hunting trip? Are you taking guns and all that? Like a real hunting trip?" She was repeating herself and needed to stop.

"Yep." He nodded a few times. She noted that his face was cleanly shaven. Maybe he was getting over her already, which was good. No… great! She swallowed down the rest of her emotions since she had no business feeling them. "Only, I don't need guns. I borrowed one. We have a ton of the things back at… you know… home."

"You do." She nodded, narrowing her eyes. "Why this store, out of all the stores in this country? You really didn't have to come here."

Rat!

She could smell one. A big-ass stinky one.

"You're the best, Angela. You know your stuff. I only want to buy from the best. Is that so bad? Also, if I'm going to spend a whole lot of money on gear, I would rather it went here than to some stranger."

She could still smell a rodent, even though it made a small amount of sense.

"You can stop calling me Angela; it's weird." It made her think about them having sex, which wasn't a good rabbit hole to go down. Not good at all.

"Okay, Angie." His voice went all deep and husky. "Anything you want, as long as you help me get the things I need. Then I'll be out of your hair."

"Once you have everything you need for this trip of yours, you'll go?" She lifted her brows. This seemed fishy.

"Yes, that's the plan." He nodded once.

Rat!

More than one of the things.

"You gents doing okay?" she asked the guys, who were now looking at rain jackets.

They nodded. Said they were fine and kept looking.

"You won't talk to me about anything other than camping gear?" she asked Cyclone.

"Nope." He shook his head, looking innocent. Forget a rat. This was fishy. *Fishy. Fishy.* A whole school of the damn things fishy!

Abort!

Abort!

Cyclone was not innocent. Not even close.

Danger!

Danger!

He was anything but innocent.

Keeping his big blue eyes on her, he blinked a couple of times. "The sooner I have the things I need, the sooner I'll be on my way."

"Fine," she finally pushed out. "Do you have warm gear? The nights have started to get cold. Days are still mostly good, so you'll need a good sunhat. Where are you going?"

"Where do you recommend I go?" he asked.

Angie rolled her eyes. "You don't have actual plans to go hunting? You *are* stalking me," she whispered. How was it that the store was so busy all of a sudden?

"Ummmmm… no, I'm really not."

Funny, she *did not* believe him.

"I thought I would ask around for the best spots. I'm looking for something remote. Out in the middle of nowhere. Somewhere that doesn't get many visitors. Off the beaten path and all that. I didn't want to pick the wrong destination."

"I guess I understand why you would need a place like that. Do you plan on… you know?" She widened her eyes. "Shifting" was what she wanted to say, but she couldn't come out and say it, now could she?

Her dad kept glancing in their direction, and another guy had just walked into the store.

"I plan on 'you knowing' a lot. Huge amounts." He winked at her.

"Okay, well, somewhere remote is important, but you'll hunt as… um… as yourself?" she whispered.

"Oh, yes." He smiled. It was so damned sexy that it hurt to watch. Kind of like looking at the sun. "I plan on hunting like this." He ran his hand down his sweater and her mouth dried up. "More fun that way."

Shit! She needed to get him kitted out, and then he needed to go. He was just too… well, too *him,* which was a problem. He did weird things to her body. To her heart, too, if she was really being honest, which she preferred not to be. It hurt less that way.

"Let me get you a cart." Angie walked to the door, wheeling one over. "Do you need cooking gear?"

"Yes. Warm clothing, cooking gear, a sturdy blow-up mattress. Do you have them in a queen or a king-size? Also, it would need to be able to take a beating."

Holy shit! Was he taking some woman on a camping trip? If so, it was really freaking rude to come to her to buy the gear. What an asshole! They might not be together, but still.

"I mean, look at me. I'm a big male." He looked down at himself. Made her look, too. *Asshoooole!* "A regular mattress will deflate before midnight."

"Oh!" Maybe he would be alone, after all. "Are you going on your own?" The question just popped out of her mouth.

His eyes brightened right up. "Would you be angry if I wasn't?"

Angie sighed. "Are you serious right now?"

"I'm not taking some female, if that's what you're asking."

"Whatever! It doesn't matter." *Crap!* She was acting all jealous.

He gave her a knowing smirk. "I'll need a tent. At least a two-man, bigger would be better though," he chuckled, "on account of my size."

She looked… again. Oh, dear lord, this had to stop.

"Okay, so you need everything for a trip away by yourself but you need sleeping gear for two." He was totally taking someone else. "No problem."

"Actually, give me everything I'll need for two people because you never know what the future might hold."

Right!

Like she was supposed to believe that. It was none of her business.

Then again, was he trying to rub her nose in it? If so, he was doing a good job. It stung.

"No problem," Angie muttered as she walked through the aisles, throwing things into the cart. Warm clothing. The mattress and bedding. Cooking gear. A head torch. Everything he needed to start a fire, including kindling. A gas stove. All of it. All the best quality. All the most expensive items, because screw him for coming here. For looking so together. So good! He didn't have to come to this particular store, and yet here he was. Wanting the best. Wanting to support her family. Yeah, right! He was taking another woman on a trip away, and he wanted her to know about it. Did he think she would change her mind?

No damned way was that happening.

"I will need some rope as well," Cyclone said as they were making their way to the checkout area.

"Excuse me?" She frowned.

"Rope. I'm going to need some." He smirked.

"Why?" She shook her head. Probably for kinky sex stuff with his new girlfriend. *Argh!*

Cyclone gave a one-shouldered shrug. "It's one of those items that comes in handy."

"We should have some down this aisle." She walked to the part of the store where they kept such things and started walking back with a coiled piece.

"I'll take two… please." He smiled, looking smug and happy.

Screw him.

Angie grabbed another coil and headed back.

"What about duct tape? Do you guys keep any of that?"

"Why on earth would you need duct tape?" She frowned. This was bizarre.

"What if a hole rips in my tent? It's called being prepared."

That made a crazy kind of sense. "If I didn't know you better, I'd say you were planning on abducting someone." She pushed out a laugh, trying to sound completely relaxed, which was impossible around this man.

Not her!

Surely not!

Back to smelling a rat.

No! Just no! Cyclone wasn't like that. He would never have come here to abduct her. That was just plain stupid. It made more sense that he was going on some trip with a woman and wanted to rub her nose in it… which also wasn't like him.

"Are you… planning on abducting someone?" She laughed. It came out sounding stilted.

Because what the heck was going on?

Cyclone gave a half-smile. He made a noise of agreement.

"Do you have any?" He lifted his brows, not denying anything. There was no way he was planning an abduction, though. That was crazy talk.

"You'll have to go to the hardware store," she told him.

"I guess I'll be somewhere remote." He gave her this look. "Then they won't hear the screams. Perhaps I don't need the duct tape after all."

"Screams?!" Her eyes widened.

"Since I'm abducting someone and all." He laughed.

"For a second, I thought you might be serious." He normally was quite a serious guy.

Cyclone laughed harder. "You should have seen your face. Anyway, this should get me through a couple of days in the wilderness?" He looked at the supplies.

"Yep. It should do the trick. Are you going soul-searching?" She really shouldn't be asking him such personal questions.

"You could say that."

"It's probably a good idea," she mumbled, stepping behind the cash register to tally up his total. She tried not to look at him too much.

The store was still pretty busy. Dad was helping the two guys who hadn't wanted help earlier, and the couple looked like they needed advice from the way they kept looking over at her. *Shit!* She needed to finish up with Cyclone so that she could get back to work.

Five minutes later, she gave him his total, which was an eye-watering amount.

Good!

Cyclone didn't blink when he handed her his credit card.

"Mr. Hamish Cyclone," she read off the front of the card. So that's what the H stood for.

Cyclone grinned. Why was he so damned happy?

"Storm apparently has a sense of humor," he said.

Okay, well, maybe it was funny, but she couldn't even crack a smile. Angie was officially pathetic. Why did he have to come here? Why? She'd managed to get five hours of sleep last night. She'd actually watched an entire television show for the first time yesterday. She hadn't had to hold back tears since this morning. She was starting to get her shit together... well, sort of. As much as could be expected, and boom... now she was at square one again.

Angie gave him the card back together with his receipt and started bagging the items. Cyclone helped. Of course he did, because being gorgeous with a shitty personality was too much to ask. He had to be the whole package. One big taunt. Once they were done, she went to the brochure stand and grabbed a few of them, handing them to Cyclone.

"These would be good options for your trip. Secluded and serene. Good hunting, too."

"Perfect." He put them into the closest bag. Then he hoisted the tent onto his back, followed by a folded-up camper chair. Then he picked up one bag after the other, leaving two on the table. "Would you mind helping me to my car?" He looked outside at where a black SUV was parked.

Angie had to hold back a deep sigh. "Sure. We need to make it quick. I've got customers who need me." She picked up the last two bags and followed him out.

Cyclone popped the trunk, putting all the items in the back. Then he grabbed the two bags from her, chucking them in too and closing the trunk with a click of a button.

"Well, good luck with—"

One second she was standing on the ground about to say goodbye, and the next, she was being hoisted into Cyclone's arms. Like "feet off the ground" hoisted. She made a squeaking noise. Then she was being flung over his shoulder.

What the—?

"Cyclone! Put me down!" she yelled as he strode to

the passenger side of the vehicle. All she could see were his glutes working as he took one stride after the other. "Cyclone, this isn't funny," she deadpanned.

Was he abducting her? Had that been his plan?

He put his hands on her hips and pulled her back over his shoulder. The big oaf was about to put her down when his whole body tensed. His hands clenched a little tighter on her hips.

"This really isn't funny!" she shouted.

Cyclone ignored her. He kept her there in midair, his face turned to the right. Then his eyes closed, and his nostrils flared.

"What the hell are you doing?" she shouted, trying to get him to let her go. He had this expression she couldn't read. "Put me down!" She kicked her legs and tried to jerk herself free, but she may as well have been trying to stop the wind from blowing. Or the ocean from forming waves. "Let me go!" she yelled, kicking her legs some more.

"Are you okay?" a woman asked. She sounded frightened.

"Don't talk to him, honey. Back away," a man said. "We'll call 911. I'm calling 911!" he shouted.

Cyclone put her down, his eyes on the people. He turned to them, keeping a hand on her hip. It looked like a husband and wife. The lady was pushing a stroller. There was a tiny baby inside. The woman's eyes were wide, and she was walking backward, both hands white-knuckled on the stroller handle. The husband had one hand on the stroller and the other on his wife's arm. His eyes were on Cyclone. He looked like he was petrified.

"Stay away from us," he said, his voice shaky. Angie couldn't blame him. He was small for a human, and

Cyclone was well… Cyclone. "Let that lady go. If you leave now, you might avoid arrest." He let go of his wife and pulled his phone out of his pocket.

"It's okay," Angie told them. "We're together. We were fooling around."

"Fooling around?" The guy stood tall. "We could've called the police." He put his cellphone back in his pocket. "Are you sure? That didn't look like fooling around. You're not just saying that because you're afraid of him?" He narrowed his eyes on Cyclone before looking back at her.

"I'm very sure. I'm fine. I swear."

"You could have hurt her," the guy told Cyclone. "It looked like… like…" The husband looked out of sorts.

"Like you were abducting her," the wife said, her chest heaving. "Are you sure you're okay?" she asked Angie. She didn't look convinced.

"I'm absolutely fine. I'm sorry we gave you such a fright." The baby started fussing. It kicked its little legs and made these choking noises.

"Oh, sweety," the lady said, fetching him out from the stroller. "He needs to be fed," she told her husband, who took the stroller. With a glaring look, they walked past, continuing down the street at a fast pace. Angie and Cyclone watched them walk for a minute.

"What was that?" Angie finally asked, turning to face Cyclone. She folded her arms.

"I… I'm sorry." He shook his head, backing away.

"Were you about to abduct me just then?" It sounded crazy.

She turned, and the couple was a ways down the road already. There was no one around. Angie looked into the store, and no one was looking their way. If he had been planning on abducting her, he could do it now, no problem.

"No… not at all. I… um… Shit!" He ran a hand through his hair, roughing it up. "I shouldn't have done that. I'm sorry! I was fooling around. Holy fucking shit! I need to go. Thanks for your help." Then he jogged around the SUV.

"Cyclone, you're making no sense," she shouted after him.

He ignored her, getting into the vehicle.

"Cyclone!" she tried again, but he started the car and pulled away. Barely braking at the next intersection, he took a left and sped off.

What. The. Hell?

Angie could barely catch her breath. Cyclone had been about to take her. He'd been about to push her into his car and drive off with her.

Rope? Duct Tape? Ha!

She knew it. The family taking a walk had scared him off. Or had they? Maybe he'd changed his mind about taking her. Maybe he'd seen them. Seen that little bundle all wrapped up in a blue cotton blanket, and that was what had changed his mind. Maybe he'd realized right then that she was right. That he wanted a family more than he wanted her.

It didn't matter. None of it did. He was gone. Maybe he'd never planned to steal her away… to try to change her mind. Or perhaps he had changed his mind. Either way, he'd left. That was that, and it was for the best. She was going to march back in there and help some customers. Then she was going to finish unpacking their newly delivered products. Just to brighten up her day even further, she was going to do a stocktake of the items in the storeroom. There was nothing like a stocktake to get a person's mind off of their troubles.

CHAPTER 24

That evening…

ABOUT DAMNED TIME, SHE THOUGHT to herself as she opened the door to her little house. It had been a long day. Too long. Especially since she kept looking at the entrance every time someone came in. There was a secret part of her that had been hoping it was Cyclone. That he had changed his mind about… what? About abducting her? Did she really want to be abducted?

Angie didn't answer the question because she didn't think she'd like her answer. She disliked how she was feeling inside even more. It made her want to give drinking a try again. *Nah!* Drinking alone was a bad idea, anyway.

She sighed. Ah, jeez, she actually hated herself right now. Hated the moping. The moaning. She hated feeling so weak and not being able to do a damned thing about it.

Screw it, she was getting into some athletic gear, and she was going to train. In fact, she was getting into an outfit that Cyclone had bought her because, screw him, she was moving on. She was going to do it. Angie pulled off her clothes, opened her closet, picked a workout outfit, and started dressing.

Who knew? She might even unpack that huge dildo later and go to town on herself. Why the hell not? She deserved it. Exercise and serious self-love; the first two steps to moving the fuck on. If she never saw Cyclone again, it would be too soon.

Her chest tightened, but she ignored it. She ignored that her eyes stung, and she picked an upbeat tune instead. She was just about to turn up the volume and get started when there was a knock at her door.

Cyclone!

Arghhh!

She had to stop thinking that way. She really was completely pathetic. Angie would get rid of whoever it was—*not* Cyclone—and then get on with moving on with her life.

"What?" she asked as she opened her door.

Oh, god!

It was him.

It was Cyclone. He wore black jeans and a royal blue sweater. The tops of his silver chest markings were just visible above the neckline. He looked good enough to eat.

"What are you doing here?" She narrowed her eyes. "Did you get some duct tape? Is that why you're back?"

Her heart raced with excitement. *Shit!* What was wrong with her? She was not letting him abduct her. *No!* She'd fight really hard, and if he happened to overpower her and leave with her, well then, it wouldn't be her fault now, would it? No matter what, she would not let him seduce her or change her mind. Angie needed to be strong.

"Relax, Spice, I'm not here to throw you over my shoulder again. Although you're tempting me with that outfit. Fuck me, I can see your nipples through that Lycra."

She sucked in a breath, preparing to put him in his place because that was just plain rude. They weren't dating. They weren't even casually sleeping together anymore. He could not talk to her like that.

"Before you say anything, I did go and buy something after leaving today. It wasn't duct tape, although I'm regretting that decision now." He looked her up and down.

"Stop that!" She pulled in a breath. "You bought me a present? Why would you buy me a present?"

"After seeing you today, I decided you needed this thing." He held up a wrapped box. The paper was off-white. There was a gold ribbon around it with a big bow. The box was too big for jewelry but too small for a whole lot of other things.

Jewelry? Why had that even factored as a possibility? It was probably a dildo. A much smaller one this time.

"You decided I needed this after seeing me today?" She narrowed her eyes on the gift.

"Yep."

"Pepper spray, perhaps?" she asked, brows raised.

Cyclone grinned. "That's cute, Spice."

"Don't call me that."

"Fine!" he growled, leaning up against the side of the doorjamb, looking all sexy. Not that he needed to try very hard. "Are you going to let me in so that you can open the gift?"

"I shouldn't." She rubbed her lips together. "I would

be insane to let you in. Crazy! I told you that I've made up my mind. I'm pretty sure that some fancy gift will not change things. It's not possible."

"Well then, you have nothing to worry about. Let me in and open the gift." He spoke in a deep voice. Holy smokes, but he sucked!

"I'll open the gift, and then you're leaving? That's the deal?" She was sure to keep her voice no-nonsense because she meant it.

"I swear. If you tell me to leave after you open that, then I'm gone." He grabbed both sides of the jamb, his biceps popping up.

He sucked so badly! "Fine!" she pushed out. "But I'm not offering you anything to drink. You're not staying that long."

He smiled. "I'm sure I'll manage."

"Okay, then." She stood to the side, and he walked in. She made the mistake of watching him as he did. Of looking at his ass in those jeans.

Crap!

Angie would open the stupid gift. Maybe it was a tennis bracelet. A whole string of fat diamonds or gleaming pearls. He should know by now that she wasn't swayed by such things.

He put the gift in her hands as soon as she sat down. Cyclone sat next to her but on the far side of the seat so as to give her plenty of space.

Angie pulled on the golden bow.

"Wait!" Cyclone said. "Before you open that. It's important that you know that I was, in fact, planning to abduct you. I was going to take you to one of those remote places you suggested and force you to believe me when I told you that I love you. That I'm okay with us never having kids."

She frowned. "You were going to tie me up? Put duct tape over my mouth so that I would be forced to listen to you?"

"Actually, the rope and duct tape were going to be used during our make-up sex, but you raise a good point about forcing you to listen to me by taping up that sexy mouth of yours."

"You are… you…" *Shit!* That was probably one of the most romantic things anyone had ever said to her. "Why didn't you do it? What changed?" she finally asked.

"First, open my gift. We'll talk afterward." He glanced at the wrapped package.

Crap! Now she would open this thing and then be forced to kick him out. She preferred the abduction route.

"Fine," she huffed out, ripping the paper since she was so pissed off.

A box fell into her lap. One she thought she recognized. She picked it up, and sure enough, it was a pregnancy test.

"Is this a joke?" Her eyes stung as tears tried to force themselves out. "If it is, it's not funny." Her voice cracked a little.

"It's not a joke, Ange. Not even close. I scented you when you were in my arms. Over my shoulder. I scented… myself. When I held you with your belly at face level, I swear I heard a heartbeat. Smaller… faster. Not yours."

"Stop that!" she yelled. "I can't have kids. You're hurting me. You shouldn't be saying these things. It isn't fair!" she spoke quickly, fumbling a little over her words.

"I swear, it's true. Please humor me! Do this one thing. Take the test." He looked at the box in her hand.

"I'm *not* humoring you." She shook her head hard. "Not when it comes to something like this. All I ever wanted was to become a mother. Especially after meeting you. It's a part of the reason why I can't withhold being a parent from you… because I understand. Please don't make me do this. It will kill me to see one line."

"There will be two lines. Trust me."

Holy shit!

She couldn't breathe, even though she was inhaling and exhaling too damned quickly. *What the hell?*

"Please." Was she begging for him to let her off the hook or begging him to make her do it? She wasn't sure at this point.

"I'll help you take the test. I'll hold your hand the whole time. If it's one line, I'm abducting you. The camping gear is still in the car. I'm almost a hundred percent sure it'll be two lines, though. I'm very serious about this."

"I can't do it!" Her hands shook, and her mouth felt dry.

"You can," he insisted. "I'll help you."

"You're not helping me pee on a stick. In fact, you're not even watching me pee on a freaking stick," she told him.

"You're right. I might get a boner."

She gasped and choked out a laugh, despite the situation. Despite her racing heart and clammy hands.

"Because of you having your Lycra pants down around your ankles and not because of the peeing part. Who do you take me for? Okay, don't answer that question." His smile quickly died. "Please do it. For me. You can. You're the bravest person I know." His eyes shone with such sincerity.

Angie looked down at the test. She never thought she'd ever have one of these in her hands. Cyclone looked so sincere, so sure, even though he was very mistaken. She could do this. It didn't change anything. It didn't because there was no way she was pregnant. It wasn't possible!

CHAPTER 25

Cyclone paced from one side of the short hallway to the other. Back and forth. Back and forth. He roughed up his hair, holding back a groan. Patience had never been a strong suit of his.

Then he banged on the door. "Tell me when you've done it. I want to see the results at the same time as you."

"I haven't done it yet," she replied.

"Why not?" Actually, it was true; he hadn't heard her peeing.

"I'm… I'm working my way up to it."

"Pee already!" he yelled.

"I can't just pee!" she yelled back. "Especially not when you're shouting at me."

"Sorry!" She was right. He was being pushy. "Did you read the instructions?" Cyclone asked, since he was being super fucking pushy already.

"Yes! I'm reading them a second time to be sure, then I'll pee."

"And then let me in." He sounded desperate. Desperate now that he was starting to second-guess himself. What if he had been mistaken? What if he'd sensed something that he wanted so badly to be true? What if it wasn't the case? What if Angie wasn't pregnant? He'd be making an infertile female take a test. He'd be giving her false hope. He'd crush her. Angie was strong in so many things, but in this… in this, she was weak. Not being able to be a mother had devastated her to the point where she didn't feel worthy of being with him. Where she didn't feel worthy, full stop. He'd read up on it. There were groups for females like her. They got together to talk it through. To help one another. There were even groups for couples who suffered from infertility. What he was asking her to do was a big fucking deal, and he might just be wrong.

He'd smelled himself on her for just a second. What if that heartbeat had been hers? He was sure there had been two. One faster but so incredibly soft. Only, now… now he was getting worried. Fucking worried. That other family had been there. What if he'd heard that baby's heartbeat? The one in the stroller. Thinking back, three or four seconds was too short to have made a decision. Why hadn't he come to see her and then found a way to get close to her belly? To smell her good and proper. To put his ear against her skin.

His whole plan had been not to get too close. Not to get too sniffy. Firstly, not to scare her off, and secondly, because he wanted to find out together with her whether they were going to be parents. Now he was regretting that decision.

Fuck!

"Did you pee yet?" There was a growl to his voice that he couldn't help.

"I was about to, and now you put me off," she mumbled. "You shouldn't have to even ask."

Cyclone sighed. "Sorry." He needed to pull himself together.

There was the sound of water, but it seemed like she'd turned the faucet on. "That doesn't sound like you're peeing."

She laughed. "I should hope not. It would mean I was an elephant or something. I'm running the water because I heard it helps make you want to go. Can you bring me some water?"

"Yes!" Good! Finally! Something he could do. Cyclone hated feeling useless. What if she was pregnant? It would mean being completely useless for the entire pregnancy, not to mention the birth.

No!

He'd cook and clean. He'd massage Angie's feet and run her baths for her. He'd carry her and rub her belly, and…

He might be wrong.

Holy fucking shit!

He might be completely wrong!

Cyclone pulled a couple of deep breaths in, leaning his head against the refrigerator. It was fine. It was all good. They'd get through this, whatever "this" was. It didn't matter. Whatever the outcome was, it did not matter.

He opened the refrigerator and grabbed a water. Then he walked back to the bathroom. The door opened just as he arrived.

"And?" he half-yelled. "Shit! Sorry!" He pulled in a breath. "All good?" He forced a smile.

"I did it!" Her face was pale. "I peed on the thing."

"Okay." He started pacing. "Okay, then. All good." Cyclone stopped. "How long do we have to wait?"

"Three minutes." She sucked in a breath, holding it in for a few beats. "I set an alarm on my watch." She held up her wrist for a second. "It said that these tests are more accurate in the morning. Maybe I shouldn't have taken it now?" She pulled her lower lip between her teeth.

"You'll be a couple of weeks along. I did the math."

"Exactly! It's early days." She licked her lips.

Cyclone gave a one-shouldered shrug. "For a human pregnancy."

Her eyes widened. "Ooooh… Yes, you're right, I hadn't thought of that. Anyway, the test said that you can get a false negative. Never a false positive. If it's negative, I'll try again in the morning." Her eyes widened. There was this hopeful edge to her voice that fucking killed him.

"Yes, that's a good plan. I have five more tests in the car. They're different brands. I mean, you can't be too sure." He widened his eyes.

"Exactly. You can never be too sure." She nodded a lot, looking so fucking sexy and so scared. So vulnerable. So beautiful that she took his breath away. He wanted to hold her. To tell her it would be okay. Cyclone wanted to give her everything, especially this… especially a child she never thought she would have.

"You need to know something." He grabbed her hands.

"What is it?"

"If you're not pregnant, I'm abducting you," he rasped.

"You told me that already."

"What I didn't tell you was that I'm not letting you go until you agree to us being together through the good times and the bad. Through anything and everything, so long as we both shall live. You need to understand that even if you grew a third tit and chest hair, I'd still be there. I love you so fucking much. Nothing else should matter other than that. You were it for me from the moment I first saw you. Even when you left me…" his voice sounded weird, but he carried on anyway, "it never changed. I missed you a whole hell of a lot. I thought my heart had been ripped out through my throat, but I still loved you. When I saw you that day at the lair, it was like the sun appearing through the clouds on a rainy day. It was like flowers opening in the desert. It was like I could breathe again. Like I was whole. One way or another…" He rubbed the back of her hands with his thumbs. "We're together now, regardless of the outcome of that test."

"That was one of the strangest and yet best things anyone has ever said to me." The alarm went off. It was loud and blaring. They let go of each other's hands so that Angie could silence it with a push of a button. "I'm scared."

"I've got you. You're not alone."

She took back his hands and squeezed. "I love you too."

"Now that wasn't so hard, was it?" He smiled.

Her lip wobbled. "I wanted you to have kids."

"And who knows? Miracles happen… people get struck by lightning all the time," he said.

She laughed through watery eyes. "You make that sound like a good thing."

Cyclone squeezed her hands. "What do you say we go and take a look at that test?"

She nodded. "I left it lying face down. Two lines mean I'm pregnant. One line…" Her voice broke, and she stopped talking. He could see that she was trying not to cry. His brave female.

"Means we'll keep on trying for a lightning strike while we live happily ever after."

She giggled softly. "That doesn't sound too bad."

"Okay, then." They headed into the bathroom and stood next to the washbasin cabinet. "I can't look," she whispered.

"Of course you can. You're as badass as they come."

Angie flipped the test over, and they both just stood there. It took several long seconds for him to comprehend what he was seeing. Angie didn't do anything.

"Two lines."

"Two lines," she whispered. "I'm not sure I can believe it. This test might be faulty."

Cyclone felt like bursting. "It might be."

His heart raced. He wanted to pick her up. To roar with joy because this was the best day of his whole entire life. The best fucking day.

He could hear her heart racing, too. He could feel her anxiety. "Wait right here. I need to fetch something from my car."

She picked the test up, looking at it more closely.

"Okay." Angie sounded like she was in shock. He could understand why. Her ass had just been struck by lightning.

CHAPTER 26

THEY BOTH SAT ON THE bathroom floor, their backs to the wall, looking up at the six pregnancy tests all in a neat row on the counter. The first one said, "Pregnant." The next one said, "Yes." Then there was a cross for positive. The rest all had two lines.

"I'm pregnant." She still couldn't quite believe it. Angie wanted to believe it so badly, but she was afraid that if she did, it would go away.

"Yep, I should have told you how potent our seed is."

She laughed. "Potent seed doesn't mean anything without an egg." Although if there was one man on this whole planet who would cause her to pop a damned ovary, it was him. "I can't believe it. I was told that I'm pretty much out of eggs."

"Six pregnancy tests don't lie. You weren't out of eggs,

Spice. I've put a little dragon bun in your oven." He squeezed her thigh.

Angie was breathing hard. "A dragon bun… I have a dragon bun in my oven. It's going to grow into a baby who will be ours." Her eyes misted up.

"Yes." He turned to her, cupping her cheek. "You're going to be a mom."

"Okay… wait, though. Wait just a minute." She jumped to her feet and walked to the cabinet. She turned to face Cyclone, who was also on his feet. He was quick and quiet for such a huge guy. "This is early days. We can't get excited." She shook her head.

"Yes, we can," he told her. "You will only be pregnant for six months. There is already a heartbeat." He dropped back down to his knees, putting his ear to her belly. She couldn't help it; Angie cupped his head, holding him close.

"Do you hear anything?" Fear gripped her.

Cyclone looked up at her, grinning. "I really should have looked harder for a hardware store. You're talking so much I can hardly hear. Yes, Spice, I can hear our baby. His heart is beating strong and true."

"A he… that's right. We'll definitely have a baby boy because I'm human."

Cyclone got back up to his feet. "I know we said two boys and two girls, but we might have to settle for one or two boys."

"Lightning does not strike twice. Get that right out of your head." She pointed at him.

He laughed. "Okay, okay. Our little one has a strong heartbeat. Please smile. Be happy. I know you're afraid, but you can do it. We should enjoy every moment of this."

"I just want him to be healthy. I need to get through this pregnancy. Oh, and the labor. And deliver a healthy baby. Okay, I'm panicking a little, which is terrifying. I don't panic. I'm not that person."

He laughed some more. "Welcome to parenthood."

Her eyes widened. "We're not parents yet."

"We will be soon enough. Our baby has a heartbeat. He's warm and safe inside his mama's belly." Cyclone touched her stomach tenderly. "I can't wait to see your belly swell with life."

She put her hand over his. "Me neither." Then she gasped as another realization hit.

"Stop it!" Cyclone warned. "You're overthinking this."

"I can't help it. I've spent the last few years ridding my brain of anything to do with babies. I cut my friends off because I couldn't stand to see them get married and have kids. I ran hard and fast. Now I'm faced with something I never thought I would have. I'm happy… thrilled even, but I'm scared shitless. Hear me out. When those goblins put silver in the water, I drank it too. I ate the poisoned food. Do you think our baby—"

"Our baby is fine!" Cyclone's eyes blazed. "You were barely pregnant at the time. Even if our baby was exposed, we do desensitization all the time. Our she-dragons go through it during pregnancy. Human females as well. Maybe not as early as you were exposed, but they all get it done. It's normal. That's why whelps are being born who are completely immune. You have nothing to worry about." He hugged her close, planting a kiss on the top of her head.

"So, I can be happy, then?" Angie sounded hopeful. She wanted to be hopeful.

"Yes, you can."

"We can celebrate. Maybe throw our heads back and howl at the moon." She hugged him tighter.

"I'm not a wolf shifter, Spice." Angie could hear that he was smiling.

"Semantics." Angie put her hands on his shoulders and leaped up. Cyclone caught her easily. She put her legs around his waist. "I'm pregnant." She finally smiled broadly, and it felt so good. "We're going to have a baby." Then she threw her head back and howled.

Cyclone laughed. "Actually, that's kind of cute. You'd make a fantastic wolf shifter."

Angie laughed so hard that her belly ached. It felt so good to let go. To be in Cyclone's arms. To know that he would have abducted her without even knowing she was pregnant. He was a keeper, that was for sure.

"What do you want to do to celebrate?" he asked. "We could go—"

She leaned in and kissed him. It was hot and hard from the word go. Angie pulled back. "I would like to get reacquainted with your cock."

"My cock would like to get reacquainted with you, too." He put both hands on her ass and squeezed. "Have you been using my little gift?"

"Little?" She snort-laughed.

"Okay, my big gift. I bought the biggest dildo they had."

"I'll bet. And no, I haven't used it. I planned to tonight, though," she told him.

"You haven't used it yet?" He shook his head, looking stunned. "Why not?" He started walking to her bedroom. "My poor, poor baby. I'm glad I'm here. Seems like I arrived just in time."

"You did! All I've done is mope around. I've been completely miserable."

Cyclone grinned. "Good! Serves you right. Don't do that again. From here on out, we're together. It doesn't matter what the future holds. As long as we tackle it as a team, we'll be just fine."

Her eyes stung. "That sounds like the best plan I've heard in a long time."

"Okay, then. Let's get you all taken care of." He put her down on the bed. They both spent half a minute getting undressed.

She forgot her line of thought as Cyclone knelt on the bed. His eyes zoned in on her shoulder.

"What happened here?" He trailed a finger over her puckered scars.

It was the first time he was seeing her completely naked since they had met up again, even though they'd had sex twice.

"I took a bullet. Had to be operated on. I lost some of my range of motion, and it hurts sometimes."

"You got shot?" His brows lifted. Cyclone kissed her scars.

"It's why I ended up getting discharged," she explained. "I thought you would have seen it when we had sex the first time." Then again, the Lycra gear might have been ripped, but parts of it were still on her when he left.

"I'm sorry you got hurt, Spice, but I'm glad you came back to me. That is the positive side to the whole thing."

She cupped his jaw, feeling his stubble under her palm. "I'm glad as well."

Cyclone's cock was fully erect as he moved between

her legs. His gaze was firmly… there. On her girl parts. His eyes were hooded. His voice was ultra-deep.

"Hook your thighs around my shoulders. I want to taste you."

Angie's insides did this flip-flop. Her belly tightened with need. She did as he said. Then Cyclone ran a finger down her slit, and Angie groaned.

"So pretty," he mumbled. "Lean back and get comfy." His jaw tightened. Then he was leaning in and licking her clit, using firm strokes that had her panting like a madwoman.

This man.

Hers!

Everything had changed.

Cyclone tongue-fucked her before moving back to her clit, where he lapped against the bundle of nerves, making her moan… hard. Her thighs vibrated. She was going to… was nearly— Cyclone sat up. He licked his lips like she was the most delicious thing he had ever savored.

"Now that you're nice and wet, I'm going to make you come using this." He palmed his huge cock, which was fully erect.

"Oh!" Her entire female area gave a hard zing of need. "Yes, please," she added.

His nostrils flared as he took her in. "My Spice," he whispered. "You are so fucking beautiful," Cyclone murmured, cupping one of her breasts in his big, warm hand. "These are fuller."

"Really?" She looked down. Then again, her bra had been feeling a little tight.

He rubbed his thumbs over her nipples, and she hissed. "More sensitive?"

She nodded.

"So damned sexy!" he groaned as he squeezed her boob again. He bit down on his lower lip and frowned, looking angry. Then he gripped her thigh, pulled it higher on his body, and lined his member up at her opening with his other hand. Cyclone swallowed thickly. It looked like he was trying to control himself.

Maintaining eye contact, he slowly pushed into her. Slowly… slowly. She was really wet. Obscenely so. Despite his huge size, he slipped in easily. His frown deepened with every inch he gained. He made a soft grunting noise as he slid all the way home. Angie bit down on her lip.

"You feel amazing. Like home," he growled.

Cyclone didn't move; sweat glistened on his brow. His muscles were out and in all their glory. His abs… Oh… things of pure beauty. Cyclone sucked on his thumb and then used it in a slow glide over her clit.

Holy shit! She drew in a breath, and her eyes widened. Cyclone was balls-deep inside her, stretching her to capacity and not moving an inch. It was just his wet thumb that slid lazy circles around her clit, which felt really swollen. She pulled in a lungful of air and let it out slowly.

"That feels… it…" she groaned. She'd been on edge for what felt like forever.

Cyclone gave her the smallest of smiles and leaned down, latching his hot mouth over one of her nipples. Her back bowed. Between his mouth and his thumb… *Oh god! Oh!* She tried to move, wanted more, but his body held her in place. More accurately, his dick held her firmly in place.

She moaned. It was a harsh sound that reverberated around the room. Cyclone nipped at her nipple, and a zing of need spread like wildfire, coursing through her whole body. His thumb barely brushed her puckered flesh. Soft little slippery circles that had her crying out with desperation. He moved to her other breast and sucked on her there, too.

"So beautiful," he whispered.

"Oh… oh, my goodness." Her voice was hoarse. Her breath coming in thick gulps. Another nip had her groaning so deeply it hurt her throat.

Then he was straightening up. His knees had to be bent, otherwise he would not be able to reach her. He gripped her thighs, lifting her legs so that they hooked over his shoulders.

"Lie back," he urged.

Angie realized she was propped up on her elbows. She did as he asked. Her clit throbbed. Her nipples were so tight they almost hurt. Cyclone leaned over her, looking her in the eyes. Her knees weren't that far away from her face—she hadn't known she was quite this flexible. His eyes bore into hers; it was intense. She'd never been more turned on in her life. She'd never been so desperate to come. When he started moving. In and out. Slow but deep yet controlled. Her mouth fell open, and it felt like her eyes actually rolled back in her skull.

Cyclone breathed in deeply through his nose. Angie only hoped that the walls of her house were soundproof. Her neighbors were only about ten feet away from her bedroom wall. She had a feeling this was about to get noisy. Right then, though, she didn't give a damn. Not when that coiling sensation had already begun deep within her belly. Not when she could feel that this might just be the best darned orgasm of her life. She grabbed hold of his thick biceps. Looked into his gorgeous blue eyes.

He kept going. Slow and gentle. Punchy little thrusts that hit her deep. They hit her just right. The lovemaking was intense, like this man. Her man. She was moaning with every thrust. Like before, Cyclone made plenty of grunting noises. It turned her on even more to know that he was enjoying this just as much as she was. His gaze drifted to her boobs, which were jerking with every strong shove inside her.

He swallowed hard, locking eyes with her. "Fucking perfect," he growled, barely sounding human. Somehow, even that was a turn-on too. He tilted his head back and closed his eyes like he was savoring her. He made a groaning noise. She touched his chest, feeling the scales that had erupted there. He was so stunning that it almost took her breath away.

The coiling sensation became almost too much. The bed made a creaking noise. Slow and deep had turned to hard and fast. His balls slapped against her with every thrust. He made this little groaning noise like he was losing control. There was a wet suction sound from where their bodies joined. Even that excited her. She dug her fingers into his arm. Her boobs jiggled so hard, but she didn't care.

"Cyclone," she sobbed his name as the coiling reached its peak. Her hips jerked, and her head fell back. A rush of ecstasy raced through her, starting in her belly. She gave a yell as everything let go. She pointed her toes and gripped his arms even tighter.

Holy shit!

Then Cyclone was groaning. Then he was roaring her name. He jerked into her. The sound of their lovemaking reverberated around the room. Slapping, sucking, panting, and moaning. The sounds they both made were laced with intense pleasure. Cyclone slowed. His hips rolled against her as he wrung out every last drop of pleasure from her. His frown was back, his mouth pursed. His eyes on hers. Locked together with the intensity of the moment. The movements slowed until he stilled altogether, staying joined with her. Cyclone was breathing hard. Then again, so was she.

He put his forehead to hers for a few moments. He kissed her ever so softly.

Then he unhooked her thighs, putting them around his waist. Cyclone rested his head on her chest. Angie ran her fingers through the dark strands of his hair.

"Do you want to go to Vegas and get hitched right now?" Cyclone asked, his voice still deep. His chest was heaving as he fought to catch his breath. "I feel like we've waited long enough."

"Is that a proposal?" She laughed.

"It sure is. We can leave right away. You can wear a poofy dress. I refuse to dress like Elvis, though." He shook his head.

"You know me so well." She clutched her chest, panting hard. "You wouldn't fit into an Elvis suit." She laughed again. "I'd love to marry you. I'm too tired right now. Can we go tomorrow?"

"Of course! One times shotgun wedding here we come." He kissed her softly, grinning.

"A shotgun wedding suits me just fine." She giggled. "I happen to like shotguns."

"Then I can officially bite you often." He nuzzled her neck, nipping her quite hard. It was the weirdest thing because it actually felt good.

Soooo good!

So much so that Angie groaned. Her girl parts gave another spasm as a zing of pleasure made her belly clench.

"You like that?" He nipped her again.

This time, she groaned harder. "Oh, my god! What are you doing to me?"

"My sweet female likes guns and biting. We were made for one another, Spice." He put his finger on her clit and rubbed a little.

Angie groaned loudly. She was already halfway to another orgasm, even though she had just come hard.

"Are you ready for round two?" He kissed her softly.

"Yes. You'd better believe it." There was no one on the planet who could do this to her. It was him. Only Cyclone. And it looked like everything had changed and for the better.

CHAPTER 27

One week later…

THERE WERE SMALL GROUPS OF people littered all around the large marquee. Fairy lights twinkled as the sun started to go down. The tables were long and beautifully decorated with the most exquisite flowers and candles. The blooms were all in different shades of rusts, oranges, and browns, all against a white backdrop. Everyone held a flute of champagne. Everyone except for Angie and Azure, who looked like she was missing at present. Probably seeing to the twins. They had sparkling apple juice instead of bubbly. Angie couldn't help but touch a hand to her belly. She found that she did it often, even when she wasn't thinking about the baby.

A mom.

She was going to be a mom.

It was crazy. A miracle was right. One she would always be grateful for.

"It's so beautiful," Amy said, grabbing her hand and pulling it closer so that she could inspect Angie's ring... again.

"You've said the same thing every time I've seen you this week." Angie laughed. "I must say, I never thought I would like to wear jewelry. This ring has changed my mind."

"This isn't just any piece of jewelry." Amy shook her head. "It's your wedding ring, you crazy chick."

Angie held out her hand, admiring her ring, moving it so that it glinted in the fading light. It had belonged to Cyclone's grandmother. It was a large, square aquamarine surrounded by tiny diamonds set in white gold.

"I love it," she whispered, more to herself than to Amy. She loved it for what it represented. She also loved it because of its sentimental value. Cyclone told her that he had planned on giving it to her years ago, that he had kept it for her ever since. Only for her. Waiting.

Sentimental shifter. He was the sweetest.

"I still cannot believe that you guys got hitched in Vegas. That you got married before Vortex and me. I had hoped to be your bridesmaid, since we really are going to be besties now that you're mated to Cyclone."

Angie smiled. "Actually, we plan on having another intimate ceremony in a few weeks, with our close friends and family here at the lair. I had planned on asking you to be my—"

Before she could finish the sentence, Amy had launched herself into Angie's arms, spilling both of their drinks in the process.

"Oh, my god!" she squealed. "Oh, my wooooord! Yes! I would love that. I've never been a maid of honor before." She pulled back. "I *am* going to be the maid of honor, right?"

Angie laughed. "You are going to be the only bridesmaid, so I guess that would make you the maid of honor."

"What are you two getting so excited about?" Cyclone put his hand on her lower back. Vortex put his arm around Amy. He gave her a kiss on the top of her head.

"I'm going to be the maid of honor at your wedding. The one we're having here, and I'm super excited." Amy did this little bounce.

"That's perfect timing." Cyclone grinned, looking so freakishly handsome in his suit that Angie wanted to steal him away so that she could jump him. Pregnancy had really turned her hormones on their head. For one, she was horny all the damned time. For another, her boobs had grown even more over the last week. Cyclone couldn't keep his hands off of them or her. "I just got done asking Vortex to be my best man. He said yes."

"That's fantastic!" Amy jumped up and down a few times, grinning like a crazy woman, which was strange since she was normally so together. "This means that we'll be maids of honor at each other's weddings. How fabulous is that?"

Amy had asked Angie a few days ago, and she'd said yes. Angie only hoped that her friend set a date quickly because she was going to look very pregnant soon.

"Yes, it—" Angie started to say.

"It looks like you guys are having your own party," Azure said as she walked up.

Ice was right behind her, pushing the double stroller. He parked it close to Azure.

"I'll be just a second." He kissed his mate and then strode from the marquee.

"We are!" Amy shouted. Then she put her finger to her lips as her eyes widened. "Shhhhh!" She made a face. "Sorry! I hope I didn't wake them." They all looked down at the stroller. It was fully covered, so they couldn't see inside.

"You didn't." Azure smiled. "I just finished feeding them, so they're both sleeping soundly. Nothing will wake them for the next two hours or so, then I get to do it all again. Feed, burp, diaper change, and nap. You'll soon know all about it," Azure told Angie.

"This 'no privacy' thing might just drive me insane before long," Angie muttered, but she was smiling all the while. So, it turned out that by yesterday, everyone at the lair suddenly knew she was pregnant based on her scent. There was no denying it. Everyone knew! So much for waiting a while before telling anyone. No wonder Cyclone had looked at her like she was crazy when she insisted on it.

Amy laughed. "You'll get used to it. It's one of those things."

Cyclone put his arm around her, pulling her against him.

"I'm going to have to," she said. "Since I'm here to stay." She looked up at her man.

Cyclone gave her a squeeze.

"Okay, so, about your wedding. Let's talk colors and flowers," Amy said. "What were you thinking?"

"Colors? Flowers?" Azure frowned. "What did I miss?"

"Cyclone and Angie are planning a small wedding ceremony for close friends and—"

"Let's welcome the mated couple, everyone!" Ice shouted from the entrance to the marquee. Everyone stopped talking and turned to the open flaps.

They all cheered loudly as Freeze and Melina walked in. Freeze wore a tuxedo. Melina looked amazing in her long, A-line dress. It was covered in sparkling crystals. She smiled brightly. They took a moment at the entrance while everyone continued to go nuts. Clapping and hollering. Freeze looked down at his mate. His eyes were filled with adoration. Melina looked back up at him, and it was clear that the feeling was mutual.

Then Melina strutted into the marquee, making a beeline for Amy. She plopped her gorgeous bouquet into the stunned woman's arms.

"There's no point in throwing this thing since you're up next."

Amy beamed, her eyes filling with tears. "Thank you," she gushed. Then they hugged tightly for a few seconds. Melina walked back to her man, who put his arm around her.

"Let's celebrate!" Freeze shouted. Everyone went nuts all over again.

Cyclone gave her another squeeze. It was true; they had so much to celebrate. Angie looked up into Cyclone's eyes. He winked at her, giving her the most beautiful smile. It took her breath away.

CHAPTER 28

Two months later…

"HI, SEXY," CYCLONE SAID AS he walked into their apartment.

Angie was in the kitchen, stirring a pot. "Hi, babe," she called over her shoulder, still stirring. "If I stop, the onions might burn," she said.

"I have good news." He couldn't keep the grin off his face as he walked toward her.

Angie turned just a little, and he caught sight of her softly rounded belly. Holy hell, but she had to be the most beautiful female he had ever seen. Her dark hair was loose. It cascaded down her back. It seemed even thicker and more lustrous than it had been before she became pregnant.

"Oh, yes?" She lifted her brows.

"I just got the go-ahead for us to move into a bigger place."

Her smile took up her whole face. "When?"

"We can move in a week, which means we can start thinking about putting a nursery together."

"That's great news." She smiled broadly, putting a hand to her back. "I can't wait. I'm not looking forward to packing, though." Angie made a face and rubbed her lower back with one hand before turning and continuing to stir.

"I will take care of all the packing and moving since you are growing our baby."

"Sounds like a good exchange." She laughed.

Cyclone put his arms around her and held her distended belly, running his hands up and down its curve. He rubbed his chin in the crook of her neck and then kissed her there.

Angie giggled. "That's ticklish."

Keeping his hands on her belly, he breathed her in. A feeling of possessiveness wrapped itself around him, and he had to fight to keep from holding her more tightly.

The baby gave a soft kick beneath his hand. It was undeniable. It was an honest-to-god kick.

"I felt it!" he yelled. "I felt him kick!" His throat clogged up instantly.

Angie gasped and covered his hand with hers. "There!" she said. "He kicked again." She looked up at him. "Can you really feel him?"

"Yes. Holy shit!"

Cyclone had been trying to feel the baby kick for two weeks. Angie had started feeling him for a while now. She said that at first, it felt like bubbles bursting inside her.

Then tiny little bumps started feeling like thumps, and now… now… he'd felt his son.

My son.

My mate.

My family.

Pride swelled inside him. Cyclone buried his head into her hair, breathing in her wonderful scent.

"I'm so happy." He sighed.

"Me too." She tried to stifle a yawn.

"You're tired." Cyclone turned her around so that he could look at her. She gave a lazy smile and yawned, making a sound of agreement.

"Growing a baby is hard work. I'm making a stew, then I'll go to bed early tonight, I think."

"Go and have a nap right now. I'll wake you when dinner is ready."

She shook her head. "Nah, I'll be fine. I'm not that tired."

He leveled her with a stare. "You know I can tell when you're lying, Spice."

"It's just that I've missed you. I wanted to find out all about your day," she said, cocking her head and narrowing her eyes. "Meanwhile, you never did tell me how you do that."

"You huff out a small breath, then bite on your lower lip for a second just before you tell a lie. It's cute, it's like you're steeling yourself."

"Now that I know about this, I won't do it anymore." She laughed.

"I'm willing to bet you that you will." He smiled. Then he kissed her softly. "You go and lie on the sofa. We can still talk about our day. I'll cook."

"Are you sure?" Angie frowned, taking the pot off the stove. "I only just started. The onions are nearly—"

"Absolutely." He took her arm. "I can take it from here. You go and lie down. Do you need a blanket?"

"That would be nice." Angie lay down on the sofa. The kitchen and living room were open-plan, so they'd still be able to talk. Cyclone went to fetch the blanket, tucking his female in.

"Do you want something to drink?" He kept a hand on her thigh.

"I'm fine."

"A snack?" He lifted his brows.

She chuckled softly. "I'm all good. Now tell me about your day. The meat for the stew is in the fridge."

"It's been crazy," he said as he headed back towards the kitchen. "Typhoon is in huge shit."

"Why? What happened?"

"You won't believe it." Cyclone chuckled. *Shit!* He still couldn't believe it himself.

Storm had been shitting bricks when he left the male's office not so long ago. He had never seen the prince so red in the face before. Cyclone grabbed his apron out of the drawer, pulling it over his head. Angie had bought it for him the other day. It was denim with "Sexy Chef" written on the front. He tied it at the back.

"Tell me already." Angie started to sit up.

"You lie down, and I'll talk," he warned.

She dropped back down. "Fine, but spill already."

"Typhoon got some female pregnant when he was last on human soil. It was a couple of weeks ago."

"What?" She lifted her head. Her eyes were wide. "No shit!"

"I'm serious."

"And the kid is definitely his?" she asked.

"Apparently, she only just found out about it and contacted him. Says that he's the only guy she's been with in a long time. He says that the condom broke when he was with her. She promised to get the morning-after pill but never did, and now he's going to be a dad."

Angie gasped again. "Why is Storm so pissed? That doesn't sound that bad."

"The female doesn't know about us. She doesn't know that she's carrying a dragon whelp. Typhoon hardly knows her. It was a one-night stand. It's a fuck-up!"

"What now?" Angie asked.

"She'll be expected to sign an NDA, and then Typhoon will have to come clean to her about what he is. About what the child will be."

Angie's eyes were wide. "I'm not sure whether to feel bad for the lady or for Typhoon."

"She might not take the news so well," he said, which was the understatement of the century. She might just flip her lid completely. She might not want the child. Hell, she might want to get rid of it. Typhoon seemed happy. He had that vibe about him, like he wanted the child. Like he might be willing to make it work with the mother, if she gave it half a chance.

"Typhoon is a nice guy. He's really good-looking too. I'm sure any woman would be happy to have him."

"This female might have only seen him as a one-time thing. She might refuse to sign the NDA. It could be a major problem for us. Storm definitely isn't taking the news well. Typhoon was supposed to have checked if the female was taking birth control before rutting her. Turns out that she wasn't. We can normally tell when a female is in heat. Storm is saying that he should have known better."

"You couldn't tell with me." Angie shook her head.

Cyclone shrugged. "Your scent drove me wild. I ripped your clothes off. There were signs. There would have been signs with Typhoon. I was less observant with you. Typhoon should have been on his guard with some unknown female."

"These things happen, though."

Cyclone nodded a couple of times. "That's true. It's just that there are protocols that should have been followed. Paperwork that should have been completed. He should never have rutted her, to begin with. Then he should have reported the broken condom, which he didn't do, and now he's in deep shit."

"I think he'll be fine. I'm sure whoever the lady is will be understanding about his scales and wings. There are worse things." She laughed. "I happen to think your dragon is cute."

"What the fuck! Cute?" Cyclone snorted, trying hard to fake disgust. "My dragon is terrifying."

"I say cute." Angie blew him a kiss, and they both laughed.

Cyclone put the pot back on the stove, throwing in the meat and some spices. His mind went back to Typhoon. He felt for the male. Hopefully, things would work out for him.

CHAPTER 29

Three months and two days later…

CYCLONE COULD SEE THAT SHE was fighting her way through yet another contraction. Angie was breathing deeply. Her belly looked tight. His female moaned. It was a guttural sound from deep inside her throat.

The pain was harsh. He could see it in her eyes.

After about another minute, she slumped back, completely out of breath.

"You are doing so well." He cupped her flushed cheek. "Do you need water? Some ice chips?"

She shook her head, swallowing thickly. Her eyes didn't focus on him properly. This is what fourteen hours of labor looked like. The last two had been fucking terrible. Forever his badass, Angie forged on. She had more strength and stamina than most of his males.

"You're doing well," the human doctor remarked, looking between Angie's legs. "It won't be long now," Doctor Michaels encouraged.

"I hope so." Angie's eyes were closed. Her hands were on her belly. She looked utterly exhausted. Never more beautiful. He only wished he could do more. "Oh god." Angie grit her teeth. "Here comes another one. It's happening more often—" Her face turned red, and she groaned while grabbing her belly tighter. "They're big. This is big!"

"What should I do?" He felt desperate. Cyclone had to do something. "Hold my hand."

Angie took his hand and squeezed.

"Breathe through it," the doctor said. "That's it. Pant." The healer began panting, and Angie followed suit.

"I need to do something," he pushed out.

The doctor looked at him. "There is nothing you can do. Nothing you haven't been doing already. The baby will be here soon. We're making excellent progress." She peered between Angie's legs again.

His female breathed as though her life depended on it. Deep inhalations. Her eyes went from being wide and anguished to tightly shut. She seemed to barely be holding it together. It seemed to last for an age before she slumped back. The shirt she was wearing was damp and clung to her body. She looked delirious. Her eyelids drooped. His female began to shake.

"I'm cold," she whispered. "I'm really c-cold. What's h-happening?" Her teeth started chattering.

"What's wrong with her?" he tried not to snarl and failed. The human doctor must be used to it because she didn't flinch.

"Calm down. The baby has entered the birth canal. This is completely normal." Doctor Michaels pointed to a blanket on the sofa. "Put that around your wife," she instructed. "You're fully dilated, Angie. You will start to feel the urge to push soon."

Cyclone nodded. He raced to fetch the woolen blanket and draped it around his female's shoulders and upper body. A few minutes later, Angie began to doze off. At least, that's what it looked like.

"What's going on?" he asked the healer. "Why has it stopped? This isn't right!" Cyclone wanted to start pacing. He wanted to shake the doctor.

"This is perfectly normal," she whispered. "The contractions will start up soon enough. Let your wife rest." She smiled. "You're going to meet your baby soon."

Cyclone hoped so. He couldn't wait to meet his son, but more than anything, he needed this to be over. Angie had coped so well. She'd been a warrior, but he could see that it was getting to her.

Not even five minutes later, Angie moaned. Her eyes popped open, and her face contorted with pain. She gripped her distended belly with both hands.

"Oh god!" she groaned. "Oh!" She pushed the blanket away. "I'm too hot," she moaned.

Too hot!

Too cold!

"Nearly there," the doctor said. "Breathe, Angie. You're doing great."

"I want to push!" Angie suddenly ground out between pants.

"You can go ahead. Put your chin to your chest and push hard," the doctor said.

Angie pushed. She made a grunting sound and pushed some more.

"That's it. Keep breathing." The doctor glanced from between Angie's legs to his female's face and back. "You're doing so great."

After about another half a minute later, Angie slumped back, breathing hard. She pointed to a glass of water on the side table. "Thirsty," she mumbled.

Fuck, but he was so damned useless. Cyclone scrambled to grab the glass and almost fell on his face.

Angie smiled as she took the glass from him. He helped her sit up so that she could drink.

"Here." He pushed the hair from her face. "You're doing so well." He kissed her forehead. "I wish I could do this for you. That I could take over."

She gave him a smile that spoke of exhaustion. "I know. I've got this."

"I know you do. I'm so fucking proud of you." He kissed her lips this time.

"A couple more contractions, and your baby will be born." Doctor Michaels gave Angie a reassuring smile.

Angie clutched Cyclone's hand. "Here comes another one."

⚓

Her break didn't last long. Her contractions were coming hard and fast. It felt like they were happening one after another, with barely enough time to catch her breath. Her whole body felt sore. Angie had never been so exhausted in her life. It was like she had just run a marathon and was being forced to drop and give one hundred pushups. It reminded her of "Hell Week" back when she was training. Women didn't realize how strong they were. They underestimated themselves at every turn. This took guts and strength she never knew she had.

There was no backing out. No stopping it. She could feel her belly tighten. Her muscles gripping tighter and tighter. It felt like her entire midsection was being ripped in half. She cried out, gripping her belly. It was better now that she could push. Pushing helped ease the pain, somehow. It was like she could finally work with her body. It felt good. She could feel her baby right there. Their son.

The overwhelming urge to push hit her. There was nothing she could do to stop it. Angie gripped the back of her thighs and pushed. Doctor Michaels was saying something, but she couldn't hear what it was. Pushing brought a strange kind of relief, so she went with it.

She sucked in another deep breath and pushed again, giving it all she had. That feeling of pressure increased down there. He was coming!

Two minutes later, her belly began to tighten, and the urge to push took over again. It felt like this went on for about ten or fifteen minutes. It was hard to say, since time blurred. Rest followed by pushing. "Labor" was the right description. This was labor, alright, and Angie had never worked this hard in her whole life. Her reserves were slowly draining. Angie kept focusing on her baby boy. She could feel that things were progressing. She knew it wouldn't be for much longer. She needed to stay focused on the prize. Their son. It wouldn't be long before they met him.

Finally—freaking finally—the doctor shouted, "I can see his head!"

Angie put her hand between her legs, and sure enough, he was there. She gave a sob of happiness.

This was it!

With renewed strength, she gave a massive push. She normally longed for the moments of rest. This time, when her contraction ended, it felt too soon. She cried out in sheer frustration.

The doctor smiled down at her. "One or two more pushes, and he'll be born."

"Oh, my fuck!" Cyclone growled. "I can't believe this." He kissed her cheek. "You are the strongest person I know. Fuck, Ange!"

It took three more contractions before his head crowned properly. Angie could feel him there without having to use her hand. She breathed in deeply and pushed like she'd never pushed before. Her nails dug into the backs of her thighs.

"That's it," Cyclone continued to whisper words of love and encouragement. She felt so much better with him there. There was something cool on her forehead. He was mopping her brow with a wet cloth.

Sweet shifter!

The doctor leaned in between her thighs. "His head is out!" Her voice was filled with excitement. "When the next contraction comes, you need to push with all the strength you have in you. You are about to meet your son."

Her heart raced. She made a laughing sobbing noise because… shit! This was big. This was huge.

Cyclone put his forehead to hers. As he pulled back, she could see that his eyes were glinting. His jaw was tense. She realized that he was trying not to cry.

"I love you," he whispered softly.

She wanted to say it back, but she couldn't because another contraction was taking hold.

"Okay, Angie. This is it. Give it all you've got." Doctor Michaels focused between her legs.

Angie pushed as if her life depended on it. It didn't take much. She felt her son leave her body, and all at once, in a rush. This is what they meant by having to catch a baby.

Doctor Michaels was busy for a few seconds. She looked up and beamed. There was a loud infant cry that had both Angie and Cyclone in tears as they clung to each other. Cyclone laughed and sniffed.

"You have a beautiful… What the hell!" The doctor's face morphed into a look of shock. Her eyes widened, and her mouth dropped open. She turned pale in an instant.

"What is it?" Angie struggled to sit up.

"What's wrong with my son?" Cyclone snarled.

"It can't be…" Doctor Michaels was looking at their baby like it might have something wrong with him. It clearly wasn't something small either.

"What's going on?" Cyclone's voice shook. "Tell us!" he growled.

The baby was squirming and gave a tiny yell. His hands were fisted. He gave another cry, louder this time. He sounded fine. His skin was pink. He looked like he had two arms and two legs. She couldn't see his face, though.

Shit!

"Does he look okay?" Angie whispered. "Please tell me that he's fine?" she asked. "Please!" she shouted when the doctor didn't say anything.

"Um…" The doctor looked down and then back at them and then back down. "You have just given birth to a healthy baby girl."

"What?" Angie choked out.

"That can't be!" Cyclone snarled.

Doctor Michaels placed the baby on her chest, still looking shell-shocked. "I thought dragon shifters, when paired with humans, couldn't have girls. I thought—"

"We can't!" Cyclone growled.

The baby made another sobbing noise. His… her… eyes were open. They were a bright blue like Cyclone's.

What the hell!

"She has a chest marking." Cyclone touched the mark. "Are you sure about this whelp being a girl? Maybe you… got it wrong." Cyclone had a stony face. Beneath his gruff exterior, Angie could see the sheer panic. The fear. He wasn't a man who was used to feeling that way.

"Look for yourself," Doctor Michaels urged with a soft smile.

Angie repositioned the tiny infant, and they both gasped.

"You birthed a she-dragon," Cyclone whispered. "We have a daughter." A tear tracked down his cheek.

"How is that possible?" she asked, looking down at all the little toes. Then at all the fingers. Her daughter's tiny little face and bald head.

"I have no idea." Cyclone said in awe. More tears rolled down his cheeks. "She's perfect."

Angie sniffed, realizing that she was crying too. "She is. We're going to have to think of a name. This is unexpected." She grinned.

"Maybe once the shock wears off." Cyclone hugged both of them. The big lug was still crying. "I'm so fucking happy. We have a whelp."

"I'm happy, too." Angie cried harder. "Oh, my god! We have a girl! A girl, Cyclone."

Her mate kissed her softly. Cyclone placed a kiss on their daughter's head as well.

Boy or girl, it wasn't important. They were a family. They were together. They had each other, and that was all that mattered.

The End

Dragon Typhoon is out now

AUTHOR'S NOTE

Charlene Hartnady is a USA Today Bestselling author. She loves to write about all things paranormal including vampires, elves and shifters of all kinds. Charlene lives on a couple of acres in the country with her husband and three sons. They have an array of pets including a couple of horses.

She is lucky enough to be able to write full time, so most days you can find her at her computer writing up a storm. Charlene believes that it is the small things in life that truly matter, like that feeling you get when you start a new book, or a particularly beautiful sunset.

BOOKS BY THIS AUTHOR

The Chosen Series:
Book 1 ~ Chosen by the Vampire Kings
Book 2 ~ Stolen by the Alpha Wolf
Book 3 ~ Unlikely Mates
Book 4 ~ Awakened by the Vampire Prince
Book 5 ~ Mated to the Vampire Kings (Short Novel)
Book 6 ~ Wolf Whisperer (Novella)
Book 7 ~ Wanted by the Elven King

The Program Series (Vampire Novels)
Book 1 ~ A Mate for York
Book 2 ~ A Mate for Gideon
Book 3 ~ A Mate for Lazarus
Book 4 ~ A Mate for Griffin
Book 5 ~ A Mate for Lance
Book 6 ~ A Mate for Kai
Book 7 ~ A Mate for Titan

The Feral Series
Book 1 ~ Hunger Awakened
Book 2 ~ Power Awakened
Book 3: Hate Awakened
Book 4: Hope Awakened

Shifter Night Series:
Book 1 ~ Untethered | Book 2 ~ Unbound
Book 3 ~ Unchained
Shifter Night Box Set Books 1—3

The Earth Dragon Series
Book 1 ~ Dragon Guard | Book 2 ~ Savage Dragon
Book 3 ~ Dragon Whelps | Book 4 ~ Slave Dragon
Book 5 ~ Feral Dragon | Book 6 ~ Doctor Dragon

The Bride Hunt Series (Dragon Shifter Novels)
Book 1 ~ Royal Dragon
Book 2 ~ Water Dragon
Book 3 ~ Dragon King
Book 4 ~ Lightning Dragon
Book 5 ~ Forbidden Dragon
Book 6 ~ Dragon Prince

The Water Dragon Series
Book 1 ~ Dragon Hunt | Book 2 ~ Captured Dragons
Book 3 ~ Blood Dragon | Book 4 ~ Dragon Betrayal

Demon Chaser Series (No cliffhangers)
Book 1 ~ Omega | Book 2 ~ Alpha
Book 3 ~ Hybrid | Book 4 ~ Skin
Demon Chaser Boxed Set Book 1–3

Air Dragon Series
Book 1 ~ Dragon Heat
Book 2 ~ Dragon Hunter
Book 3 ~ Dragon Avalanche
Book 4 ~ Dragon Overlord
Book 5 ~ Dragon Cyclone
Book 6 ~ Dragon Typhoon

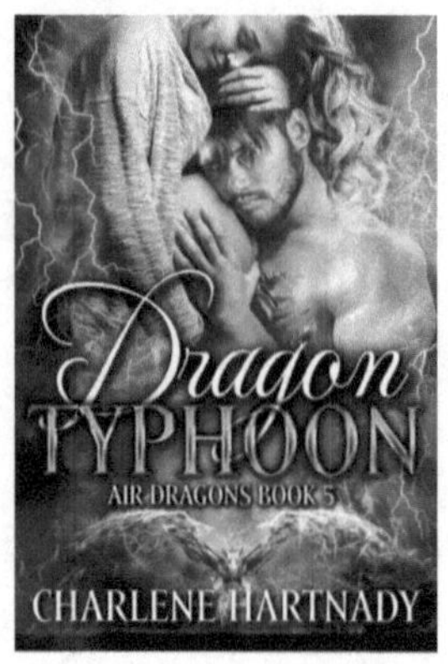

CHAPTER 1

THE DOOR SLAMMED, AND THE whole trailer shook. "Hi, Tay!" Natalie tried to sound bright and breezy. She gave the pot a final stir before putting the lid on it and switching the burner off.

Her sister dropped her school bag on the floor with a loud clunk and sighed. Her shoulders hunched. Her eyes were clouded.

"Is everything okay?" Natalie asked, eyes narrowing on her sister. This could not be good.

Taylor shook her head. Natalie could see that she was trying hard not to cry.

"What is it, sweetie?" She went over to her sister. There was a time, not so long ago, when she would have wrapped Taylor up in a big old hug, but not anymore. Her sister was on the brink of being a teenager. Natalie knew that she wouldn't take kindly to the show of affection. Certainly not when something was bugging her like this.

"I asked you to buy me new sneakers last month." Taylor sniffed. "I begged." Her lip wobbled.

"We didn't have the money, and these ones still fit you." Natalie was too afraid to look down. "We agreed it could wait a little while."

"Turns out that next month was too late." Taylor's voice hitched.

"What happened?"

"They broke." She sniffed again. "In front of everyone. The whole front ripped open like a gaping mouth. I tripped and fell." A tear tracked down her cheek. "Right in the cafeteria while I was walking to go and have my lunch." She wiped her nose with the back of her hand.

Tay's lunch had consisted of a peanut butter sandwich. No jelly. In fact, it had been the last of the peanut butter. Tomorrow would be dry bread, emphasis on the dry. More like stale. It was on days like this that Natalie second-guessed herself. Perhaps it would have been better to have allowed the state to put Taylor in foster care. She was doing a terrible job of raising her little sister.

"Everyone laughed at me." Another big tear rolled down her face. "Then Mrs. Clarkson stepped in and decided to help me." By now, Taylor was swiping frantically at her tears, which fell in earnest. She kept sniffing. "Look." She held up her foot.

Natalie looked down and winced. Mrs. Clarkson had

used duct tape to close the gaping sole. It was silver and gaudy.

Poor Taylor.

"I'm so sorry!" Natalie whispered. She gripped her sister's arm and squeezed.

"What am I going to do tomorrow? I can't go like this." She pointed at her sneaker.

"Wear mine."

"Your feet are two sizes bigger. I'll look like a clown. Besides, what will you wear?" Her voice was filled with anxiety. Her blue eyes shimmered with tears.

"I'll wear your sneakers." Natalie shrugged. "It's no biggie. I'll go to the thrift store. I'm sure they'll have something."

Taylor's eyes widened. "No! Please, Nat… they have weird shoes at the thrift store."

"They sometimes have gems. Until we find a gem, you might need to wear a fake diamond in the rough."

"More like a lump of coal," Taylor muttered. Nat's sister wasn't trying to be difficult. Most days, she was as sweet as they came. Some days were overwhelming.

Nat knew that better than most. She felt her throat clog up and her eyes sting. "I'm sorry, Tay-Tay! You know I'm doing my best. I wanted to keep us together. I—"

"I know." Taylor's voice cracked, and she threw her arms around Natalie. "I'm so glad you did. I know I complain sometimes, but… I wouldn't want to be anywhere else. Sisters have to stick together, right?" She pulled back, looking terrified.

"Absolutely, kiddo." Natalie pulled Taylor back into a hug. "I wouldn't have it any other way." It was something that Natalie had told Taylor after the accident. She used to say it all the time. It still held true six years later, even if their situation was dire. They hugged each other tightly for a while.

"Thank you, Nat," Taylor said as they pulled apart. "You're the best big sister I could ever have asked for."

"I do my best, kiddo. I'll find you something to wear… I promise." She ruffled Taylor's hair.

Her sister stepped back, smoothing her long dark tresses. Taylor looked like their mother more and more as she grew up.

"I'd better get going, or I'm going to be late for work." Natalie ran a hand down her uniform, checking to see if everything was in order. Her manager could be a tyrant. Maybe she'd get lucky, and someone would leave a tip out for her today. It happened from time to time.

For a five-star hotel, they paid terribly. There were still three days to go until she got her next paycheck. Natalie had been worried about making it to the end of the month before Taylor's shoe had broken. Now… it was hopeless.

Emotions thrashed around inside her. Anger, frustration, anxiety… lots of that particular one. She could do this, though. They would get by. They still had a roof over their heads; even if it wasn't a fixed structure, it was home. Most importantly, they had each other.

"I wish you didn't have to work the late shift," Taylor muttered.

"Me too, kiddo! My boss promised to try to get me onto the day shift, and I'm off on Saturday, so we can hang out." Camilla had been promising for over six months, and Natalie prayed her boss would come through at last. Although she wouldn't be holding her breath.

Taylor nodded, not convinced, and Nat couldn't blame her since she wasn't convinced herself.

"Do your homework and be in bed by 9."

Taylor nodded again, looking over at the tiny kitchenette. "I will. What's for dinner?"

Natalie held back a flinch. "It's your favorite," she joked.

"Beans and rice?" Taylor asked.

Her sister hated beans, but they were a cheap protein source.

"Yep." She made a face. It was the second time this week. Yesterday had been boxed mac and cheese. Natalie doubted that there was any real cheese in it.

"Okay. I don't mind it so much anymore." Taylor smiled.

Sweet girl!

Natalie felt her eyes sting, but blinked back the tears. "I'll see you in the morning." She would see Taylor off to school, do whatever chores needed doing, and then nap before the late shift.

Her sister really was growing up fast. She only wished she could give her more. A new pair of sneakers for one. Natalie wished she could finish her college education. That she could get a better-paying job. The fact of the matter was that they were barely scraping by. If one thing went wrong, they would be out on the street.

No!

Don't think like that.

Natalie was determined to come up with a plan. There had to be something she could do to get them out of this situation.

CHAPTER 2

THEY HUDDLED IN A GROUP in the tiny laundry room in the basement of the hotel. Washing machines whirred, and tumble dryers vibrated.

"You've got the tenth floor." Camilla had to speak up over the noise. The housekeeping manager pushed her glasses more firmly onto her face, looking down at Natalie. Even though the woman was five-two, she still managed to somehow look down on people. "There are five late check-outs that require a full room turnaround, two general cleans, and fifteen turndowns." She handed Natalie a keycard and a printout of the numbers and the order in which she had to do them. "Do the—"

Her manager's words sunk in. "Fifteen?" *Holy shit!* "Did you say fifteen?" That was crazy. The nine cleans would already take up most of her shift.

"We're short-staffed. Everyone needs to chip in," Camilla huffed.

By chip in, her manager meant to take a short dinner

break and no tea break. There were plenty of days they had to stay late after a shift to get the job done. Backbreaking stuff! It wasn't fair. Not when they were earning minimum wage with no extra pay.

"When is the hotel going to replace the three ladies who resigned?" she asked.

Camilla narrowed her eyes on Natalie.

"A decision was made at in the board meeting last week that they wouldn't be replaced." Her voice was clipped.

"What?" one of the other room attendants blurted. "They said that the new budget would be approved for next month. What happened?"

"Yes, that's what they said," another of them chimed in. There was a whole lot of grumbling.

"This isn't right," someone else remarked.

"It wasn't approved because," her boss spoke loudly, drowning everyone out, "the board felt that you were doing a fantastic job, despite being short-staffed," Camilla said. "They didn't think we needed the extra hands."

"Surely you told them otherwise? We've been working overtime without pay to get the job done," Natalie pointed out. That whole thing about budget approval was bullshit. The budget was there; they'd decided to use it for something else.

"I think that all of you should be grateful you have jobs." Camilla folded her arms. "You know what you have to do. Now, get it done, and I don't want any more complaints."

They all fetched their carts. It wouldn't do any good to complain. It fell on deaf ears. There was a shortage of work in Brixton. Particularly for this type of position. There were twenty more willing ladies to take each of their jobs. Camilla made sure they all knew about it.

Natalie made her way down the hall, pushing the heavy

cart. She'd packed her linen, toilet paper, and cleaning supplies. There were still sufficient amenities and gold-wrapped chocolates. She had one room to clean for a late check-in. Then she needed to get the general cleaning done before turndowns, which couldn't be left too late.

Natalie knocked on the door.

"Housekeeping," she announced. As was customary, she waited ten seconds before repeating the process. This time, she added, "I'm here to clean your room." This guest had already checked out, but one could never be too careful.

Natalie groaned as she pushed her cart into the upended room. What a mess. Crumpled-up wet towels lay strewn around the room. The bed was a disaster. There were pillows on the floor. The coffee station looked like a mini hurricane had blasted through it. The bathroom would be disgusting too. Natalie knew this from experience. Best she get to it.

It took her fifty minutes to get the room done. *Great!* She was already behind. She prayed that there would be one or two Do-Not-Disturbs. She didn't hold her breath. Most of the guests would be out to dinner soon. They'd want their turndown service.

First, she needed to get the two cleans done for guests still staying at the hotel. Those were normally quicker. A DND was far less likely, as well. Room 1010 was just to the right. She pushed the cart, already feeling the strain in her lower back.

This couldn't be her life.

She went through the routine of knocking and announcing herself.

"Housekeeping."

"Come on in," she heard someone yell.

Great! There was a guest inside. Hopefully, they were

on their way out, and if they were staying, with any luck, they wouldn't feel much like talking.

Natalie huffed out a breath. Since when had she become so jaded? She used to enjoy chatting with people. She used to enjoy life.

Enough with the self-pity already!

This had to stop.

She plastered a smile on her face and entered the room.

"Good afternoon." Natalie faltered when she saw the woman putting a jacket on. "Anna?" she asked, sounding bewildered. "Wow! Hi!"

"Nat!" Anna beamed, closing the distance between them. They hugged, laughing.

"Oh, my word!" Natalie said as they pulled apart. She looked down at her friend's belly. "Things have changed a little since I last saw you." It had been a while.

Anna nodded. "They have."

"Who's the lucky guy? When did you get married?" she gasped. "I can't believe you're pregnant." There was an obvious bump at her midsection.

They used to work together three or four years before as waitstaff over at the Irish pub. Their boss, Simon, had paid them less than dirt. He liked to keep a whole line of ladies employed. Since they mainly relied on tips, it just wasn't worth her while to stay, so when a position at the hotel came up, she took it. It was more work for not much more pay, but at least the money and the shifts were steady, which wasn't the case at McGinty's. Natalie hadn't seen her previous colleague in a while.

Anna gave her belly a quick rub. "Yep! I'm pregnant, alright, but it's not what you think." She dropped her voice as if someone might be listening in. "There's no husband."